ASHES

SERAYA

Author's Note

Readers discretion advised. *Ashes* is a dark, contemporary romance and contains strong language, explicit sexual content, and topics that may be sensitive to some readers.

It is my hope that I've handled these with the care they deserve.

For a detailed list, click here or scan the code below.

Playlist

◄ ► ►|

"War of Hearts" by Ruelle
"ICU" by Coco Jones
"Snooze" by SZA
"Mastermind" by Taylor Swift
"DMFU" by Ella Mai
"anatomy" by kenzie
"Worship" by Ari Abdul
"Still Don't Know My Name" by Labrinth
"Arsonist's Lullabye" by Hozier
"Frozen" by Sabrina Claudio
"Water" by Tyla
"Do or Die" by Natalie Jane
"We Go Down Together" by Dove Cameron, Khalid
"Lost in the Fire" by Gesaffeltstein ft. The Weekend
"Lose Control" by Teddy Swims
"Very Few Friends" by Saint Levant
"BESO" by Rosalía, Rauw Alejandro
"Superpower" by Beyonce ft. Frank Ocean
"Skin & Bones" by David Kuschner
"Hymn for the Weekend" by Coldplay

*To finding the person who will create better
memories to replace the bad ones.*

And to my independent girls who have a praise kink,
be a good girl and start reading.

Sibaya
Bemes
Azilah
Adrar
Bab Al Mansour
N
E
S
W

enya Island
Blackwell
untains

PROLOGUE

TEN YEARS OLD

"All right, *mon ange*, I think it's time to say good night," my mother whispered while smoothing a hand over my tightly curled hair.

I peeled my heavy-lidded eyes open at the sound of her voice. I looked up and found her still lying next to me in my bed.

"Please, Mama. One more time," I pleaded, fighting back a yawn.

She playfully flicked my nose up and chuckled. "Jamal, you were barely listening. Your eyes closed before I even got to the second verse."

The sound of her light laugh bounced against the walls, enveloping us in a warm cocoon. I loved the sound. It always made me feel safe and loved, and I often found myself doing everything I could to hear it again.

But my all-time favorite sound of hers was when she was singing.

Angelic, that's how I would describe it because her voice was the most peaceful melody.

I wanted her to stay longer, I always did, but sleep kept tugging at me.

"Is Baba still working?" I asked and her smile dimmed from its usual brightness.

I immediately regretted asking and fought the urge to reach and rub away the worried line that was forming in the middle of her forehead.

I was about to apologize for asking about Baba's work when she nodded.

"*Oui, mon amour*. He got caught up at work, but hopefully, he'll be home soon."

She pulled my plush blue comforter up to my shoulders and tucked the sides tighter, just how I liked it. I gave her a small smile and sneaked a hand out from under my blanket to rest it on her cheek, reassuring her.

"Baba always comes home. He's putting away the bad guys, right?"

My mother nodded, a small smile curving her lips again. "Yes, baby boy. He is."

My heart swelled with pride.

When I was old enough, Baba explained to me that there were both good and bad people in this world. That he tried to be one of the good ones and his job was all about putting the bad ones away. He did it to protect us and the people of Sardenya, the island we lived on.

He'd been working more these past few weeks because he was tasked with an important mission and it needed all of his attention to make sure everything went well.

Although I was really proud of my dad for saving so many people, Mama had been more worried these past few weeks, especially when he came home late.

"*Bonne nuit, mon ange. Je t'aime,*" she said quietly before kissing my forehead.

"*Je t'aime aussi, maman,*" I replied.

"*Jamais autant que moi,*" we finished in unison.

"*Jamal, fi9 a weldi!*" Baba called out from a distance.

I was in the middle of a very nice dream and wasn't ready to wake up for school yet. Baba was always the one in charge of waking me up in the mornings since Mama had to work early, but the tone of his voice was different today.

It wasn't annoyed that I was late again.

Instead, he sounded in a hurry, panicked.

I opened my eyes and sat up in bed, only for a strange smell to tickle my nose, making my stomach swish around.

The smell was so strong, I could almost taste it.

Why is it so warm in my room?

I quickly pushed my blanket off my body and jumped down my bed. I walked to my door and reached for the knob, but when my palm made contact, I jumped back.

Ouch.

It burned me.

"Jamal!" This time it was Mom calling my name.

That's weird. It's Dad's turn to take me to school this week. She should already have left for work.

I reached for the door again, but this time, I decided to use the sleeve of my pajama shirt to open it.

I opened the door fast, a loud thud resonating from it hitting the wall.

All at once, a large cloud of smoke poured into my room and the smell from before was now even stronger. My eyes started burning and I rubbed them forcefully, hoping it would help get rid of the burning sensation.

It didn't, only made them sting more.

"*Mama? Baba?*" I shouted, confused.

I was barely able to see, but I tried looking toward where I heard my parents' voices, only to see them running around the corner where their room was.

But they weren't alone.

Bright waves of red flames were following closely behind them, closing in on them. Before I knew it, Baba reached for me and rolled me into the small blanket he was holding, then scooped me up into his arms. He held me tightly with one arm while his other hand reached behind for Mama's hand.

I coughed, the smoke filling up my lungs and making it hard to breathe.

"It's going to be okay," Baba reassured me.

He bolted for the stairs at the other end of the hallway, but they seemed so far away.

The heat of the fire was so close.

I looked up into my father's eyes, the harsh flames illuminating his deep brown skin. When our gazes locked, I noticed an expression I'd never seen there before.

Fear.

No, it couldn't be. Baba wasn't supposed to be scared of anything.

"I-I can't breathe," I cried through the fabric covering my mouth.

"It's okay, baby. I'm getting us out, I promise," my father choked out as we reached the top of the stairs.

He only made it down one step when a loud boom exploded behind us.

Then, suddenly, the ground below us was gone and all I could feel was the air being sucked out of my lungs as my body hit a hard surface.

My head was hurting. I couldn't see anything through all the darkness surrounding me, couldn't feel Baba's tight grip around me anymore.

Where am I?

I tried to move, but I was tangled and wrapped up too tight into the blanket that I couldn't get out.

"Mama? Baba? *Finkoum*?" My heart was beating faster

and I could feel hot tears rolling down my cheek. I wiggled around again, but there was something heavy on top of me.

I couldn't move. I couldn't breathe.

I tried screaming again, but I couldn't even hear myself.

Something wet trickled from my ears and my back was really, really warm.

I thought I heard a noise, but everything was muffled, like when I was underwater because of the annoying ringing in my ears.

Then, I finally heard a voice through all the muddiness.

"Nina…Ayoub…Jamal! Make noise if you can hear me."

Uncle Noah?

I tried to open my mouth to answer him but couldn't. It was too much effort and I just wanted to sleep.

I let my eyes close, hoping the horrific sight of our home burning changed back into the nice dream I was having.

I felt the pressure of strong hands gripping my body and heard the echo of my name being called over and over again, but I was still *so* tired. I didn't have enough energy to open my eyes to see who it was.

I let the warmth at my back and in my insides lull me back to where everything felt better.

Maybe this was just a really bad nightmare and Baba would wake me up tomorrow like he always did on Tuesday mornings.

CHAPTER 1

TWENTY YEARS LATER

"Time of death: 19:26," I announced to the now quiet room. After a moment of silence, I heard the staff move around me, but I tuned them out, my gaze fixed on the unending flatline on the cardiac monitor.

When you grew up dreaming of being a doctor, you always imagined how great it would be to help people, the rush you would get working as an emergency medicine resident, the thrill of stepping onto the floor and not knowing what lay ahead.

But rarely did you imagine what it would be like to face the other part of the job. How numbing losing a patient was despite doing everything right.

Those days were rare and far in between, but when they happened?

They were devastating.

Shake it off, Sienna, you still have work to do.

I gripped the edge of the bed, my knuckles turning white, and pulled myself out of my thoughts. I stared down at my patient's closed eyes, the intubation tube now hanging limp on his pale face.

Craig was just sixty years old. I'd cleared him and he was being discharged today, but when the nurse started her rounds, she'd found him unresponsive.

He was supposed to go home.

But now, he was *gone*. Just like that.

We'd done everything we could, but it wasn't enough.

I swallowed the knot in my throat and quickly thanked everyone in the room. I turned around to find one of the senior nurses, Leena, staring at me, her expression grim.

We'd been working together for the past two years and, ironically enough, we'd met under similar circumstances on my first day here.

I gave her a small nod, hoping it would be enough to reassure her that I was okay. After that, I walked out and headed down the hall, straight for the family room where Craig's family was waiting for his discharge.

Tap.

Tap. Tap. Tap.

Everything around me felt far away except for the feel of my index finger drumming against the side of my thigh.

Tap.

Tap. Tap. Tap.

My steps faltered outside of the room where his wife, Jamie, was waiting on the other side. I knew I should take a moment before notifying her, but I decided to ignore the voice in my head and walked into the room.

His wife stood up from her seat. She looked behind me, waiting to see her late husband appear with a smile gracing her face, but it dimmed with every step I took toward her.

Tap.

Tap. Tap. Tap.

This part of the job was never easy, especially when it wasn't expected. But as time went by, you got better at breaking the bad news, the words flowed out easier because you quickly learned that to carry out your job effectively, you needed to learn how to detach yourself from giving in to high emotions.

For me, learning this had been quite easy since I'd been doing it my whole life with everyone around me.

Lucky me, I guess.

Despite that, having to announce to a family their loved one was no longer with us just weighed on you. And it never quite went away.

You always tried to remember every patient you helped, but the ones you lost… those stuck with you the most vividly.

I remembered my first time like it was yesterday. It was my first day at Monte Claro Hospital and we'd received a patient who'd been stabbed during a robbery.

She'd died within minutes of arriving in my care.

There was nothing I could've done because the assailant had removed the knife from her wound and nicked her aorta in the process, but I still carried the memory with me to this day.

Tap.

Tap. Tap. Tap.

Craig's wife quietly sobbed while I did my best to explain what happened and what we did until I ran out of useless words and got up, leaving her with her grief.

Once in front of the door that led back into the ER, I shook my hands out, swiped my badge, and stepped back onto the main floor.

The ache in my chest was quickly stored away by the chaos of the ER and I continued working, dealing with the back-to-back wave of patients flooding into the hospital until my shift ended.

After grabbing my things out of my locker, I made my way out of the hospital, but as soon as I stepped outside, my adrenaline quickly faded and was washed away by a bone-deep exhaustion.

Pushing it away once again, I walked over to my car and drove home.

I parked my car in my parents' driveway and shut off the engine, then threw the keys into the passenger seat.

Just one minute.

I leaned back into my seat and closed my eyes.

Tap.

Tap. Tap. Tap.

All the pressure that had built throughout the day and that I'd kept storing away finally swept over me.

You're going to be okay, Sienna, you always find a way to be.

I stayed silent until my minute was over. Then I wiped the streaks off my face, took a deep breath, grabbed my bag and keys, and made my way inside.

It was almost 10:00 p.m., so I knew my sisters and mother were already in bed since tomorrow was the *big* day, but I prayed my father had done the same and hadn't stayed up waiting for me instead.

I let out a sigh of relief when there were no signs of him.

Thank God.

I made a quick detour to the kitchen to grab a bowl of whatever my mom had made tonight. I quietly opened the cupboard above the stove and grabbed a large bowl. I scooped a few ladles of rice and added the *habichuelas guisadas* on top.

I skipped on heating it up to avoid waking anyone and retreated to my room. I was almost at my door when my name was called out.

Guess I spoke too soon.

"Sienna," my father called me from his office.

I peeked my head inside.

"Yes?" I asked grudgingly.

He gave me a small smile and gestured for me to come in.

I had a long day and wasn't up for any niceties, but I didn't want to seem disrespectful, so I pushed the wooden door farther open and walked in, my duffle bag in one hand, food in the other.

"Tomorrow's the big day," he stated as if I wasn't aware of my own wedding.

"I am aware of that fact, papá," I responded coldly.

His smile faltered and it drove a phantom fist to squeeze my middle.

Great.

He was the one who'd messed up, but I was the one who felt guilty for reminding him of it.

I wasn't a dreamer. Truthfully, I never had the chance to be, so I never imagined a fairy-tale wedding or being swept away by Prince Charming.

It always felt like true love wasn't in the cards for me, but despite that belief, I thought that if I decided to settle down, it would at least be with someone I respected and loved.

Someone I at least *knew*.

But tomorrow, I was marrying a stranger to ensure my family's safety because my dear father gambled it away.

"You know I'm s—"

"Don't," I said firmly, cutting him off.

It was too late to apologize now. The damage was already done.

He opened his mouth to say something else, but I stopped him before he could.

"If there's nothing else, I've had a long day."

When he didn't speak, I quickly told him good night and left his office. Once in my room, I locked my door and backed into it, a loud thump ringing in the space.

My phone pinged with a text. I set the bowl on my desk and placed my bag on the floor to reach for my cell phone in my back pocket.

I opened the thread in our group chat.

Kenna: Meet us at Fenice.

Me: It's late and I just got back from the hospital... I'm tired.

Esra: It wasn't a question, so, kindly, get your ass over here!

Kenna: Besides, you're getting married tomorrow so we must celebrate your last night as a single lady.

Me: Ugh, fine.

Esra: YAY! See you in a bit.

I had no desire to go out and had a strong dislike for packed spaces, but I knew if I didn't, they would both show up at my doorstep and haul my ass out whether I liked it or not.

Kenna and I had gone to medical school together. It had been a long and draining four years, but she'd made it bearable. She was currently in her final year of residency in Family Medicine at North Western, our competing hospital.

We'd met Esra during our third year of medical school after one of our intense study sessions. It had been late at night and we'd been walking out of the library when she'd bumped straight into me.

All of her stuff had fallen down, so both Kenna and I had bent down to help her pick up her things when she'd broken down in tears.

We'd barely heard a word she said, but all we'd needed to hear were the words ex and cheating. We'd gathered her things and had sat on the ground with her until her sobs had quieted down.

Then we'd all walked to the diner around the corner that was open 24/7 and ordered milkshakes and fries. We'd spent the rest of the night cursing her ex-boyfriend who'd cheated on her with her best friend and talked about anything and everything.

We'd been best friends ever since. They were family and my reprieve from home. Our relationship was one of the few aspects of my life that brought me any type of joy and peace.

Although I loved my family, being the eldest daughter came with a weighted anchor that was drowning me every day I spent in a place that I was supposed to call home.

I guess this union has a slight positive side to it.

I liked to believe my parents' intention wasn't to burden me, but the constant responsibility of taking care of everything they needed on top of raising kids I didn't give birth to, might I add, because they didn't care enough to do it themselves was becoming too much.

Every day, it was a different story to handle and that was a lot to ask for one person to deal with.

I scarfed my food down, hopped into the shower, and quickly got dressed before heading out to meet my girls.

Kenna and Esra were both waiting for me outside of Fenice, a new club that had opened a few weeks ago and had been the talk of the island.

My best friends looked like they could've stepped off a runaway. Kenna wore a burnt orange midi dress that complemented her dark skin, gold block heels strapped to her feet, and her box braids were in a half-up, half-down style.

Esra, on the other hand, wore a one-shoulder ruched maxi dress, the fabric molding to her curves, her brown hair falling over her shoulders in soft curls.

Esra threw her arms around my neck, hugging me tightly.

I chuckled and huffed out, "Easy, babe." But that only made her squeeze me tighter.

I wasn't much of a hugger, but you could never say no to an Esra hug, so I wrapped my arms around her and embraced her back.

"I haven't seen you in forever, so let me get my Sienna recharge," Esra said, smiling against me.

Kenna wasn't a hugger either, but she joined in, wrapping her arms around both of us. "She's right, you know. How long has it been since we last saw you? Like four weeks?" Kenna pointed out.

"We FaceTime almost every day."

Esra sighed, letting me go. "Yeah, but that doesn't count."

"I've just been busy with work. You know how residency is."

"Yes, but you've been working yourself to exhaustion, babe," Kenna said gently.

That was the point. If I was exhausted, I didn't have time to dwell on the shitshow that was my life.

Exhausted was good, safe.

"I'm fine, I promise," I dismissed, walking toward the main door to avoid dwelling on the look of pity they were both sporting.

The deep bass of a reggaeton song thrummed against my skin as we stepped into the packed bar. The entryway opened up to a dance floor that covered half of the first floor, the rest set up like a cocktail den. Red velvet booths with wooden round tables were scattered on the far walls, dim-lit lamps placed on top of each table.

Fenice was three stories tall, the famous private party rooms being on the top floor, a glass wall covering the front. The mixture of red-and-black walls along with the dark wooden accents behind the bar gave the place a secretive and forbidden atmosphere.

After ordering our drinks, we found our reserved booth along the back wall.

"So," Kenna started, pausing as she moved a few of her braids back before taking a sip of her martini.

"Ready for tomorrow?" Esra finished, her faint Turkish accent peeking through when she got nervous.

"As ready as I can be," I said, hoping I sounded convincing enough.

They both looked at me skeptically. I took a sip of my wine to avoid talking.

"Let's just hope he's good in bed."

My eyes darted to her and I swatted her behind the head. "Esra!"

"What?" She squeaked, rubbing the back of her head. "I mean, you've waited all these years. You deserve a little pleasure."

"*Or* you could find someone tonight," Kenna added.

Esra turned to her, scowling.

"Don't look at me like that. Mateo might be good-looking, but he might suck in bed."

An uneasy pang rang through my body at the thought of also having to give that up. It wasn't that I was particularly attached to my virginity or waiting for *the one*. I'd always been too busy to meet anyone and when I did, I just didn't want to go any further.

I never felt that *spark* or the intense desire to *be* with someone like everyone seemed intent on. Most times, I was indifferent to the men I dated, so it never felt right.

I didn't want my first time to be out of obligation. My marriage already was.

"Can you both stop talking about me like I'm not here? I'm not sleeping with Mateo or with anyone tonight for that matter."

"Sorry," they said in unison.

"You just work so much," Kenna started, her eyes filled with pity.

"We want you to be happy," Esra finished, wrapping her arm around my shoulder and giving it a small squeeze.

"I know, and I will be."

Eventually.

I didn't come here tonight to let self-pitying thoughts swarm in, so I downed the rest of my drink, plastered a smile to my face, and stood up.

"We need another round," I stated despite them not having made a dent in their respective drinks.

Before they got to answer, I spun on my heels and headed toward the bar. As I wove through the crowd, I felt the weight of being watched, but every time I looked up, no one was in sight.

Finally, I reached the bar and flagged down the bartender. "Another round for table three, please."

"Coming right up," he said, giving me a wink before turning around to prepare our drinks.

I watched him work when suddenly, I felt the woosh of

a breath skating over my bare shoulder. I turned around and tilted my head up to look at the culprit, giving him a once-over.

Blond slicked-back hair, a fitted three-piece Armani suit, and a shiny—fake—watch adorning his wrist.

By the look of it, he seemed to be in his mid-thirties. He was probably one of those investment bankers who worked a few streets over. They always came to Fenice to unwind after a long week of numbers, in search of someone to bring back home with them.

"Can I buy you a drink?" He gave me a smile that he probably thought was smoldering, but it was just creepy.

Men.

I pondered on the best way to brush him off but quickly decided that a direct approach would be best since most men rarely got the message when you were nice.

"No, I already got it. Thanks." I gave him a tight smile and turned my attention back to the bartender who was preparing our drinks.

Instead of leaving, he crept closer and placed his hand over my lower back.

"Come on, now. At least let me buy you another after you finish it." His hand inched farther down and it was now brushing the swell of my ass.

I shook my head to myself. What was it with men and them not processing the word "no"?

I subtly whipped around and grabbed his hand. Twisting it behind his back, I pulled him closer. "Listen, when someone says no, it means no. It doesn't mean maybe or later, it means *no*. I made a vow to save people, but I won't hesitate to break your radius because you don't know how to respect boundaries and want to impress your *buddies*."

He swallowed, his throat bobbing down, and nodded.

"Now, off you go," I said, releasing the hold I had on his wrist.

He pivoted around and left, finally getting the message.

I was glad the music was loud enough because our little *interaction* didn't seem to draw any attention.

I turned back toward the bar and sat on a vacant stool. While I waited for our drinks, the same feeling of being watched reappeared, but I brushed it off when the bartender came back, placing my order in front of me.

I grabbed my glass of wine and Esra's beer in one hand and held Kenna's espresso martini in the other. I walked back to our table and placed them down before sliding back into the booth.

"Thank you," they both said before they resumed their previous conversation. I didn't know when I'd zoned out of it, but I found myself perusing the floor, people watching.

The place was filling up by the minute. The previous remix shifted into a popular R&B song and the room came even more alive. A group of girlfriends with bachelorette party sashes were dancing on the main floor and belting out the lyrics while couples were sensually gyrating against one another.

They looked so carefree and I envied that. I didn't even remember the last time I felt like that, the last time I felt *free*.

I was in the midst of my musing when I felt the heat of someone's stare over my skin. I lifted my head and that's the moment I saw *him*.

He was sitting at the bar, a tumbler in hand, his arm lazily hanging on his thigh.

It was difficult to see him properly considering how packed the club was and the sultry lighting, but I didn't need to. His presence exuded an intoxicating aura that you couldn't help but be drawn to. It felt like an invisible line threaded between us, pulling me to him.

Like a moth to a flame.

When our gazes collided through the moving crowd, something swarmed in the pit of my stomach. Shivers of anticipation rushed down my spine and the hairs on the back of my neck lifted.

The brutality in his gaze sprouted goose bumps all over my skin and I shifted in my seat, crossing my left leg over my right. Heat swarmed over my body the longer his penetrating gaze roamed over my skin.

My mind wandered to possibilities.

What if I followed Kenna's advice?

I couldn't tell how long we kept looking at each other until Esra snapped me out of my haze. "Sienna, what do you think?" she asked and I broke eye contact and looked over at her.

"Sorry?" I said, startled.

Kenna leaned back against the leather booth, assessing me. Her eyebrows winged up at the expression my face must've been sporting. "Who were you looking at?"

I glanced back at where he was sitting, only to find him gone. I scanned the room, but there were no signs of him. "Oh, no one," I said, unexpected disappointment delivering a punch to my stomach. When I saw Kenna gearing up for a deeper interrogation, I changed the subject. "What were you saying?"

Kenna didn't push me any further and continued her previous train of thought. I pushed away the regret of not walking up to the stranger and joined their discussion.

Since I was off work tomorrow for the big day, we spent the next few hours catching up and talking about Kenna's upcoming wedding until it was almost closing time.

When I lay in bed later that night, I wasn't thinking about how I was signing my life away to a stranger tomorrow, but rather about how a different one had set my skin ablaze with a simple look.

CHAPTER 2

On. Off.

On.

Off.

My flicks were steady as I let the voices of our team fade into the background. They were discussing our newest potential client and I was only attending this meeting because I *had* to.

I always preferred delegating this part of the job to Kai since he was better at talking to our employees, whereas I preferred demanding, but we'd agreed to take turns on these meetings when we started the company and today was mine.

I pressed my finger down on the button, releasing the flammable gas and letting the flame dance against my skin.

It was something I'd been doing out of habit ever since I was a little boy.

Ever since that night.

My gaze was hypnotized watching the flames fold into themselves, feeding on the surrounding particles to burn brighter, hotter, *stronger* until it fulfilled its intended purpose. But at least this time, I was in control of how close it could get.

Control what it consumed.

I learned early on that life could change in the flick of a match. All it took was one little spark for everything to go up in flames until it was the only thing left standing on top of a pile of ashes.

How ironic was it that I craved the feel of fire in my hands when it had destroyed everything I'd ever loved. When twenty years ago, it had brutally murdered my parents and I'd barely escaped it.

Flames almost suffocated me, but now the flicker of a flame felt like the only effective balm for my nerves.

Before the fire, my father had been working on his latest case for months without any breakthrough when his director asked to bring on a fresh pair of eyes to help solve it.

Noah, who was well-known as the academy's prodigy at the time, had been assigned as my dad's new partner after successfully helping in a similar case during his training.

They had both been working on the case for a few

weeks when they'd found discrepancies that could finally lead to tangible grounds for an arrest. That same day, my father had left the office early to come home since it was my mother's birthday. Noah had, unsurprisingly, stayed behind since he had been—still was—married to his work.

In the middle of the night, he'd received a tip from one of his informants about a hit that had been ordered on our family. Despite him rushing over to our house to warn my father, it had already been too late.

He hadn't been able to go back for my parents, but he had got me out just in time before more damage was done.

Pressure.

That's the first sensation I was aware of as I regained consciousness. My head felt like it might explode.

I peeled my eyes open to see where I was, but the fluorescent light seared into my pupils, so I pinched them shut. An incessant beeping got louder, so I lifted my hand to shut my alarm, but tightness in my back prevented me from doing so.

My entire body ached.

Noah's voice broke through the fog I was under. "Jamal?"

I opened my mouth to answer him, but it was bone-dry.

"Let me give you some water," he said gently.

A straw poked at my lips and I sucked. The cool water soaked my parched throat and felt like the best thing I'd ever had.

I opened my eyes again and looked at my father's

partner and friend through blurry eyes. I tried to remember why he was here, and then, a flood of memories assaulted me.

The flames. Dad running. Mom right behind.

I looked behind Noah and around the room, but they didn't seem to be there.

"Where's Mama and Baba?" I asked, panicked.

I moved to sit but instantly collapsed, wincing in pain. My head fell back on the pillow.

"Don't move," he said sternly.

"Why are they not here?" I asked again.

"Jamal." *His voice trailed off, but the look on his face told me everything I needed to know.*

They were gone.

I stretched my back, my shirt suddenly feeling heavier against my skin.

On. Off. On. Off. On. Off.

The increased speed of my flicks matched my escalating heartbeats.

"Boss." Dania's voice cut through the thudding in my ears. "What do you think?"

I blinked away the unwanted memories before they swarmed in and clicked my Zippo's lid shut. The room came back into focus and I glanced up to find a room full of anxious and expectant expressions on our team's faces.

"I'll take this information to Kai to make the final decision," I announced, my eyes flicking to Dania, who looked like she was gearing herself for me to chew her head off.

"Mr. Gao is already up to speed on the client," she said hesitantly.

Then why the fuck am I here?

I checked my watch and noticed that it was almost time for another one of my meetings. I pushed my irritation down and turned my attention back on Dania.

I lifted a brow and muttered, "Any material that can be held against him?"

"Already sent to your inbox, sir," Dania answered, her knuckles almost turning white with how tightly she was gripping the notebook she was holding in her hands.

"Send the contract over to Mr. Williams and make sure that he understands what it means to sign with us."

"Yes, Mr. Brown," I heard her say as I left the conference to retreat to my own office for the rest of the evening.

Although I'd changed my last name a long time ago, I still felt a pang in my chest anytime someone called me by Noah's surname instead of my father's.

While I was stuck in a hospital bed for months, hooked to multiple machines and healing from the burns marring the entirety of my back, Noah had kept working on the case, trying to find legitimate proof to bring down whoever they were after since the lead he and my father had been working on had been shot dead immediately after his passing.

However, after weeks of unsuccessful raids, the bureau had removed him from the case because they deemed him unfit to remain objective on the matter. That's when we'd moved to Blackwell where Noah had been offered a training position at the academy.

On top of the relentless hours of self-defense and martial arts training, I'd never fully understood his insistence on changing my last name and staying hidden. He'd always just say, *"in case you find yourself in a bad situation."*

That belief only remained until I left for college and learned the real reason why.

The ding of the elevator doors opening pulled me from my thoughts. I didn't even remember working for the past few hours or even leaving my office.

The door slid open and I stepped out and into the private parking garage to head toward my car. Once inside, I turned the engine on and the screen of my dashboard flashed with an incoming call.

Kai.

Kai Gao was not only one of my partners, but he also happened to be a royal pain in my ass. But despite how aggravating he could be with his smart wits, he was one of the few people I trusted.

I grew up surrounded by agents and quickly learned that our world wasn't always what it seemed because people often wore masks to conceal their truths. Everyone had their own agenda and would do whatever it took to find themselves on the winning side because let's be honest, no one liked to lose.

And sometimes the people you love most are the ones keeping the most secrets from you.

Kai and I both attended the same university to get our computer engineering degrees. He'd only been there on an international student visa and originally planned to move back home to Taiwan to take over his father's company, but all of that changed when he sat next to me during one of my late nights I pulled at Navarra's library.

A night when he showed me that there were still a few selfless people out there and not everyone had a hidden agenda.

He'd lent me a helping hand during a period of my life when I needed it the most. But I'd never admit that to him because he'd never let me live it down.

My screen flashed again and I finally answered.

"Why did you make me attend the meeting if you already knew about the client?"

"Thought you needed to make an appearance at the office. After all, you do own half of the company," he answered, chuckling.

Ignoring him, I diverted his attention back to the reason for his call. "Why are you calling?"

"Guess who's getting married?"

"Enlighten me."

"Antoni Bruni is marrying off his eldest daughter to Mateo Barrera," he announced as my phone pinged with a notification.

Interesting.

"This is quite…" I paused, pulling my phone out of the breast pocket of my jacket to look over the details Kai had just sent me. "Unexpected. When's the wedding?" I finally replied in a clipped tone.

"Tomorrow evening at the Plaza."

Already?

"Start prepping. We have a celebration to attend," I ordered before ending the call.

My fingers traced over the steering wheel as I leaned back into my seat, contemplating what to do next.

When I learned the truth about my parents' murder, I knew the only way to get answers would be to somehow immerse myself into their world.

And money always talked.

Most of the people who dealt with the cartel were in serious debt, which was how I became known as The Collector. My deals were simple. I loaned money to whoever needed it and they needed to repay me by the time our term ended.

If that wasn't met, I had the right to collect a favor.

That's how Antoni Bruni landed on my radar.

A year ago, Bruni had requested my help to get out of his crumbling debts and our deal had been simple. I'd lend him the money he'd needed to pay back the client he'd *borrowed* from and he had a year to pay me back.

Instead of doing the right thing, he'd taken that money and gambled it away, probably thinking he would double it.

Such a pitiful man to let something so insignificant as money and pride ruin his family's future.

But he seemed to have forgotten what he owed me if the terms of our agreement weren't fulfilled.

He is about to find out just how good I am at keeping my promises.

I put my car into reverse and headed out onto the quiet streets, my thoughts inundated with the opportunity presented to me.

My other meeting would have to wait.

I looked out the floor-to-ceiling windows, searching through the crowded club for what I came here for.

I leaned a hand over the one-way mirrored glass, brought the whiskey tumbler in my hand over to my lips, and took a long pull from my drink.

There she is.

Sienna Bruni hadn't been too difficult to track. She rarely ever went out, and when she did, it was either for work or here at Fenice, which just so happened to be one of the many properties I owned.

Sitting with two of her friends in one of our reserved booths, she sipped from her glass of wine every once in a while, sporting a smile while the brunette next to her carried the conversation.

Nearing the end of her glass, she swiftly slid out of the black booth and made her way to the bar on her own.

She was wearing a black dress that softly hugged her curves, a drastic change from her usual blue scrubs. Her hair was pulled back from her round face into a ponytail, stranded curls escaping like she'd rushed while doing her hair.

Même à distance elle est magnifique.

But she didn't stay alone for long. As soon as she reached the bar, a man in a three-piece cheap suit pounced on her, a leering expression on his face.

The sight lit a match in my blood and an unwanted feeling flared in my chest. I left my office and made my way downstairs, reaching inside my pocket.

I settled on a barstool not too far from her to watch, but not close enough for her to see me.

On. Off. On. Off.

I kept going, but the feel of the metal flicking open strangely wasn't relieving the tension tightening my shoulders.

I couldn't hear their interaction over the loud music, but by the annoyed expression on her face, she was clearly not interested. She fended him off and turned her attention away from him to gesture for the bartender to place her order. But the unwanted man didn't seem to get the message.

Instead, the creep moved his body closer, this time placing a hand on her lower back. I was halfway out of my seat when she whipped around, grabbed his hand, and discreetly twisted it behind his back.

She pulled him closer and forced him to bend down to hear what she had to say. Although I didn't know exactly what she was saying to him, the look on his face told me everything I needed to know.

He finally got the message and quickly left, his bruised ego following sloppily behind.

The bartender refilled her glass and set our signature beer and an espresso martini on the counter with a napkin. I kept watching her in awe as she made her way back to her table and handed her friends their orders.

On. off.

I flicked my lighter's lid shut, then pocketed it.

I only realized I was still watching her when our gazes clashed. She shifted in her seat, crossing her left leg over her right.

A myriad of images of ways I could make her bend to my will flashed in my mind, but I pushed them aside, knowing the opportunity would rise again very soon.

She briefly turned her attention back to her friends and I took the opportunity to slide out of my seat and leave.

I would see her again soon enough.

Sienna

CHAPTER 3

I FELT SICK.

Today should be described as one of the happiest days of my life, but unfortunately, fate hadn't dealt me with the greatest card.

Or should I say my father hadn't.

He'd sealed my destiny when he'd decided to put his needs for prestige and recognition at the top of his priorities instead of protecting his family.

Instead of protecting *me*.

Growing up, I admired my father. He was loving, hard-working, and the best at his job. He'd worked for a small company for years before he'd been offered a promotion to work for one of the most influential families.

As a ten-year-old child, being moved into a bigger house and attending a fancier school with the best teachers the system could provide just meant I was one step closer to my dream of becoming a doctor.

Then, two weeks ago, I'd learned that my father had lied to me my entire life because when he got that famous promotion, everything went downhill.

Over the years, greed slowly consumed his intentions and he started skimming money from offshore accounts set up for his employers' more *private* business endeavors.

What's worse was that he firmly believed they wouldn't find out a few thousand were missing from their billions of dollars stashed away.

As if cartels don't closely track the ins and outs of their money.

But there was one thing my father learned a little too late.

You didn't cross the Barreras.

When they confronted him, he chose the easy road for him and blamed it on the authorities. They *were* in fact relentless in wanting to bring down the Barreras for the last twenty years, but they'd never found enough evidence to bring them in. So it couldn't have been them.

How did a twenty-six-year-old emergency medicine resident know all of this?

Well, my father not only sucked at covering his tracks, he also wasn't very aware of his surroundings when he spoke on the phone.

One night, after an already long and draining day at the

hospital, I came home to find out that my father wasn't the man I thought he was.

I never thought *my* father would turn out to be a coward.

My relationship with my parents wasn't the best by any means, but I always let go of their deceits, forgave them, and moved on. What else was I supposed to do?

They were my family.

Yes, I had Kenna and Esra, but they weren't blood. Family was family, even if they ended up being the people who'd hurt me the most.

But hearing him give me up so easily to pay his debt shifted something in me. That decision became one too many to forgive.

The course of my life was upset by simply overhearing a phone call where I'd discovered my father had been living a double life.

I could've said no, but who else would've taken on the responsibility? I couldn't let my mother and sisters bear the repercussions of my father's actions, let alone allow the Barreras to kill my father for betraying them.

So here I was, about to marry the son of the head of the Moroccan cartel to fix my father's mistake.

A soft knock came to the door.

"Sisi, are you ready?" my mother asked, walking into the small room where I was getting ready for the ceremony.

"As ready as I can be." I tipped my chin up and tried

mimicking her smile to soothe the worry etching the two deep lines on her forehead.

She sighed and caught my eye in the mirror. "I know this isn't how you pictured your wedding, but I'm sure Mateo will take good care of you."

Tap.

Tap. Tap. Tap.

Although I had my trials with my mother, I'd heard her fight with my father over his careless decision. But it was useless. We all knew there was no other choice.

I was sure my father hadn't shared the full ins and outs with her, but it didn't take much to figure out that I wasn't marrying into one of the most influential families for *love*.

Tap.

Tap. Tap. Tap.

"I know," I said, forcing my voice to sound surer than I felt. "As long as it keeps you, Akari, and Iris safe, that's what matters."

With a heavy sigh and a concerned gaze, she came up closer behind me.

"*Oh, mi hija hermosa.*" Her voice trailed off and she rested her hand on my shoulder.

Tap.

Tap. Tap. Tap.

I'd made my peace with this being my future, but the finality of knowing this would become my new normal never failed to nip at my chest.

My tapping slowed when fleeting memories of last

night and the ephemeral connection I had with the stranger flooded back into my mind.

It was so unusual and *tempting*.

What if I had gotten up and walked up to him? What if I had stopped overthinking about making the right choices and just *lived*?

I placed my hand over hers. "*No pasa nada, mamá. I've* made my peace with it."

She opened her mouth to say something, but I spoke before she could say anything else. "I'm almost done getting ready and will be right out to meet Dad at the entrance."

She placed a kiss on the top of my head. "All right, *mi amor. Te amo.*"

The words nipped further at my heart. I'd rarely heard her say them and hearing them in a situation like this was bittersweet. But I pushed it aside and said them back to her.

"*Yo también te amo.*"

She paused at the door and her eyes searched mine in my reflection in the mirror. She tried offering me a comforting smile, but all I could muster was a sad one.

When the door closed behind her, I stared at myself.

Today should've been described as one of the happiest days of my life, but it wasn't, and I didn't have it in me to pretend any further.

I finished applying a coat of mascara and dabbed some clear lip gloss over my brown-lined lips to complement my tanned skin. I usually didn't wear much makeup and decided that today shouldn't be any different.

Getting married already wasn't much of a choice, so I wanted to at least feel comfortable during the ceremony.

I gathered my curls and pulled them tightly off my face and into a taut bun at my nape before putting on small, chunky gold hoops that would match my shoes. Then I slipped into my dress—a simple off-white gown with a scoop neckline and dainty straps that effortlessly hugged my curves in all the right places—and stepped into my favorite gold heels, then strapped them to my feet.

I looked at myself in the mirror one last time to secure my veil right above my bun before stepping out of the room. I made my way to the main reception room where everyone was waiting for me, but my steps halted when I felt a presence behind me.

I whipped around to see who was there, but no one was in sight. I was about to round the corner when I noticed a shadow at the other end of the hallway, but it was only for a brief moment that I convinced myself I was imagining it.

No es nada, Sienna.

I was probably overthinking things, especially after hearing my parents argue when I came home late after my night with Kenna and Esra.

"¿Estás seguro de esto, Antoni? *What if he comes back?*" *I heard my mother say, her tone panicked.*

"Mia cara, *there's no need to worry. I promise I've got it all under control, Yanira,"* he said confidently, but I could hear the wavering fear beneath his words.

I wasn't sure which "he" they were referring to since I could barely hear the rest of their conversation after they moved farther into his office, but I just assumed they were talking about my future in-laws.

"You look beautiful," my father whispered once I reached the closed double doors of the ballroom.

I glanced over at him to find his eyes filled with unshed tears, his hands smoothing down over his tux. I'd never seen my father cry, and it chipped at the walls I'd put up when I learned about his deceit.

But this was his doing, so I looked away from him. Hooking my arm into the crook of his, I squared my shoulders and said, "Let's get this over with."

I knew I was being harsh, but I was getting tired of being nice and sparing everyone's feelings in spite of my own.

As I looked through the glass doors and down to the other side of the aisle where Mateo was waiting for me, my throat threatened to close up. I knew this day would come, and yet, standing here, it felt like I was diving head first off a cliff.

I wasn't ready, but I didn't have the privilege to be ready. I just had to be.

The ceremony was being held at the Plaza, one of the many hotels the Barreras owned. A cream carpet served as a segue from my old life and toward my husband-to-be. A few chairs flanked both sides of the aisle, flower arrangements decorating them. The setup was small and simple, but that's how I insisted for this wedding to be.

Both of our families wanted a much bigger ceremony, but I didn't see the point in spending money we didn't have on an event that didn't have a meaning beyond ink scribbled on a piece of paper. I'd become a master at masking my emotions, but I knew this day would already be draining, so the fewer people I had to put on a show for, the better.

The music started and two guards swung the doors open.

Then I walked toward my unwanted future, each step I took toward him setting my new reality in stone.

My free hand found the side of my thigh.

Tap.

Tap. Tap. Tap.

I felt the heat of everyone's stare and my plastered smile faltered under their perusal.

Tap.

Tap. Tap. Tap.

It'll be over soon, I reassured myself.

I tried looking for Kenna and Esra for support but remembered I'd told them to skip the wedding since this wasn't real. So instead, my gaze landed on my younger sisters.

Akari & Iris were both beaming at me because they

thought this charade was a happy event. That I was in love and about to marry the man of my dreams.

Sometimes, I wondered how was it that younger siblings seemed to never share the same weight of duty as the eldest did. Was it because we took it all upon ourselves or because it'd been imposed on us?

I forced my gaze away from them and shifted my attention to the Barreras' side where everyone looked at me with hope.

At least one side is excited about this union.

Omar Barrera, the head of the family, watched me expectantly from his front seat as my father handed me over to his son.

My father dropped a kiss to my temple and met Mateo's gaze, a pleading look in his eyes. "Please take care of my daughter," he whispered before clearing his throat and moving to his designated seat next to my mother.

I swallowed my emotion down and willed my trembling hand to stop shaking as Mateo wrapped his fingers around mine.

The room blurred out of focus and I finally fixed my gaze on my betrothed. He was wearing a simple black suit, a crisp white shirt underneath, and a black bow tie. His dirty-blond hair was combed back and he was wearing a small smile.

In other circumstances, I might have found him pretty, but being forced to marry him was kind of ruining his appeal.

The officiant cleared his throat and started the ceremony.

"We are gathered here today to witness the union of Sienna Bruni and Mateo Barrera."

He started babbling about the sanctity of marriage, its power, and the beauty of true love. I shut him out, not needing to hear him any longer. I was only here to say the two words that would seal my fate.

I do.

The urge to take my hand out of Mateo's and drum my finger against my thigh surged through me, but I couldn't do it without attracting attention. My heart thumped heavily against my rib cage, gearing up to make a run for it.

A sigh of relief escaped me when the time came for our vows.

"Do you, Mateo Barrera, take Sienna Bruni as your wife, from this day onward, for better or for worse, for richer or poorer, in sickness and in health to love and cherish until death do you part?"

"I do," he said without hesitation.

The officiant then turned to me. "Do you, Sienna Bruni, take Mateo Barrera as your lawful husband?"

My gaze met his.

Eyes glittering with fabricated lies, I opened my lips to add to the deceit by saying *I do*, but a voice erupted from the back of the room, interrupting me.

"Well, well, well," the intruder started, each word punctuated with a short clap. "Isn't this lovely?"

The smooth, deep voice sent a deadly thrill through my body. It had the barest hint of a French accent and I slowly turned my attention to where it was coming from.

Murmurs broke out from the audience while my eyes narrowed to try and find who was interfering before I was able to get this over with. I stared at the back of the room to find someone—a man—leaning against the doorframe of the exit door to the far left.

"Who's this?" my father and Omar asked simultaneously, both rising from their seats to face the intruder.

A dim light flickered and I watched the voice materialize into one of the most dangerously attractive men I'd ever laid eyes on.

He made his way toward us. Something about his presence consumed the room, something that went beyond his height and considerable bulk.

Power.

Precision.

Brutality.

My lips parted on a gasp, and for a long moment, all I could do was stare. My eyes swept over his features. Dark brown hair buzzed short, soft and inviting lips, and a stubble darkening the ridges of his strong jawline.

He was dressed in a dark navy suit that showcased his smooth brown skin. His pressed white shirt clung to his physique and the top three buttons of his shirt were undone, a small golden chain nestled around his neck. His thighs strained against his tailored slacks as he inched closer.

It was only then that I realized he was staring straight at me.

Dark piercing eyes locked with mine, daring me to defy them. Suddenly, something stirred in me, his familiarity demanding to break free in my mind.

The newcomer's gaze roamed over my body, searing my skin like he'd just set it on fire. I frowned, urging my brain to remember where I'd seen this man.

My eyes widened when the memory finally surfaced.

Him.

The man in front of me was the same man I'd seen last night at Fenice.

He shoved his hand into his pocket and fixed his gaze on my father as he delivered another blow to my life.

"Such a shame you don't remember me, Antoni. Especially after everything I've done for you." He paused and smirked. "I'm here to collect what's mine."

CHAPTER 4

"ARE YOU SURE YOU WANT TO DO THIS?" KAI ASKED, HIS brow furrowed with concern.

I stepped out of his gray McLaren and bent down to look at him. "Yes, I am," I said, closing the door and leaving him behind with his tools to run surveillance.

After coming home last night, Kai, Valentina, and I had met where they'd debriefed me on how we would infiltrate today's ceremony so that I could claim what I was duly owed.

We'd been watching over the ballroom where the ceremony was taking place over the last few hours. The few guests invited were already seated and Mateo was dutifully standing at the altar, waiting for his bride.

Not for long.

Kai and I had driven our own cars here—mine currently parked in the underground parking of the hotel—but we'd stationed in his since he had all the equipment installed in his car.

I attached my earpiece, turned it on, and headed toward the back entrance. Pausing at the door, I spoke to my sniper through the intercom. "Valentina, are you in place?"

"Am I not always?" she replied, her tone bored, while pointing the red dot at my heart.

Kai let out a soft laugh in the background.

"Just checking," I said, shaking my head. "Now, could you please divert your aim before you accidentally shoot me?"

"Why would it be accidental?" she stated, no ounce of humor in her tone.

Kai and I both met Valentina a few years ago when she'd tried to hack into our system to infiltrate one of our clients' files.

Although her hacking skills were—still are—remarkable, Kai's were better the day he found a loophole in her iron-clad firewalls and tracked her location. Knowing she'd be an asset with her wide array of skills, we'd offered her two options when we showed up at her doorstep.

Come work with us or turn her in to the authorities.

She'd immediately accepted when we mentioned the word authorities.

Now, years later, she was part of the only people I trusted with my life. *Literally*. She'd take down anyone before the thought of harming us crossed their minds.

I kept my circle small because in this world, it was the only way to stay alive.

I walked inside the hotel and cleared the other rooms on the floor before I headed for the side door of the ballroom. I stepped inside just in time to hear the first "I do." I leaned against the doorframe, gently closing the door behind me, and waited for the officiant to ask *her* the infamous question.

Unlike Mateo, she hesitated, which gave me the perfect opportunity to make my presence known.

"Well, well, well," I started, punctuating each word with a clap of my hands. "Isn't this lovely?"

"Who's this?" Antoni and Omar asked simultaneously, shooting out of their seats.

The dim light of the exit sign flickered above me and I stepped out of the shadows. As I walked toward her, my breath strangely caught in my throat when I took her in.

I'd caught a glimpse of her earlier when she came out of the room she used to get ready, but it didn't do justice to what was now in front of me.

Her simple off-white dress hugged her curves beautifully and fell to her feet. The neckline, although modest, molded and pushed her breasts in a way that had me salivating for more.

Her eyes found mine and a peculiar sensation slid up my spine.

Her brows furrowed and slowly, her eyes widened as she recognized me.

I stopped in the middle of the aisle and shoved my right hand into my pocket, letting the cool metal ground me. Then I flicked my gaze away from her and onto her father.

"Such a shame you don't remember me, Antoni, especially after everything I've done for you." I paused, the corner of my lips hiking up into a smirk. "I'm here to collect what's mine."

The temperature in the room plummeted.

Omar's hands curled into fists at his sides and Antoni's shoulders stiffened as he braced himself for what was about to unfold.

Barrera broke the silence first. "Antoni," he bit out, his eyes narrowing as he looked over at Sienna's father. Barrera's body was exuding rage in waves and the tension in the room could be cut with a blunt knife.

Before Antoni could respond, his daughter chimed in once my words finally filtered through her mind. "Collect?" she questioned, her gaze going back and forth between me and her father.

Dread settled over Antoni's features.

J'ai hâte d'être témoin du chaos que sa confession va créer.

"Sienna, forgive me," he said, giving her an apologetic look, his tone full of remorse.

"Forgive you for what, *Father*?" she muttered, spewing that last word. "What is he talking about?" she asked, furrowing her brows, attempting to put the pieces together.

I noticed movement at her side and looked down to find her index finger drumming against her thigh in a sequenced motion.

Interesting.

"You, love," I answered in his place, turning my attention to her.

Her tapping paused and she whipped her head around, glaring at me. She clenched her teeth and the drumming resumed. "I wasn't talking to you," she snapped right as Barrera's men came out of their hiding places and pointed their guns at me.

I tsked and fixed my gaze on the man who might be the answer I was looking for. "I wouldn't let your men do that if I were you."

"You don't know who you're dealing with," Omar replied in a cold tone.

Being face to face with Barrera made me want to put a bullet into his brain, but Kai's voice nagged at me to remind me that killing the head of the Moroccan cartel wouldn't bode well for me.

I'd never been told much about what had happened the night of the fire and since I had hit my head pretty badly that night, my concussion had caused the majority of my memories before then to grow blurred and distorted.

But throughout the years, fragments of the past, of

whispered arguments between my parents fought back to be remembered.

Noah had always reassured me that there was nothing to worry about and that the fire was accidental, but something deep inside pushed me to look further into it because things weren't adding up.

Their case files were sealed, but since the media was in a frenzy back then at the bureau coming after such an influential family, I was able to find who my dad and Noah were after.

The Barreras.

However, the cartel was only a piece of the puzzle. I needed to find out exactly who had ordered to turn my family into ashes.

"I know exactly who I'm dealing with, which is why the more you prolong your little"—I waved my finger around the room, pointing at his men—"theatrics, the worse it'll be for you."

Omar nodded at his men and their fingers twitched over their respective triggers. "I—"

I cut him off. "Why don't I save us some time and tell you exactly how this is going to go. I just need to grab Sienna, since her dad owes me, and you can all go back to enjoying the rest of your evening."

"And what if we don't?" Omar's tone was condescending. He thought he had the upper hand, but he was about to find out just how wrong he was.

Let's toy with him a little.

"Open your accounts and see for yourself."

He laughed at me. "What accounts?"

I didn't dignify his foolish question with a response and quirked a brow up.

He laughed at me again, but it quickly died down when I didn't react to his patronizing behavior. He gave me an incredulous look. "You're lying."

I tilted my head. "Why don't you see for yourself."

Barrera took his phone out of his suit pocket and I watched him log into his banking accounts. His eyes flew to my face and the blood drained from his complexion once he realized what was happening. He wasn't laughing any longer.

I gave him a sly smile.

"You son of a bitch."

"Oh dear, no need for such foul language. Now." I paused for dramatic effects, enjoying watching him squirm. "Every minute that passes, a hundred thousand will be withdrawn from your account."

Mateo's eyes narrowed. "You can't take her. There's an agreement in place," he said, his voice attempting to be threatening.

Comment je déteste quand quelqu'un me dit quoi faire.

My patience started slipping and I propped my foot over one of the empty chairs on the side. Then I rested my right elbow on my knee and crossed my other arm over it, leveling him with a stare. "I can and I *will*."

Mateo lunged for me, but his father's hand gripped his shoulder before he could move an inch. "Stand back," Barrera told him through gritted teeth. Then he pinned me with a glare and added, "She's not worth that much money."

Mateo reluctantly listened and shrugged his father's hand off him, straightening his suit back in place.

Sienna finally seemed to be catching up to what was happening because she finally broke her silence. "You never stopped, did you?" she asked through gritted teeth, glaring at her father.

If looks could kill, he would be completely incinerated by now.

"Sienna…" His voice trailed off.

She took a step back as if his unspoken confession had physically slammed into her. Her eyes drifted closed for a moment and she winced. When her eyes popped back open, the hurt expression on her face morphed into a dark hatred in a matter of seconds.

She stepped toward her father and pointed an accusatory finger at him. "You fucking sold me twice."

His eyes widened. "Sienna, language," he said sternly.

Her intense gaze bore into his. "Do *not* Sienna me. You don't get to do that."

"I didn't sell—"

"Then what the *hell* do you call this, *papá*? I was already marrying Mateo to save our family, but you're telling me this isn't the first time you gambled my future away because you couldn't take care of your family on your own."

Mateo had long since moved away from Sienna's side, cowering behind his father, leaving her all alone at the altar. So while she was distracted yelling at her father, I came up behind her.

"Your father isn't a very clever man, is he, love?" I whispered.

She swung around and her amber irises flared with irritation. "I won't be going anywhere with you," she bit back. "And do *not* call me that."

I loomed over her and she canted her chin up. "I will call you whatever I please, *love*," I drawled. "You're mine."

"I am not yours," she retorted, raising her hand to hit me.

I caught her wrist before her palm made contact. The warmth of her skin seared into my palm, branding me. I didn't know what overtook me to do what I did next, but I brought her flush to my body.

I lowered my head to hers, my mouth brushing the shell of her ear. "What is it? Am I not to your liking?"

I pulled back and our gazes locked. A dark flush spread over her cheeks and her eyes blazed with a fire that matched the one igniting my insides from her proximity. Her throat flexed with a swallow when my thumb softly brushed against her erratic pulse point.

"No," she said, tilting her chin up in defiance, but the word came out strained.

She struggled against my grasp, but I held her tighter against me. A muscle ticked in my jaw at her response and my pulse roared, sweeping every ounce of logic or rationality aside.

I curled my free hand around the back of her neck, hovering my lips over hers. "Let's fix that, shall we." My voice came out so low and dark, I barely recognized it.

"What?"

I turned my attention to the officiant, who had been standing still this whole time.

"Finish the ceremony," I ordered.

He rubbed the back of his neck. "Sir, this is—"

I reached inside my suit with my free hand and interrupted him before he could finish by aiming the barrel at him. "I wasn't asking for your opinion."

She yanked her wrist out of my grasp and put distance between us. She stared at me for a long moment before a laugh bubbled up her throat.

"You are completely delusional if you think I'll marry you."

I cocked an eyebrow and took a step forward until her front grazed mine again. I grabbed her chin between my thumb and forefinger and slightly tilted her head back.

I leaned in and whispered low, only for her to hear, "Now, listen very carefully because I strongly dislike repeating myself and my patience is already running quite low, love. Either you do as I say, or your family will pay the price I'm owed." I pulled back to look into her warm brown eyes. I wiggled my gun in her family's direction. "One way or another."

She tried masking her reaction but couldn't disguise the shiver rippling through her. Her defiance was only superficial.

She was afraid of me.

And I liked it.

After a moment, her resolve vanished and she nodded. "If I do this, you have to promise me that you'll protect them from the Barreras."

I gave her a curt nod before letting go of her chin.

She shook her head. "You have to say it."

"I promise."

She gave me a curt nod at my assurance. I holstered my gun and looked over at the officiant again. "Proceed."

"What's your name, sir?" he asked, his eyes locked on Sienna.

"Jamal."

He cleared his throat and whispered, "Jamal…" His voice trailed off, waiting for me to give him my full name.

"Just Jamal. And skip straight to the I dos."

Then he finally started the impromptu ceremony.

"Do you"—he paused, his forehead wrinkling with uncertainty—"Jamal, take this woman to be your wife?"

My gaze trailed over to my future wife. "I do."

The officiant turned his gaze to Sienna, giving her a compassionate look before asking, "Do you, Sienna Bruni, take this man to be your husband?"

There was a small pause before she took a deep breath and nodded. "I do."

Her answer strangely rattled a sentiment of satisfaction within me.

Mine.

We were finally pronounced husband and wife. "You may…um, you may kiss the bride," the officiant said hesitantly.

I dipped down and gently brushed my lips against hers. It was only meant to be a chaste kiss, just enough to seal our union, but the moment my lips touched hers, any restraint I was holding on to snapped.

My body felt like it had been asleep for the past thirty years and all of a sudden, every single sense in me had been awoken.

Sienna placed a hand on my chest, and her kiss was hesitant, but I grabbed the back of her neck and yanked her closer, swallowing her protests by deepening the kiss.

My tongue slipped into her mouth and I could feel her giving in, her arguments turning into a delicious moan.

Fuck, she tastes good.

I gripped her harder, losing track of where we were and who was watching.

Her tentative tongue met mine and I found myself craving every single one of her tastes, desperate to savor her in every way possible. Which was when I pulled away because this was a simple business transaction and I couldn't allow myself to want *anything* when it came to her.

I hadn't intended to kiss her like that, but there was no stopping me. As soon as our lips connected, I reacted on instinct. And the only thing my body was directing me to was claiming what was mine.

Our gazes met for a brief moment and the hint of lust hiding behind her eyes wasn't lost on me.

The officiant cleared his throat and hesitated before saying, "The bride and groom, everyone."

We turned to face a befuddled crowd.

I heard a slight click fill the room, but before I reached underneath my suit jacket again, the glass on the far left window broke and a scream of agony filled the space.

Well done, Valentina.

I pushed Sienna behind me, covering her with my body. Then I grabbed her wrist, pulling her behind me toward the emergency exit as everyone brought out their weapons again.

After I'd gotten Sienna out safely, I gave the altar one last glance, finding Mateo on his knees with a bloodied hand held to his shoulder.

He looked up, rage transforming his features. "*N3al—*"

I shut the door behind me, cutting the rest of his sentence.

Sienna tried to wrench herself free from my grip, but I held her tighter, walking toward my car.

"I have to go back in there," Sienna shouted, resisting.

"No, you don't. You're coming with me."

"But my fam—"

I turned around so abruptly, she flinched backward.

"Would you just stop fighting me already?" I groaned.

What had I gotten myself into?

This is why you don't make rash decisions, my mind reprimanded me.

I sighed and loosened my grip. "Your family is just fine. It was someone on my team who took the shot and they won't do anything to your family unless I say so."

She finally stopped her fighting enough for us to make it to the parking lot beneath the hotel.

I let go of her hand, unlocked my car, and lifted the door open for her.

"Get in the car," I ordered. "And do not force me to make you, Sienna," I added before she could protest.

She muttered something inaudible in Spanish under her breath and got in the car, settling into the passenger seat.

Kai spoke into my ear as I rounded the car. "Jamal, what the hell was that?"

"I'll see you guys at home," I said, dismissing him. I cut communication before they said anything else, turning off and throwing my earpiece into my pocket.

I was well aware that hasty decisions never led to

anything good. I'd never made a decision unless I analyzed every angle of a situation as well as its probable results.

But for the first time in my life, I let impulse take over.

I let *someone else* dictate my next move.

But Sienna Bruni was infuriating and all I wanted to do was infuriate her even more.

Guess I'm a married man now.

CHAPTER 5

I was married.

And I didn't even know his last name.

I watched my new *husband* as he pulled out of the parking garage. He had one hand on the steering wheel, the other on the gearshift as he shifted and flew through the city's streets.

This, *he*, was my new reality.

Everything in me screamed to fight it, but I couldn't bring myself to let my younger sisters get caught in the crossfire of my father's poor judgment.

I'd made the decision long ago that I didn't want to take part in the world my father had thrust us into when I saw what it did to others. But that didn't change the fact that it still relied on alliances that stemmed from three things—money, power, or like in this case, marriage.

But alliances always came at a cost.

I knew I was the only thing standing between my family and their safety when I'd agreed to this, so I went into today with one task to accomplish.

Get married to Mateo Barrera.

But I hadn't expected *this*. My father had used me as a pawn to fix the consequences of his own selfish mistakes.

Again.

I felt blindsided.

Betrayed.

Was I ever his daughter or just an object to barter with for protection?

I shook myself out of my thoughts and after burying my surging resentment deep inside as I always did, I took a closer look at the man sitting next to me.

There was no denying how infuriatingly beautiful he was. I was starting to resent it, to resent how dominating his presence was, how it flooded the space around us until it was the only thing I could think of.

But unlike last night, Jamal felt completely closed off. I noticed the tightness in his grip over the steering wheel, the tic in his jaw, and the slight pinch between his brows.

Annoyance clawed at my chest from his suddenly cold demeanor. *I* was the one forced into this, not the other way around.

I flicked my gaze back to look outside, only to realize that we were driving out of the city. "Where are we going?" I asked, breaking the tense silence suffocating the air.

He slid a brief glance in my direction before focusing his attention back on the road. "Home."

The foreign word made my stomach churn. Although I'd lived in a house with my family all my life, it never felt like a home. It never felt like a safe place for me to just be. Instead, as each year passed, it became a place where something was always expected of me.

A place where I only existed when it was beneficial to them.

"You don't say," I snarked, wanting to rid myself of the growing sorrow. "And where is that?"

"You'll see when we get there."

That's informative.

I opened my mouth to ask more questions, but he turned his gaze on me, this time pinning me with a cold stare. "Listen, Sienna. I have no desire to argue with you right now. Either you remain quiet or I'll find something to occupy that mouth of yours until we get there."

An unfamiliar warmth spread through my body and pooled at my core in response to the low tone in his warning. Flashes of discarded clothes and frenzied touches rapidly blazed through my mind. Despite my lack of experience, my imagination always loved to run wild with scenarios.

I cleared my throat and managed a low scoff as I nodded.

I fixed my eyes back on the road ahead and watched the city blur before my eyes. The drive to his place seemed to drag on, but when the car slowed to a stop in front of heavily guarded black steel gates, it didn't feel like long enough.

How does it always seem that I get dealt the worst cards?

Jamal reached into the left side of his seat. My gut tightened as I watched the doors swing open, waiting for what they would reveal.

Once opened, he drove up a strip of concrete with tall topiary trees on either side covering what was beyond. The road eventually thinned to a driveway and my breath caught in my lungs at the sight that came into view.

Holy shit.

The two-story house, or should I say mansion by the size of it, was a mix of dark stone and black beams. The large floor-to-ceiling windows had black frames encasing them and modern lights were scattered over the house, accentuating the dark structure.

The carport under the left side of the house had two identical cars to Jamal's already parked under it, one gray and the other a deep red. He swung into the empty parking space next to them and climbed out of the car, then rounded it to open the door for me.

"I could've done it," I grumbled under my breath.

My instincts were always geared toward being agreeable, but something about this man made me want to fight him at every turn. I knew it wasn't rational, but nothing about our situation or how he made me feel was.

He ignored my comment and closed the door behind me once I'd slipped out. He started heading for the door, but for some reason, I couldn't seem to move. I stayed rooted in place, watching my *husband* walk toward what would now be my new home.

The thick, wet air washed over my skin and I inhaled sharply, the salty air filling my lungs. Suddenly, reality seemed to finally crash into me.

I snorted, letting out a startled laugh.

This was far from being funny, but I seemed to always laugh at the most inconvenient times. I looked over at Jamal, only to find him watching me with a puzzled look on his face from the front door.

That only seemed to spurt more laughter out of me until wetness blurred my vision.

"Are you done?" he asked, his brows furrowed.

I cleared my throat and wiped the corners of my eyes with my ringless ring finger. "Yeah, sorry," I said, recovering from my fit of laughter. I took another deep breath and walked over to him.

I expected him to reach into his pockets for a set of keys, but when I peered over his side, I watched him place his thumb on a screen above the handle.

"Little much, don't you think?"

He glanced at me over his shoulder and rolled his eyes. "That way the only way for someone to get in is with my dead body."

Well, that's... intense.

A click resonated in the air and he swung the door open, leading us inside. I followed right behind, then stopped in my tracks. If I thought the outside was impressive, the inside was even more so.

An enormous entryway, dark wooden floors, and charcoal blue walls with molding accents. The ground floor was an open-floor layout with a dining room on the right and a lounge room at the center. The open-floor plan gave a straight shot all the way to the back of the house where floor-to-ceiling sliding glass doors opened to an infinity pool overlooking a hill of greenery.

My eyes flitted to the left, under the U-shaped staircase, where an open entryway led to a shadowy hall that had what looked like a glass door at the end. The right was similar, but this time, you could barely make out the end of the simple straight hallway.

Everything here was large. I'd seen luxurious houses before, but this was beyond what my imagination could've conjured. I was too lost in admiring the fine furnishing and artwork that I'd barely noticed the addition in the room.

"Hello," someone said, the voice drawing my attention to the man now standing in front of me.

What are these men consuming to look this fucking attractive?

The man in question was at least a foot taller than my five-foot-three. He had thick dark hair, high cheekbones, and short subtle covering his jaw. He was wearing a navy blue cable knit sweater and dark gray slacks, hints of tattoos peeking through the hem of his sleeves on his wrists.

After briefly glancing at Jamal, he finally turned his attention to me. He gave me a warm smile, his dark brown eyes glinting with amusement. "It's a pleasure to meet you, Sienna. I'm Kai, Kai Gao," he said, his hand outstretched.

Unlike my new husband who radiated a callous energy, a light, more playful wave emitted off this one.

For the first time today, my lips formed a genuine smile. "It's nice to meet you too, Kai," I responded, shaking his hand.

I felt Jamal tense beside me.

"When you're done, come see me in my office. We have things to discuss," he ordered. Then, without waiting for a response, he walked away and stepped into what I assumed was his office, already dialing someone on his cell.

This is going to be fun.

I rolled my eyes at his retreating form. "*Qué agradable*," I murmured under my breath while lifting the skirt of my dress to take off my heels, then held them in my right hand.

"You get used to it," he answered, chuckling.

My eyes widened in surprise as I asked, "You know Spanish?"

"Yes, among other languages," he said matter-of-factly.

Before I could ask him to elaborate, he kept going, "Now come, I'll show you around."

"You both live here?" I turned around slowly, taking everything in while Kai stood in the middle of the living room.

"Yes, we each have our own wing. You and Jamal will be living here while Valentina and I share the other side of the house."

Valentina?

I must've said the question out loud because Kai answered, "You'll meet her soon enough."

"Is she your girlfriend?" I asked, since he didn't have a band on his ring finger.

A deep flush bloomed across his cheeks. "Oh no, we're just colleagues," he said, clearing his throat and turning his back to me.

Interesting.

I smirked to myself and returned to my previous perusal. Although the place was well-decorated with expensive furnishings, I noticed how every item was displayed in a calculated manner.

The couch was leather and looked like the most comfortable place to nap on but appeared to have never been used. Even the large TV sitting above the fireplace seemed brand-new.

The only room that looked remotely used was the kitchen.

He stepped into it next and placed his elbows over the

island, tapping his finger against the black marble counter-top. "You're welcome to anything in the kitchen, but there's usually meals ready in the fridge for the week. You just need to warm them up. If you have allergies or preferences, let us know."

"Oh, that's okay. I can manage myself."

"I'm sure you're more than able, but Jamal doesn't like it when we mess with his kitchen. It's better if you let him know, and he'll prepare it for you."

My brows knitted in confusion. I met his eyes with a surprised look on my face. "Wait, he's the one who cooks? I just thought that with all of this," I said, gesturing around the room, "someone else who would've done it."

"It's just us here," he said, but his tone seemed different this time. He quickly gave me another smile and placed a hand on my elbow, guiding me toward the large staircase that led upstairs. "Let me take you to your room," he proposed.

"It better not be the same as his," I scoffed, which drew a laugh from him.

He shook his head once, then said, "Don't worry, you'll have your own space."

Menos mal.

My shoulders relaxed. Being married to Jamal was one thing, but sharing a bed with him wasn't something I was ready for. Especially since I'd never shared a bed with anyone before.

"This way." He led us up the steps and once we reached

the upper floor, he veered to the left and headed down the long hall. He opened a door on the left and I trailed inside after him. "This will be your room."

Unlike the darkness that the rest of the house seemed to bask in, this space was anything but. Cream-colored walls, matching lush silk bedding, and white oak floors. But despite the lightness in the colors, the room also felt devoid of life.

It was clear no one had ever stayed in here.

My gaze roamed over the room as I drifted farther inside. A massive bed sat in the middle of the room with a large bookcase along the opposite wall, a sliding ladder attached to it.

Putting a hand in his pocket, Kai said, "There should be everything you need here, but we can also have your things delivered if you'd like."

"Thank you," I said solemnly, offering him a smile.

"If you need anything, you just have to ask. We work most of the day, but we'll be around."

"I'll need to drive to the hospital," I said, hoping to segue into being able to have my car back.

"You can use one of o—"

"I'd prefer my car if that's okay," I cut him off. It might not be the luxurious kind they drove, but my car was my little safe haven and I'd worked hard to get it.

He dipped his head in understanding. "I'll take care of it."

"Thank you," I said, appreciative.

Kai turned around to leave, but he halted when his hand rounded over the doorknob. He was quiet for a moment, his brown eyes working over my face. It wasn't until our gazes met that he pleaded, "Just give him a chance, will you?"

The door clicked shut behind him before I could ask him to elaborate, leaving me alone for the first time since this morning. His words didn't come as a shock because they were friends, but I couldn't imagine Jamal and me ever getting along.

Besides, it'd be easier to hate him. At least, that's what I chose to believe.

I counted to ten before finally letting out the breath I'd been holding since I'd said "I do." I looked up at the ceiling, blinking as I rubbed the knot in my chest. "*Qué carajo?*" I cursed out loud as the adrenaline running through me slowly faded and reality hit me like a sledgehammer to the chest.

I dropped my heels next to the door and fell onto the bed. Onto *my* bed.

In my new room. In my new *home*.

I breathed in and out to get my heart rate down. I was surprised I hadn't had a fucking heart attack after what just happened.

We can't lose it. Distract yourself.

My eyes floated over to the bookshelves, noticing they were filled with various genres of books and even medical textbooks. Two doors were on either side of it, so I slid off the bed and ventured to the one on the right, the one closest to the entry door.

Holy shit.

This was by far the biggest walk-in closet I had ever seen. Even Esra's massive closet was nothing compared to this.

Who needed this much space for clothes?

The room was plastered with large floor-to-ceiling glass doors and a mirror decorated the far wall, making the room look even bigger. A plush white carpet lay in the center of the closet with a cream bench with golden legs atop it.

I glanced inside through one of the glass doors and surprisingly found it was filled with clothing. Dresses. Shirts. Pants. Everything was color-coordinated and organized to perfection. I explored further until my eyes landed on clothes that I hadn't expected here. My eyebrows lifted.

Are those scrubs?

I opened the glass doors and sifted through the clothes, wondering who they belonged to, only to realize they were all *my* size.

A reminder of what he'd said at the wedding resurfaced.

I'm here to collect what's mine.

He'd prepared for my arrival. I didn't know whether I should be furious at him for stampeding into my life or flattered that he'd taken the time to cater this room to have things that would be familiar to me and have a closet full of clothes that fit me.

Shaking my head, I took a deep breath. I slipped into

the en suite bathroom from the door connecting both spaces and hopped in the shower to rinse this day off.

This morning, I knew today would be one of my least favorite days.

What a fucking understatement that was.

Sienna

I RUMMAGED THROUGH THE DRAWERS TO FIND SOMETHING more comfortable to wear before I faced my husband again.

I let out a disgruntled huff.

Husband.

I couldn't believe I had one of those now.

Out of the few casual clothes in the closet, I went with an oversized black T-shirt and a pair of wide-leg navy blue yoga pants. After slipping on long black socks, I took one last look at myself in the mirror and headed downstairs.

As I walked down the hall toward Jamal's office, I noted an opening farther down to the right, which I assumed led to a basement, but I pushed my curiosity away and faced the door he'd pointed at earlier.

Sucking in a deep breath, I straightened my spine, rapped my knuckles against his door as a courtesy, and cracked it open, revealing the dimly lit office.

Dark oak standing shelves ladened with books adorned the entire back wall of the room, glass doors encasing each of the opposing ends. My attention snagged on a picture frame sitting on one of the lower shelves in the middle.

It was a photo of Jamal and Kai, the scenery behind suggesting they were at the beach. Kai's arm was slung over Jamal's shoulder and it had to be a few years back because they both looked much younger and Jamal was sporting an expression I had yet to see on him.

Not that I think he could be capable of exhibiting anything remotely similar now.

The boy in the picture was a complete contrast to my now husband. There used to be a lightness to his features, but the man sitting in front of me seemed like he held the weight of the world on his shoulders.

A flicker of sorrow always flashed behind his hardened mask.

Maybe Kai was right. Maybe there was more to the man than what he showed the world. Maybe…

"I'll call you later," he said harshly to whoever was on the other end of the line.

Never mind.

The chair swiveled around and his dark eyes landed on mine. I tried very hard not to find him attractive.

Tried being the keyword.

I tried and kept failing because my husband inexplicably made my heart stutter.

I didn't like it.

It never did that before, so why all of a sudden did it beat faster for a man I was supposed to resent? Besides, he was looking at me like he wanted to rip my head off, and that's what I should be focusing on instead of my traitorous body's reaction to him.

"You wanted to see me."

He stared at me for a few seconds, then ordered, "Sit."

I sat rigidly on one of the two black leather accent armchairs opposite his desk.

Jamal's eyes roamed over my bare face, studying and examining every inch. I shifted in my seat at his scrutiny, my right hand moving to rest on my thigh. His eyes narrowed on me and my fingers found a stray thread peeking at the side seam of my pants.

I twirled it around my finger and watched my index finger blanch to avoid his searing glare. Then I released it and repeated the action.

Finally, he cleared his throat then said, "I have some rules you'll have to abide by while you're here."

I abandoned the thread I'd been playing with and my eyes snapped back to him. "Rules?"

"Yes, rules."

I let out a disgruntled huff. "Listen, if you're about to order me around, I'll leave now." I jumped to my feet, but before I could storm out of the room, he'd gotten out of his seat and rounded his desk, sitting at the edge.

I stood still.

His annoyance bubbled in the air. "Sit down, Sienna. I wasn't finished," he ordered, his voice hard.

The way he said my name, his voice dipping on the last syllable, made my stomach clench and my eyes moved instinctively to his mouth.

No! No, no, no, Sienna.

I needed to leave the room. Immediately. I turned around, but his hand wrapped around my wrist. I faced him and tried to yank my wrist out of his grip, but he only held it tighter.

He tilted his head to the side and pinned me with a glare. "I said. Sit. Down," he repeated with the same tone.

A small chill traveled down my spine at the sound combined with the feel of his touch. He hadn't touched me since, well, earlier, and I thought it was an anomaly then, but his touch still made my skin prickle in goose bumps.

I smothered a hard swallow, my eyes never leaving his. "Wasn't marrying you enough?"

"The rest of our lives will be pretty entertaining if my wife is this easy to rile up," he said more to himself than to me. He let go of my arm and I pulled it closer to my chest, my other hand rubbing where his hand previously was, trying to get rid of the residual sensation his touch left behind.

He propped himself against his desk, crossing his arms above his chest. "But to answer your question, you were mine, so it doesn't count." He motioned for me to sit down with a flick of his hand.

I broke our eye contact and sat down. My gaze landed on the envelope opener on the corner of his desk, imagining what it would be like to stab him with it to try and distract myself from what him calling me 'his' made me feel like.

I took my eyes off the envelope opener to look at him again, only to find him looking me up and down, appraising me.

"Then talk," I said, unable to bear his scrutiny any longer.

"My rules are simple. Number one. Since we're married, we'll need the outside world to believe we're actually happily married. Which means you'll be required to accompany me to any social event I need to attend."

Required? Who does he think he is?

"I'm a resident. I can't just fit my schedule to your needs."

"We can work around it."

Well, that was easy.

"Fine, anything else, *sir*?" I say, stubbornly crossing my arms over my chest.

"You're free to come and go as you wish, but I need to know where you'll be at all times. And before you argue, it's for your safety."

"But—"

He chuckled, and the sound was entirely patronizing. As if me wanting agency over my own life was amusing. His gaze turned dark as he placed his hands over the arms of the chair I was sitting on.

"No buts, love. Displease me, and I'll punish you. Defy me, and I'll punish you. Do you understand?"

I shifted in my seat, his proximity rousing something inside me that I would have rather not defined right now. But his scent of musk and a hint of vanilla warped my senses, and I fought the urge to grab his tie and bring him closer, to discover what type of punishment he was threatening me with.

I didn't know how long we stayed that way, but I finally shook myself out of the haze he'd induced me in and replied with a strained, "Yes." Then I blurted out, "No kissing, unless it's absolutely necessary."

He loosened his grip on the right arm of the chair and twirled a strand of my hair around his finger before tucking it behind my ear. He dipped his head toward me until his lips found the shell of my ear, his breath teasing my skin.

My heart was beating wildly in my chest, my breath halting as I awaited his next move. I'd never kissed anyone before. Well, before him. And I found myself wanting to repeat what happened earlier.

I felt myself tilt my chin, but his next words sent a cold shiver down my spine, bringing me back to reality.

"I wasn't intending to," he whispered, his dark eyes dropping to my mouth.

My palms connected with his chest and I pushed him off, embarrassed that I felt anything for this infuriating man. "*Cabrón.*"

There's a small frown that formed between his eyes

when he caught the expression on my face and his face momentarily softened, but the sound of the door opening cut off whatever he was about to say.

"Everything okay in here?" Kai asked, looking back and forth between us with concern.

I shot out of the chair, straightening myself. "I was just leaving." I stopped beside Kai, dropping a hand over his shoulder. "Good night, Kai. Thank you for everything."

Then I made my way back to my room, pushing what just happened to the back of my mind and focusing on my upcoming shift tomorrow at the hospital.

Jamal

CHAPTER 7

"You okay?" I heard Kai ask.

Thank you for everything.

Thank him, why did she thank *him*? She was *my* wife.

I swallowed harshly, trying to rid myself of the acidic tang on my tongue. I cursed under my breath before straightening my spine and looking up at Kai. "What do you want?" I snapped at him from behind my desk.

He watched me warily and I didn't blame him. I rarely lost my temper or even raised my voice at anyone, but Sienna seemed to have rattled it out of me.

I let out a slow breath, propping my fists over my desk. "Yes, everything's fine," I huffed out.

He raised a brow, conveying he didn't believe me.

I hated how well he could read me. It usually was quite helpful since we worked so closely together and I didn't particularly enjoy talking to people, but it was rather inconvenient in moments like these.

"Drop it," I said. "Please."

"Fine, but you know you don't have to be an asshole." He took a seat in one of the leather chairs on the other side of my desk. Propping his ankle on his knee, he said, "She's a very sweet girl."

I glanced up at him, my irritation flaring back up. "How would you know how sweet she is?" I gritted through my teeth.

He lifted a brow. "Jamal, don't start. You know what I meant."

I ran a hand over my face. "I know. I'm sorry."

He chuckled. "You're lucky I'm used to your tantrums by now. Wanna talk abo—"

"There's nothing to talk about," I cut him off, knowing he would dig close enough to uncover how she made me feel. Changing the subject, I asked, "Did you get it? Did Valentina get the device on their vehicle?"

Kai shifted in his seat and by the expression on his face, I already knew the answer. "She followed his car after they left the church but couldn't get close enough to get a clear shot and lost him on the highway."

"What do you mean lost him? That was our best opportunity," I bit out and slammed a fist on top of my desk. Running my hands on top of my head, I turned away from him, trying to rein in my irritation. "He was *right* there. How did she fucking lose him?"

Valentina chose to walk in at that exact moment. "I'm working on it."

I whipped around to see her glaring at me. She was still in her black long-sleeved unitard jumpsuit, her dark auburn hair in a ponytail.

"Well, you better since you might have blown our only shot," I gritted out.

"He might put up with you, but I'm not dealing with your attitude," she said before shutting the door on her way out.

Neither of them deserved my aggravation, but after my impromptu nuptials and being in the same room as Barrera, I was on edge.

That's an understatement.

Kai studied me for a moment before he finally spoke up, "Listen, if you don't want to talk about what happened today, that's fine. I know better than to push you." He stood and glared at me. "But don't you dare take whatever you're feeling out on Valentina. This is the last time you'll raise your voice at her. She did her job and you know it. Shit happens."

He was right.

I groaned and said, "I'm sorry."

"Like I said, I'm used to your little tantrums. But I'm not the one you should be apologizing to."

"It's just, he was finally in our reach. I could have gotten the answers I've been waiting for."

"And you will. But, Jamal, you need to stop going a

thousand miles an hour. It'll get you killed, and now, it might get *her* killed. You might be willing to jeopardize your safety, but I know you don't want anything to happen to her. So get your shit together. We'll get them. Just be patient."

I knew he was right, but after waiting all these years, I finally had my in. Being so close, only to lose the opportunity to be able to infiltrate their systems knocked some of the hope I had to finally find the iron-clad proof I needed to go after who was behind my parents' murder.

The near-constant gnawing in my chest flared up again. It'd gotten worse since I found out that my parents' death wasn't accidental. It'd been four years and waiting in the shadows for the right time to get revenge was nearly killing me.

The Barreras were old-school to a fault. They made their money through extortion, smuggling, and drugs, and that unfortunately didn't involve much of my trusted friends, computers. Which meant that finding what I needed was more difficult than I anticipated.

Although I'd been mixed up in more than my fair share of crime, I would never take an innocent life just to reach my goals. My gut screamed that Barrera was responsible, but until I had tangible proof, I wouldn't make a move.

But we had to find out sooner rather than later because after my little entrance earlier, it wouldn't take long before they connected the dots and figured out who I really was.

And when they did, the only thing that remained was when they'd strike.

I slipped off my jacket and rolled my sleeves up. Then I pulled on the picture of Kai and me of the summer we graduated and waited for the mechanism to click in place. Once it did, the shelves pulled back and opened sideways, revealing a staircase that led to our headquarters.

"Time to apologize," I muttered.

He placed his hands on my shoulders and gave them a squeeze. "Good luck," he said, chuckling.

I made my way downstairs and he followed close behind. Once at the bottom, I entered the code to our workroom then stepped inside.

My office as well as Kai and Valentina's side of the house were the only ways to get here. Computer monitors lined almost every inch of the right side of the room, some of the screens projected over the walls. On the left was our equipment storage room and a training ring.

Although we all worked here, this was mainly Valentina's space. She barely ever left the room, unless it was absolutely necessary.

Speaking of Valentina, she was bent over her desk, sifting through documents and furiously typing on her keyboard. If she kept going at that rate, we'd have to buy another keyboard even though I'd just gotten her this one last week.

Hopefully, she doesn't bite my head off.

"Valentina?" I asked tentatively.

No answers.

Kai stayed behind, propping a foot on the wall, watching the scene unfold with a smirk on his face.

Bastard.

I drifted closer to her. I knew not to touch her when she was this focused on her job, so I said her name a little louder.

She removed her noise-canceling headphones. "What do you want?" she asked, never taking her eyes off the screen.

"To apologize?"

"Was that a question or a statement?" she asked, spinning her desk chair to face me.

Kai chuckled, the sound of his mockery reverberating off the walls. I glared at him over my shoulder before turning my attention back to her.

"A statement," I replied hesitantly. I shouldn't be this nervous and I was technically her boss, but she wasn't one to cross. Besides, I'd stepped over the line by taking my issues out on her. I huffed. "Listen, I'm sorry. I was mad and took it out on you."

She pushed the bridge of her glasses back into their position. Then she shrugged, which was her way of accepting my apology. "Let me show you something."

I let out the breath I was holding.

Dieu merci. I was back in her good graces.

Kai made his way to us and we both loomed over her. I

placed a hand on the desk and the other on the back of her chair to watch her screens.

"I lost Barrera's car before I could attach the device, but I was close enough to ping a signal from his cell phone. These documents were in the latest email Barrera received. I already sifted through them and initially, I thought this was just a document marking their newest real estate acquisition. But I found this." She paused, swiping through the pages until she stopped on one in particular. "At first glance, it seems like another segment of the contract, but if you look closely, it's a date and coordinates to a meeting. All we're missing is the time."

"Who's the meeting with?" I asked.

"Bianchi," she answered, looking at me over her shoulder.

"Bianchi as in the Don of the west side?"

"Yes," she confirmed.

"That's unexpected," Kai said, and I thought the same.

The Italians rarely dealt with anyone outside of the three other Italian mafia families on the island. So for them to be in discussion with the Moroccan cartel was quite out of the norm.

"The Moroccans are trying to acquire more land in Sardenya, and Bianchi owns the majority of the real estate in that corner of the island. The goal is still to get to Barrera and find what we're looking for, but for now, this is a good start."

I pulled back, crossing my arms. "So the meeting's in three weeks," I concluded.

"Yes," she said, looking back at us.

I looked over at Kai, a slow smile creeping along both of our faces.

"Let's get started, then."

Barrera, I'm coming for you.

We spent the rest of the night planning for the meeting.

We looked over the building blueprints and security system, narrowing down the best access route we could use without being seen. There wasn't a building in the vicinity where Valentina would be able to best use her skills, but she'd still be able to help me out on the grounds.

I knew she could handle herself, probably more than I could, but I never liked having neither her nor Kai there, especially him. Let's just say Kai's strength wasn't in the combat department. He wasn't much of a hands-on participant in all of this, but Valentina volunteered to train him, which was surprising in itself, but I didn't dwell too much on it.

I needed the extra hands. Especially if things were to go south.

The only thing missing was the time of the meeting, but we figured out a window where Barrera would be in town, so we'd simply have to be on alert that day until the time was set.

I woke up the next morning and headed downstairs to get breakfast started.

Strangely, over the years, the kitchen became a place where I could turn my brain off from everything that had it spinning a hundred miles per hour.

I went over to the pantry and grabbed all the ingredients I needed to make pancakes, then stopped by the fridge to get the rest. I was almost done when Kai walked in and took a seat on one of the bar stools behind the kitchen island.

"Oh, I'm hungry," he whined. "What's for breakfast?"

"Pancakes. Make yourself useful and get everything else set up."

"I thought you said no one else could cook in the kitchen."

I glared at him over my shoulder. "That's not cooking."

He laughed. "Okay, grumpy." He got up and walked over to the fridge to grab an assortment of berries. Moving over to one of the cabinets next to me, he picked up three separate bowls to fill them with each kind. "You know your mood has been more sour since she showed up," he said, his tone teasing.

I flipped over the pancake cooking in the pan. "No, it hasn't."

"She's affecting you."

"No, she doesn—"

Someone cleared their throat behind us. I swung around to find Sienna standing a few feet away, wearing the same yoga pants she was wearing yesterday that hugged her body perfectly.

Even in the morning, she was quite the sight.

When we both didn't say anything, her mouth hesitantly lifted at one corner. "Um, morning."

Words continued to elude me, but Kai intervened, cutting the awkward tension.

"Good morning, Sienna," he said, his voice a little too cheerful for my liking. "How did you sleep?"

"It was fine," she answered, shifting on her feet. "I'm surprised to see you guys here. I didn't think anyone else would be up yet."

The smell of something burning brought my attention back to the stove. "Fuck," I muttered, cursing under my breath. I hadn't burned anything since my early days of learning how to cook, but apparently, that was another thing Sienna disrupted.

Kai brushed past me and murmured, "Told you," only for me to hear.

"We have an early work meeting, but what are you doing up so early?" Kai answered for both of us.

I hated that it was so easy for him to talk to her when she was *my* wife. I'd never been good at talking to people, much less to strangers. I wanted to, but it was like something physically stopped the words from coming out of my mouth.

And the only ones I managed to get out were aimed to rile her up.

"I'm using the free time I have before my shift later today to do some research for a presentation I have," she explained, leaning her elbows against the kitchen island.

"What do you do again?" Kai asked as he filled the bowls with strawberries, blueberries, and raspberries.

Before I could hear more of their conversation, I turned off the stove and stacked the last batch of pancakes to the side. Then I washed my hands and tossed the towel resting over my shoulder aside.

"There's pancakes and a separate pot of decaf coffee for you," I said to her before leaving them and retreating to my office.

Being married to her might be the death of both of us.

CHAPTER 8

BEING MARRIED TO JAMAL WAS LIKE HAVING psychological whiplash.

My poor brain was running in circles, scrambling to land on whether I should give him a chance or shut him out like I knew I should.

I was still trying to grasp how he knew I only drank decaf and what they were talking about before I walked into the kitchen when I remembered Kai had asked me a question before my husband rushed out of here.

I looked over at him, finding him perched at the kitchen island. "Emergency Medicine," I finally replied with a small smile. "Is he always like this?" I asked, pointing to where Jamal had disappeared to.

With a shrug, he handed me an empty plate. "You get used to it."

"I doubt it," I mumbled under my breath as I stacked a

few pancakes on it, which I drowned in blueberries and syrup. In desperate need of coffee, I stood in front of the coffee machine, looking around to try and figure out where the cups were.

Seeming to read my mind, Kai directed me. "Right above you," he said, pointing to the cupboard.

I muttered a "thank you," picked out a large mug, and poured myself a cup. Then I stood across from Kai, preferring to eat standing.

"Have you known each other for a while?" I asked, picking up my fork and taking a bite.

Holy shit. These might be the best pancakes I've ever had.

"You could say that," he simply said, not offering any more details.

Silence fell between us, and I continued eating. After a while, my curiosity sparked to know more and I asked, "Where did you guys meet?"

"We went to school together," he said, reaching for his mug to take a sip.

"Valentina, too?" I questioned, curious as to how their arrangements came to be.

He opened his mouth to say something, but a voice cut him off.

"No."

A woman appeared in the kitchen out of thin air.

She had long, dark auburn hair pulled back by a claw clip. She wore a black romper that hugged her strong, lean body. It had a low scoop back with a straight neckline and she had long white socks and black slides on her feet.

She was petite and quite frankly stunning, but her aura was intimidating. Not in a way that meant she was mean but rather in a way that she would kill you in a heartbeat.

That single word was the only thing she said before leaving the kitchen, a cup of coffee in hand.

My brain finally caught up to the present. "That's decaf," I warned her, but she was already gone. I turned my attention back to Kai, only to find him watching her retreating form, a longing look on his face.

I wonder if she's aware he has a crush on her.

"Was that…"

"Yeah," he confirmed in a hushed tone.

The sound of a door slamming shut snapped him out of whatever trance he was in. He cleared his throat and brought his gaze back to me, giving me a wide smile. "So what's it like to be a doctor?" he asked, changing the subject.

We kept making small talk about my journey through med school and the most interesting cases I'd seen while working in the ER. I didn't like talking about myself, so I tried veering the conversation toward him, selfishly wanting to learn more about my husband, but every time I did, Kai would find a way to bring it back to me.

I guess I might have to go to the source if I want answers.

A few hours later, I was out the door. As Kai had

promised, my old gray Honda CR-V was waiting for me in the driveaway, a sharp contrast to the three McLarens lined in front of it.

I climbed into my car, threw it into reverse after a few stuttering false starts, and pulled onto the long stretch of gravel, praying that today would be a good day.

Today was in fact not a good day.

As an ER resident, I thrived under chaos, but after everything that happened yesterday, I'd just wanted a simple shift.

Guess I jinxed myself wishing for a quiet day.

Barely an hour into my shift, I'd already treated a broken arm on a kid who fell off his bike, stitched a deep cut on a construction worker's hand, and had to lead a code blue since I was the senior resident on duty.

And I had eleven more hours to go.

It was nearing the end of my shift and I was finishing up my notes when a nervous presence loomed over my shoulder. I glanced up to find Marissa, one of our fourth-year medical students, fidgeting next to me. She was one of our most promising students, so the nervous expression tightening her features made me weary.

"Yes?"

"So…" She hesitated a moment before rambling on, barely taking a breath. "I was just with a patient in Room

3 and they've requested an actual doctor for the assessment." The pitch in her voice climbed with every word coming out of her mouth. "I did inform them that I was competent to do it despite being a medical student, but he insisted."

Her notebook slipped through her fingers, fluttering to the floor. "Oh my God, I'm so sorry."

I tried to rein in my annoyance at whoever made her feel less confident and got up out of my seat, then bent to pick it up. I handed it back to her with a reassuring smile. "Marissa, there's nothing to apologize for. It's okay. I'll go check on him," I said, knowing the interaction probably overwhelmed her. "Why don't you go check on your next patient and we can debrief after, okay?"

Clutching her journal to her chest, she nodded and made her way to the next room. Once she was inside, I quickly pulled the patient's chart and looked over the nurse's notes and his vitals.

He was a thirty-five-year-old male coming in for shortness of breath. His vitals were stable and he was also known to have asthma, making a straightforward case, so I was confused as to why he wouldn't let Marissa examine him.

Brushing it off, I grabbed my stethoscope from the table, placed it around my neck, and walked over to Room 3.

I pushed the door open. "Hi, I'm Dr. Bruni. What brings you to the ER, Mr.…."

He looked me up and down and smirked. "Kane. Ryan Kane."

"What brings you here today, Mr. Kane?"

"I've been feeling a little out of breath recently and thought I'd come get it checked," he explained. "And you can call me Ryan, Dr. Bruni," he added, his smirk growing wider.

Overly friendly patients weren't always a bad thing, but the way he said my name felt like sludge was poured over me. I shook the feeling off and grabbed my stethoscope, walking over to him to examine him close.

"Can you take a deep breath for me," I asked while listening to his breath sounds.

"You have to tell me, what's a pretty thing like you doing here?" His tone was flirty and I could feel his gaze burning into my face.

I tried to rein in how uncomfortable I was and remained professional. "Take another, please."

"Are you single or has a lucky man claimed you already?" The way he said claimed made my skin crawl.

After I was done listening or trying to at least, I stepped back a healthy distance and placed my stethoscope back around my neck.

He was almost spot-on in regards to how my wedding went, but he didn't need to know that, so I gave him a tight smile and said, "I'm happily married." The lie rolled off my tongue, but again, he didn't need to know that. He raised a brow at my bare finger, but I ignored it. "Mr. Kane, I don't hear anything abnormal. Can you tell me when your shortness of breath started?"

I could tell my use of the formality and how I didn't play into his flirtation irked him. He crossed his arms over his chest. "You should wear a ring if you're that *happily* married. It would help a guy out."

Keeping my professionalism was becoming harder by the second. I swallowed the lump of unease that formed in my throat and continued my train of questioning. "In your chart, it mentioned that you have asthma. Is that correct?"

"Yeah…" He trailed off, unsure where I was going with my question.

"Have you been taking your inhaler whenever your shortness of breath occurs?"

His brows furrowed. "My inhaler?"

"Yes, the blue one?"

"Oh yeah." He hesitated. "That one. I, um, I don't think I have any left."

"That's okay. I'll take a look at your previous prescription and write you a new one. Is there anything else you were concerned about?"

"I don't think so," he replied. His tone was polite but cold.

"Great, well, let me get that going for you and you should be good to go." I gave him another tight smile. "The nurse will be back shortly," I said, closing the door behind me and walking away.

I could feel his eyes still on me and a shiver ran down my spine, but I ignored it.

After renewing his prescription and signing off on his discharge, I spent the last thirty minutes of my scheduled shift with Marissa, hearing about her patients and signing off on anything she needed. Then I caught up on my notes since I'd been off work yesterday.

It was already past midnight when I finally left the hospital.

During the entire ride back to the house, I couldn't shake how unsettled the interaction with my last patient left me. Patients who flirted weren't uncommon, but this one felt different.

Especially with his insistence on discussing my marriage.

My fingers started drumming over my steering wheel before I realized it. I didn't know how long I'd been driving until the GPS on my phone directed me to take a right onto the street that led to Jamal's.

The gates swung open as I drove toward them, recognizing my license plate.

Guess that's why Kai texted me earlier this afternoon asking for a picture of it.

I still couldn't believe this was my new reality. Living in a mansion, married to a stranger, and in the process inheriting two roommates—one who I'd only met once, if you could call that a meeting.

It was almost one in the morning when I finally parked

my car at the side of the driveway and made my way to the front door. Right before I left to get ready for my shift, Kai had asked to take my fingerprints and showed me how to use the device.

Should be easy enough.

I placed my thumb on the screen, waiting for it to unlock.

Error. Unrecognizable fingerprints. The screen read, so I tried again.

I was almost about to call for someone when it finally clicked open. I stepped inside to find the living room and kitchen empty. Not that I expected anyone to be up at this time, but for some reason, I just assumed they were night owls.

I placed my shoes to the side in the entryway and fought a yawn. I was so tired and just wanted to crash into my bed, but my stomach growled at that same moment, reminding me that it had been a while since I last ate.

I walked into the kitchen and dropped my purse on the counter. The remnant smell of food hit my nose and I spotted a plate sitting on the counter next to the stove. I made my way over to find my name written on it and was about to unwrap it when I heard a thud coming from upstairs.

What is that?

I waited for more, but everything went quiet again. Thinking my mind played tricks on me, I picked up the plate and marched over to the microwave when I heard someone yelling, "Mama? Baba?"

Suddenly, I was out of the kitchen and halfway up the stairs.

"Mama? Baba? *Finkoum?*" He sounded so scared.

I followed the sound of his voice, guiding me closer and down the hallway. I'd never explored this side of the hallway, my room being on the right, but I knew his bedroom was somewhere toward the other end.

Noticing a door ajar at the very end, I walked faster toward it.

A cry echoed and I stilled, unaware of what I would be walking into. Walking into his bedroom was probably a bad idea, but it was a bad idea I wanted to do.

I tentatively pushed the door farther open.

Nothing could have prepared me for what I found.

His room was dark, but the moonlight streaming from his window highlighted his body. Jamal was on his side on top of his dark sheets, his hands rigidly clutching at the fabric in front of him.

I couldn't see his face from my viewpoint, so I approached the side of his bed and finally saw his expression. It was contorted in pain and a whimper of agony left his lips, sweat covering his forehead.

Every inch of him was taut and another anguished cry tore from his throat as he gripped the sheets even tighter.

My heart clenched at the sight, the urge to comfort him growing stronger.

I kneeled next to his bed. "Jamal," I whispered gently. "Jamal, it's me, Sienna. You're safe. I'm right here."

I tried his name louder this time, but he was still in a deep slumber. His breathing was shallow, his chest rising and falling faster. My mind was screaming at me to do one thing while my heart was pounding furiously, telling me another.

A la mierda.

Hesitantly, I climbed onto his bed and placed a gentle hand on his arm, shocked by the heat of his skin through his long-sleeved shirt. He was burning up.

He cried out again and the vice grip around my heart squeezed tighter at seeing my husband in this state. I shouldn't care, but I'd rather have him angry at me for being in his room than leave him like this.

I slowly reached for his hands, loosening his grip on the silk sheets. His body tensed, but I kept repeating "you're safe, I'm here" until I found myself next to him, my back resting against his headboard.

The idea of how often this happened to him and who took care of him when it did crowded my thoughts.

I brushed my hand back over his silk head wrap repeatedly, whispering, "*Te tengo.*"

My heart was beating so fast.

With every minute that passed, his body relaxed further, his strained muscles loosening under the brush of my fingertips. He eventually nuzzled his head under the crook of my arm and one of his arms shifted across my lap, his fingers splaying across my thigh.

His body stirred and my name left his lips in a small murmur, causing my breath to halt. I glanced down and watched his features, waiting on bated breath for him to wake up.

He never did, his breathing evening out.

I watched over him thoughtfully, studying him closely. Every part of me wanted to reach out and trace the sharpness of his cheekbones, the slope of his straight nose, the curvature of his chiseled jaw.

But I fought the urge to trace the lines of his face, instead settling on brushing the fingertips of my right hand over his shoulder.

Although I wouldn't admit it to myself, I was enjoying being able to look at him—soaking in this moment— without him knowing. There wasn't a single wrinkle on his face as he slept.

A shocking fact especially with the amount of frowning he did. I'd expected at least a few frown lines.

More moonlight poured in from the window, illuminating the rest of his bedroom and distracting me from my perusal. I didn't know whether his space was bigger than the room I stayed in because of how empty it was or because it *actually* was larger.

His bed sat in the middle of the room, a large crystal chandelier hanging right above us. The only other furniture I could make out were the nightstands on either side of the bed and the small armoire in the left corner of his room, right next to the large window.

The en suite bathroom door was ajar and the only thing I could make out from where I was sitting was the outline of a clawfoot bathtub and the beginning of a vanity sink, a mirror sitting right above.

My thumb was still idly drawing circles on his shoulder when I traced the edge of something raised under his shirt. I narrowed my eyes and looked closer, only to find a jagged scar peeking through at the edge of his shirt.

It seemed to travel farther down, but what I saw was so small, it was hard to notice until you were this close to him. My fingers itched to trace over it. To wake him up and find out what it was from, but I once again refrained.

Instead, I watched his chest rise softly, up and down, his expression much softer than when I'd walked in, however long ago.

Eventually, my adrenaline faded and the exhaustion from earlier took over. My eyes fell closed, the steady beat of his heart lulling me closer to sleep.

A few minutes later, I fell into a slumbered sleep.

CHAPTER 9

Why is it so warm?

I knew it wasn't one of *those* nights because I would've woken up feeling the opposite, my body shivering from the cold sweats.

I could also feel the early morning rays of sunlight brushing my skin through the cotton shirt I wore to bed last night, but this was a different type of warm.

It was nice.

I knew I should probably wake up and get ready for work, but I wanted to bask in this comfortable nest for a few more moments.

Yesterday, Kai, Valentina, and I spent over eighteen hours in the basement running through simulations of how we'd interrupt Barrera and Bianchi's meeting in three weeks. We were almost there, but our timing was still not efficient enough to avoid being seen.

The building was heavily guarded and their guards only changed shifts twice a day, giving us a tight window to navigate. Plus, Kai still wasn't ready to fight by himself. He and Valentina were still sparring when I left for bed.

I tightened my grip on the pillow I'd apparently been cuddling throughout the night.

It stirred beneath me.

I frowned, the sensation abruptly waking me. My eyes shot open, but I was too close to whatever I was lying on, so I carefully pulled back to discern what or who it was.

I didn't sleep around, or at least, I hadn't since I left college, so I knew it wasn't that. Besides, I was married and it might not have been out of love, but I would never do that to Sienna.

Besides, she was by far the most beautiful woman I'd ever laid eyes on and I just didn't care to pay attention to anyone else.

I looked up and my breath caught in my lungs when I realized who I was sleeping with, or on if we were being technical.

My face was resting on her lap, my right arm thrown over her thigh, the other growing numb under my body. My slight movement caused her to stir, and the hand she had resting over my shoulder instinctively rubbed it back and forth.

I closed my eyes and took a shaky breath.

Why is she here? What happened last night?

It suddenly dawned on me that I must've had a nightmare and she heard me when she got home last night because she was still wearing the same clothes she'd left with yesterday. She most likely came straight to my room because even her hair was still in a tight ponytail when I knew she wore it loose under a bonnet to sleep.

I knew I needed to get up because I was becoming entirely too comfortable with the feeling of her arms wrapped around me, but when I looked at her again, I couldn't tear my eyes away from her.

I'd forgotten to draw the curtains closed last night and the morning sunlight spilling in from my windows illuminated her soft features.

I'd studied her features before, but I never really took a moment to *look* at her and now, I understood why. I never let myself because if I did, I would've grown distracted.

My wife was simply beautiful.

Thick brows, a sharp nose, full, inviting—*no, not inviting*, I reminded myself—lips. Her eyes were still shut, her dark lashes resting on her soft skin.

But they fluttered open and her gaze clashed with mine.

My eyes captured hers and I momentarily got lost in her brown irises.

"Um, hi," she said hesitantly, her voice hoarse from sleep.

"Yes, hi," I replied, lowering my gaze.

Yes, hi? Good job, Jamal, smooth.

I groaned and when I looked at her again, she gave me

a small smile and cleared her throat, shifting under me and revealing that I was still holding her.

"Sorry," I mumbled, detangling myself from her body and moving into an upright position to put distance between us. Which was when I noticed I was only in a shirt and underwear, my usual sleep attire, while she was fully clothed. But I sighed in relief when I realized the only part of me that I didn't want her to see was concealed.

Silence hummed between us and she pushed a stray lock of hair behind her ear.

She was the first to break it. "Are you…" She paused, hesitating on her next words. "Do you remember what happened last night?"

The concern in her tone seemed to snap me back into reality, reminding me of the real nature of our relationship. She was a transaction, a payment for a debt not settled.

She wasn't *actually* my wife.

"You should leave," I said harshly, looking away.

"Jamal," she said softly.

Her hand reached for me, but I jerked away from her touch.

"I said *leave*," I repeated, my tone even colder this time.

"Fine," she huffed out.

She cursed under her breath in Spanish. I didn't understand everything she'd said since my Spanish was rusty, but I understood enough to know it was something about me being an ungrateful asshole.

She wasn't wrong, but I couldn't let her get close.

I'd expected her to slam the door, but when she simply shut it closed behind her, it only made me feel even worse.

I groaned, running a hand over my face.

Why do I do this to myself?

I let out a deep breath and headed to the bathroom. After brushing my teeth, I washed my face and grabbed a facecloth to dry my skin.

I still couldn't believe I'd slept all night without being aware that she was there.

I rarely remembered when *they* happened. The night terrors had started when I'd come back from the hospital and started living with Noah at his new place. The first time it happened, I'd woken up the next morning drenched in sweat with Noah kneeling next to my bed, a horrified look on his face.

He'd looked like he'd spent the entire night watching over me, and I'd later learned that he indeed had. Since waking me up wasn't a solution, he'd stayed up to make sure I didn't injure myself from all the trashing I did during my sleep.

He'd asked if I remembered what happened and I'd looked at him confused, unaware of what he'd been talking about. That's when I learned about them.

I had them frequently and every time I did, I woke with Noah by my side.

We'd eventually gotten them under control, but I

guessed the recent events must have stirred them back to the surface.

I combed my hair then made my way to my closet and changed into one of my suits since Kai and I had to make an appearance at the office for a new acquisition.

When I came downstairs, Kai was sitting on one of the island chairs, typing away on his laptop. "Morning," he said cheerfully, too cheerful for my current mood.

I grunted in response and walked over to grab a mug from the cupboard. Then I grabbed the carafe and was mid-pour when I asked him, "Where's Sienna?"

I knew I shouldn't have asked, especially after I'd kicked her out of my bedroom when she'd only tried to help me. But I couldn't help myself.

"She left for work. Man, I don't know what you said to her, but I've never seen someone be so eager to go to work, *especially* after the day she had yesterday."

Wait, what?

I almost spilled coffee all over myself when I whipped around to face him. My brows furrowed and anger exploded in my chest. "What do you mean 'the day she had'? What the fuck happened to her yesterday?"

He took a sip of his tea, then said, "Calm down. We were talking and right before she left, she mentioned that she hoped none of her patients today would hit on her like the last one she examined yesterday."

As soon as I heard the words *hit on her,* my mind went on a whirlwind and started planning how I could infiltrate the hospital's records, find this man, and show him what happened when he made my wife feel uncomfortable.

"Hit on her?"

He shook his head and rolled his eyes at me. "Have you seen her?"

"Do not talk about my wife," I said through clenched teeth as I glared at him.

He held both of his hands up, feigning innocence. "Hey, you know what I meant. She's a beautiful woman, but she's not my type."

The more he talked, the more irritated I became. "Tell me what happened."

"Listen, we're late for our meeting with Williams. All she told me was that a patient flirted with her yesterday and it made her extremely uncomfortable."

"She's married to me."

"Trust me, *I know*. But she doesn't wear a ring, so my guess is he thought she was available."

Ah putain, j'ai oublié de lui donner une bague de mariage.

"Fuck, I forgot," I chastised myself.

"Yeah, well, we can discuss that later. We need to get going if we don't want to be late."

"Yeah, I'm coming."

I transferred my coffee into a to-go cup, rinsing the empty mug before retrieving my car keys from my pocket and walking out the front door.

God, I hated meetings.

I didn't see the point in having them after our clients had signed the contract, but Kai thought it was a nice personal touch to our business model. He'd insisted that if we were more hands-on with our clients, they would be more likely to trust us.

Thank God for Kai and his love for talking because if it weren't for him, I'd barely make it through these. I'd most likely send them away after the first few minutes in their company.

Don't tell him I said that I was grateful for him.

My mind drifted to this morning again and how it felt to be in her arms before I ruined it and made her flee. I thought about her more than I wanted to, especially after what Kai told me earlier this morning before we left the house.

I wanted to reach for the inside pocket of my suit to settle my thoughts, but we were at a café and I wouldn't be able to conceal my playing with fire.

Williams's voice snapped me out of my thoughts. "So it's settled?" he asked us, eager to have us as his new security firm.

"Yes," I replied curtly, wanting to be done with this already.

Kai chuckled nervously, kicking my shin under the table. "What he meant to say is that we've installed the software into your company's system and should be able to find out who's been leaking your data to your competitors."

Yeah, what he said.

"Good," was all Williams said before we shook hands to say goodbye and he left Chez Arthur, the Belgian café that was a few blocks away from our office building.

The owner was a sweet older woman, Marianne, and she made the best waffles I'd ever tasted in my life. Well, except for my mom's. Although I hated these meetings, the only good thing about them was that the smell in this place reminded me of her.

Marianne was not only an angel, she also happened to be from the same town my mother grew up in. I'd never been to Spa since my father's job didn't leave much time for out of the country vacations, but the various pictures of the city plastered on the walls here were the closest I could be to my mother's roots.

Kai kept his wide smile fixed in place until Williams stepped into his car and his personal driver veered into the busy streets.

Then his smile faltered, quickly replaced by an annoyed look. "Why do you always have to be like this?"

"What do you mean? You know I don't do people."

He groaned. "Of course I do, but you're insufferable. Even more so since becoming a newlywed."

I got out of my seat, not wanting to venture more into this topic of conversation.

"I have some things to do, but I'll meet you at the house

later," I told him. I didn't wait for his answer and walked over to the parking facility next door, waiting for the valet to bring my car around.

Then I slid in and pulled away, joining the afternoon traffic.

I was ten minutes away from the boutique when my dashboard flashed with a phone call. Noah's voice boomed through my speakers. "I heard congratulations are in order," he said playfully, the loud chatter I heard behind him dimming to a quiet hum.

I slowed to a stop at a red light. "Yeah," I grumbled.

"What's with the 'yeah'? You get married and don't invite your favorite uncle?"

"How can you be a favorite of anything when you're only competing with yourself?"

"Because I know I'm the best," he said and I laughed, which was a rarity these days.

His voice then turned more serious. "I didn't know you were dating anyone."

"Well, it's not like you've been around and besides, I don't always tell you everything," I said, turning defensive.

Just like you haven't told me everything either, I thought, but I immediately regretted it. Noah was the only family I had left and despite the secrets he'd kept from me, that would never change.

"Sorry, it's been an adjustment and I've just been a little on edge," I apologized.

"No, you're right. I have been busy with work, but I

should've checked in more often on my *favorite* nephew." His emphasis on the word favorite made me chuckle.

"Are you happy?" he asked, concern shadowing his tone.

I pulled into a parking spot in front of Amara, a popular jewelry store on the island, and shut the engine off.

"I am," I lied to him, not wanting him to worry or dig further into it.

I knew he most likely kept the Barreras' involvement from me to protect me and I was doing the same. I'd chosen to take this path, and I wouldn't bring him down with me.

Judging by the silent pause he took before saying more, I knew he didn't believe me.

"That's all that matters, then," he replied, not questioning me further.

There was a knock at his door. "Agent Brown, we need you for debriefing," I heard a voice say.

"Listen, I have to go, but I'll call you soon. Okay?"

"Okay," I replied before hanging up.

I spent a total of fifty-three minutes in the store, much longer than I was planning, but once I got what I came here for, I climbed back into my car and headed home.

CHAPTER 10

It was almost nine in the evening when I pulled into the driveaway. Voices drifted from the kitchen as I dragged my heels into the house.

I was exhausted.

I'd just spent the last nine hours running around between patients. North Western hospital, where Kenna had matched for her residency, had suffered a flood after a pipe burst in their emergency room, so all of their emergency calls were directed to our ER.

And I'd barely slept last night.

I'd stayed awake for hours, watching over Jamal, only to wake up to his ungrateful ass. Not that he had to kiss my feet, but a simple thank you would have sufficed.

Instead, he'd kicked me out of his room like I'd been an intruder.

All I wanted right now was a hot shower and an eternity

of sleep. And my mother's *yaniqueques*, but the people in the kitchen reminded me that wouldn't be possible.

Jamal's back was to me while Kai was leaned up against the island, his elbows propped on it. I was in the process of taking off my shoes when suddenly, a foreign laugh echoed against the wall.

Was that… Jamal?

Before I could register if it was or not, it abruptly stopped when he noticed I was here. I walked inside the kitchen and Kai, as usual, was the first to greet me. "Hey, Sienna," he said, giving me a warm smile.

This marriage and living arrangement had been thrown at me, but I was grateful to him for making it an easier transition.

"Hi," I said back to him, also giving him a smile in return. I stood next to Jamal and could feel his body tense, but I ignored it and kept my attention on his friend.

"How was your day?" Kai asked.

I could hear Jamal's internal groan at his question. I chanced a peek, only to find his jaw flexing in something—anger, frustration, or maybe it was in annoyance. I could never tell. He seemed to always be in a mood, so I figured it was better to just ignore it.

I set my tote bag on the island and propped a hand on it, the other resting above my hip, my fingers discreetly rubbing at my lower back.

I never paid attention to how much it pained me while I was working since I was too busy running everywhere to care, but as soon as I was off the clock, the pain manifested itself until it came on at full throttle.

"It was exhausting," I huffed.

He winced. "That sucks."

I laughed softly at his comment and said, "Comes with the territory." I loved my job, but a bed sounded like the best thing in the world right about now, especially since I had another shift tomorrow morning.

"I should probably head up and catch up on some sleep." I smiled warmly at Kai, but before I was able to move, Jamal's voice halted me in my tracks.

"Have you eaten?"

"I did quickly at lunch, but I should be fine until tomorrow," I replied curtly.

"Sit," he ordered.

I hated when he told me what to do.

"I'm fine, I—"

"Sit, Sienna. I'll make you something," he said, his voice softer this time.

I was about to gently decline, but I couldn't find it in me when I saw the pleading expression on his face. So instead, I nodded in agreement and took a seat on one of the stools next to Kai.

"Okay."

Jamal shot a look at Kai, prompting him to say, "I have, um, I have some work to do," Kai announced hesitantly. "Have a good night, Sienna."

I shook my head and looked up at Kai. "Yeah, you too."

Once Kai was out of the room, I turned my attention to Jamal, who was staring at me. "Good to know you're not an asshole just with me," I said, teasing him.

He frowned.

Guess it's too early for jokes.

"Do you want to eat something in particular?"

"Unless you know how to make *yaniqueques*, anything is fine with me. I'm not picky with food."

"Give me about an hour."

"You know how to make it?"

"I do."

"How?"

He shocked me by chuckling. It wasn't quite a laugh, but it was progress from the constant grumpiness he was carrying. "I'm a quick study," he responded confidently as he pulled his phone out of his pocket and gathered everything he needed.

I smiled to myself. *Let's see what he's got.*

He spent the next fifteen minutes moving through the kitchen with grace, looking over at his phone every once in a while. My gaze stayed stuck to him, curious to know how this would turn out.

I'd never had a man cook for me and never thought it would be attractive, but watching Jamal kneading the dough was a sight to see.

I must have been staring too hard because he glanced over his shoulder and caught me. I blushed and averted my gaze.

After a few minutes, my gaze drifted back to him, hoping the coast was clear. And once again, I became entranced by my husband and became hyper aware of every inch of his body.

The bead of sweat trailing down the side of his forehead, the way his shoulders strained the fabric of his long-sleeved shirt, the way his hands worked the dough.

My thoughts wandered to what those hands would look like on something else. On someone else.

On me.

Jamal was becoming a temptation I didn't know how long I could resist.

The sound of a loud smack snapped me out of my thoughts. He placed the mixture back into a bowl and went to the sink to wash his hands.

With a towel in hand, he looked over at me. His lips parted and I waited for him to say something, but instead, he turned away, placing the towel back over the handle of the stove.

Then he whirled around and blurted out, "I have something for you."

"Okay?" I asked hesitantly.

He slid onto the stool beside me, spread his knees, and I shifted to face him, my legs now fitting between his. He rubbed his hands up and down on his thighs, his eyes focused on anything but me, as if he was mentally preparing himself to give me whatever it was that he had for me.

He was *so* close. If he shifted, his hands would be skimming *my* thighs.

Something I wouldn't be opposed to.

No, Sienna. No puedes pensar en eso.

He reached for my left hand and slid something around my ring finger. The way his fingers grazed over my skin sent a shiver running down my spine and I hoped he hadn't noticed.

The look on his face was a mix between uncertainty, frustration, and something I couldn't determine just yet.

I was too focused on his face to realize what it was until I looked down. My eyes widened at the sight.

Holy shit.

A gold band with a marquise cut focal diamond, a flurry of diamonds surrounding it, was now sitting on my ring finger.

It was simple and elegant.

I'd never spent much time imagining what wedding ring I'd like since I was too focused on landing in an ER, but this was beautiful. And surprisingly, *me*.

His thumb brushed over my knuckles and I finally looked up at him, the expression on his face knocking the air out of my lungs.

Our gazes locked and the air hummed with a dangerous energy swirling around us and wrapping us in a suspended cadence.

My body found itself compelled to be closer, leaning toward him.

My knee brushed against his thigh and the slight movement was enough to snap the tendril that connected us. He dropped my hand like it was on fire and jerked back, clearing his throat.

"Keep this on," he grunted.

And he's back.

He moved out of his seat and went back to the counter where he had let the dough rest.

Still puzzled by what just happened, I settled on watching him finish cooking the *yaniqueques*, mindlessly playing with my ring. I shouldn't have felt anything when he slid the ring on my finger because this *wasn't* a real marriage.

But somewhere deep down, I knew I was lying to myself.

Once he was done, he set them to rest on a plate with a paper towel underneath. After that, he grabbed the small saucepan from the stove and poured whatever he'd made into a cup. Then he made his way over, set the plate in front of me, and slid me a mug of what I realized was hot chocolate.

"Thank you," I murmured, trying to push away the unwanted feelings his care and the ring invoked inside.

He hummed in response. Without another word, he went back to the counter and started doing the dishes.

I focused my attention on the food in front of me, my stomach rumbling at the mouthwatering smell. I picked a *yaniqueques* from the plate and dipped it into the chocolate, which was the best part, and brought it to my mouth.

I almost moaned at the taste.

Oh, coño, esto esta buenísimo.

I would have never guessed this was his first time making it if I hadn't seen him research how to make them. He wasn't kidding when he said he was a quick study.

I was almost done with the last *yaniqueques* right as he dried the last plate and placed it back in one of the cabinets. I got up to walk to the sink when a jolting pain shot from my lower back.

"*Fuck*," I muttered under my breath. I gripped the edge of the counter to hold myself up, the other landing on my lower back.

This day just keeps getting better.

Jamal ran to me. "Sienna, what's wrong?" His voice had an edge of panic. "Are you hurt?" His hands were hovering over me, not sure if he should touch me or not.

"I'm fine," I gritted out as I rubbed over the tense muscles. Tears sprang to my eyes at the spasms of pain rolling up my back.

"You're clearly not fine. Let me see," he demanded, his voice harsher this time.

"I told you I was *fine*. I just need to let it pass." I tried to stand tall to prove to him I was okay, but that wasn't the greatest of ideas because I moaned in pain.

Being doted on wasn't something I was used to, so I didn't know how to react to his worry.

He muttered something in French under his breath.

"Stop being so stubborn and let me help you," he huffed out.

My protest died on the tip of my tongue when he gently wrapped an arm around my waist and the other under my knees, lifting me so I was now cradled in his arms.

I whooshed out a breath. "What are you doing?" I asked, surprised.

He ignored me and walked toward the stairs that led upstairs. I instinctively wrapped my hands around his neck to avoid falling, but I knew he wouldn't let that happen. He carried me up the stairs, but instead of veering right toward my room, he turned left.

"Where are you taking me?"

"Would you just please stop arguing with me for once?" He pushed the door of his bedroom open with his foot and walked us into the dimly lit room.

It wasn't the first time I'd been here, but the memory of this morning hadn't exactly made me eager to return. He hadn't apologized for his earlier outburst, especially when I was just trying to help him, but I wasn't about to bring it up again.

So I chose the easier route. Fighting him.

"I will talk if I wish to talk."

He ignored me once again and carefully placed me at the edge of his bed and propped a few pillows behind my back. Then he walked into his en suite bathroom.

I heard the sound of a faucet being turned on and a few

minutes later, the smell of lavender drifted past the confines of the bathroom and slowly enveloped his bedroom.

The sound of water filling the tub eventually stopped and Jamal walked out with a large white robe in hand. He dropped to his haunches in front of me, placing the bathrobe on the bed right next to me.

"Are you able to undress yourself?" he asked, his eyes locking with me.

"What do y—"

He looked up at the ceiling and groaned, running a hand over his face. "Sienna, it's a simple question. Can you undress yourself or do you require my help?" he spelled it out for me.

I contemplated both options for a moment and then went for the safest route.

"I can do it." I didn't think I could bear more of his touch, especially after what a simple brush of his fingers on my skin did to me earlier.

And this felt too intimate already.

He got up and turned his head sideways, holding the robe open to shield me and allowing some sort of privacy.

I hesitated for a moment, my anxiety spiking.

I'd never undressed in front of a man, but my options were limited. Jamal wouldn't take no for an answer and the pain wasn't subsiding like I thought it would.

I shook the tremble that rippled down my spine and took a deep breath and slowly pulled my long-sleeved cardigan over my head, wincing. I let it drop behind me and moved to my wide-leg yoga pants. I slowly tilted my hips to get the elasticated band over my waist and tried to bend to get them off, but the pain was growing stronger.

I stifled a whimper and tried using my feet to push them down my legs, only managing to get them halfway there before I had to pause to wait for the wave of pain to ease.

But it didn't.

"Jamal…" I whispered, the request dying on my tongue. But he must have heard the underlying plea in my tone because he chanced a look.

There was a flicker in his eyes when he noticed my state, but it quickly vanished and he kneeled in front of me, draping the robe over his shoulder.

"I've got you," he promised, his words seeming to carry a weight beyond just our current circumstances. He grabbed the waistband of my bottoms and gently pulled down, his eyes roaming my face for any signs of discomfort.

Once they were off, his gaze locked with mine.

"We need to take everything off." His tone was lower and it sent warmth spreading over my skin.

I slowly nodded, my eyes never leaving his.

Tension crackled in the air, suspending the moment in an infinite time.

He grasped at the fabric over his shoulder and wrapped the soft cotton around my body, concealing me as much as he could.

"Okay," he muttered more to himself than to me.

His fingers brushed against my middle as he reached for the clasp at the back of my cotton bralette, deftly undoing it. Then he moved higher to slip the straps off my shoulder.

Not physically reacting to his touch was becoming harder by the second.

I tried to look away, but I feared that if we broke eye contact, the bubble we were wrapped in would burst and I would realize that he was in the process of undressing me.

As the fabric fell off my body, he wrapped the robe tighter around my body to hide it.

He muttered something in French before resting his hands on the side of my thighs. Then he tugged at my boy shorts and sucked in a sharp breath as he pulled them down my legs.

Goose bumps erupted all over my skin and my stomach clenched with a sensation I'd never felt before, my body feeling heavy with need.

A need for more of his touch.

A need for his fingers to explore somewhere no one has ever been.

A need for *him*.

I thought the first time I'd be naked in front of someone, I'd be more nervous. But it was quite the opposite.

Strangely, I felt safe in his arms.

He averted his gaze from mine and helped me stand, loosely tying the robe at the front. Then I wrapped my left arm around his neck to hold on.

It was only a few steps to the bathroom, but each one was more excruciating than the other.

"We're almost there," he said softly in encouragement.

Heat steamed up the mirrors and drenched the room in an alluring haze.

We stopped at the edge of the tub and Jamal's eyes were on mine once again. I didn't have a ton of experience in the department, but his gaze was drowned in lust.

"I'm taking this off now," he warned before he untied the loose knot and pushed the fabric off my shoulder, letting it pool down at our feet.

I thought he'd take the opportunity to look, but his eyes never wavered from mine. His intense gaze was becoming too much, so I looked away and tried to grab onto the edge to get in, but he stopped me.

"I'll do it."

Without bothering to remove the jacket of his suit, he wrapped an arm around my back and lifted me into his arms.

I hissed when my body broke the hot water.

He delicately helped me inside the tub until I was fully seated, not caring that his shirt and sleeves were now fully soaked.

I closed my eyes and dropped my head against the back of the tub. The warmth slowly seeped into my muscles and the sensation combined with the feel of his skin searing into mine was enough to work out a small moan off my lips.

He removed his hands and despite being submerged in

hot water, I suppressed the shiver running down my spine at the loss of his touch.

"Is the temperature okay?" he asked, his voice sounding strained.

I hummed in agreement.

I thought Jamal had left when I felt his fingers gripping my nape and it sent my pulse and mind into overdrive.

I could get used to this.

Despite how much I didn't—*shouldn't*—want to, I let him massage the back of my neck and my shoulders.

The pain in my lower back slowly subsided and the tone of his voice paired with the gentleness of his actions flooded my system with a different type of warmth.

I let myself revel in the way his hands kneaded the tense muscles in my neck that I hadn't noticed had been there.

I didn't realize I'd drifted off until I heard my name being called out in a hushed tone. I opened my eyes and tilted my head back, only to find Jamal's face barely a few inches away from mine.

He slightly pulled back, putting more distance between us. "You should get out," he said gruffly.

"Yeah, okay," I murmured.

He moved over to the other end of the tub, removed the drain, and turned his back to me, waiting. While the water drained out, I slowly got on my feet and rinsed myself off with the small detachable showerhead.

After, he shifted to face me and quickly averted his eyes

this time, holding the same robe open for me. I climbed out of the tub and slipped into it.

Then he cinched the belt, tighter this time, which elicited a small gasp out of me.

Before I could register what was happening, I was back in his arms as he carried me out of his room and headed for mine.

He gently set me down on my feet at my doorstep. "Get some rest," he said and turned to leave.

I nodded although he couldn't see it and watched him retreat back to his room.

I was about to close the door when he halted in his steps and glanced at me over his shoulder. I watched him war with his next words.

He dipped his head and said, "Good night, Sienna."

I gave him a small smile. "Good night, Jamal."

I closed the door and leaned against it, letting out a soft sigh.

We'd only been married a few days and the man he was right now was completely different from the one who'd threatened to kill my family if I didn't agree to marry him.

Maybe this is what Kai meant when he said to give him a chance.

After changing into a comfy set, I climbed into bed and pulled the soft duvet cover over my body, trying to fall asleep, but instead, I found myself staring at the ceiling, replaying what just happened on a loop in my head.

He'd taken care of me and well, I'd never been taken care of.

A deep ache settled in my chest, but I quickly shook myself out of it.

As the minutes went by, my earlier exhaustion settled back into my bones.

You were in pain. He had to help you. It doesn't mean anything, my mind chimed in right before I dozed off.

Jamal

CHAPTER 11

I FLICKED MY LIGHTER OPEN, WATCHING THE SMALL FLAME dance against the sensitive skin of my palm as I tried to burn the images of her branded in my brain. But it wasn't working.

Nothing seemed to work.

Not even the thirty-minute cold shower I just took to calm the fire inside me.

She had been naked in my room. In my bathroom.

Under my touch.

Having to undress her had been pure torture, images of how I would have drawn pleasure out of her assaulting my mind with every brush of my fingertips against her skin.

They still did.

I stared at the ceiling, aiming curses at the universe for the situation it put me in. It took everything in me not to memorize every inch of her, everything in me not to say 'fuck it' and claim her.

Especially when she stood up, water drops sluicing down her delectable body.

A need for her had scorched my veins, but I'd looked away before I did something we would both regret after.

I'd so *desperately* wanted to because she was irritatingly embedding herself under my skin, but I had to shake her away. I *needed* to. She was a distraction I couldn't afford.

No matter how much I would love to lose myself in her.

I rubbed a hand over my jaw, my aggravation at war with my blazing desire for her. I snapped the lid shut, my thumb mindlessly running over the engraving in the back.

A memory from the anniversary of my parents' deaths crept in.

"Jamal?" Noah's voice was getting closer.

I brought my knees closer to my chest, hoping he wouldn't find me. I didn't want to talk to anyone, let alone him.

I knew I should be grateful for everything he'd done for me. I mean, he'd saved my life, but I was so angry at everything, I couldn't see past it.

If it weren't for him, I wouldn't have been in so much pain and discomfort for the last two years.

I wouldn't have been in so many surgeries, I lost count.

If it weren't for him, I wouldn't be alone without a family.

The door to my closet slowly creaked open.

"Found you," he teased me, giving me a warm smile, but it dimmed once he saw the expression on my face. "Jamal, what's wrong?"

"Go away," I shouted at him. Instead of leaving, he switched on the light and stepped into the closet and sat next to me.

"I said go away."

"No."

I turned away from him, facing the wall on the left. "Why don't you ever just leave me alone?" I spat out, tears brimming my eyes with how angry I felt.

"Because I'll always be by your side," he replied softly.

A tear fell down my cheek and I angrily wiped it away.

"Jamal," he said, gently placing a hand over my shoulder.

I shrugged it off, not wanting him to feel the scars under my sweater.

"Jamal, look at me," he persisted. "Please."

I shifted to face him. "What do you want?" I asked, still angry.

He gave me a small smile despite my attitude. "I have something for you." He reached into his pocket and extended his hand in front of me.

I glanced down, looking at the small object in his hand. He pressed it into my palm and closed my hand around it.

I opened my hand and explored the object, flicking the lid open. It was a small gold Zippo lighter. My finger flicked down on the wheel on the side and I watched a flame form.

I flinched, almost dropping it to the floor.

Noah wrapped his hand around mine and placed my thumb on the wheel again. I tried again and watched the flame come to life.

"This is a reminder. You might not understand what it means right now, but I want you to remember this. Don't let fire consume you because you can always rise from its ashes."

I leaned the Zippo to the side, moonlight reflecting on the inscription at its back.

I closed my eyes for a brief moment, reminding myself of my goal.

Find out who started the fire and kill them.

I sat tucked back in the corner of the dimly lit hotel room and watched the elevator doors open to an older man with two much younger women flanking his side as they stumbled in.

The majority of men seemed to lack originality, but collectively, they always made themselves easy to trap.

From my seat in the living room, the suite's bedroom

door was opened enough to give me the perfect vantage point to capture this while still being hidden.

The brunette on his right giggled as he nibbled on her earlobe before whispering something in her ear. She playfully swatted his chest. "You've got such a filthy mouth," she said, her speech slurred.

"And I can do even filthier things with it," he teased.

I rolled my eyes at his lame innuendo.

"Oh yeah," the redhead on his other side countered.

"There'll be plenty for both of you," he said, moving to sit on the bed as both women stood in front of him. "Get undressed," he ordered them, his voice taking a huskier tone.

I stifled a disgusted shiver. I hoped they would hurry so I could get back to actual business instead of having to witness this.

Both of them started unzipping their dresses as he reached over the bed and behind him to turn on the light in the room.

The brunette had lost her dress but left her heels and underwear on. As for the redhead next to her, she was in a similar state, but she'd left her red corset on while the brunette was topless.

Uninterested, I sat back in my chair and pressed a finger in my ear.

"You're getting this?" I whispered under my breath to avoid making my presence known. It wasn't the time just yet.

"Can't get a better angle than that," Kai said and I could hear the smile in his voice.

Once the one with the red corset unbuttoned his shirt, he grabbed her upper arms and pushed her on her knees. "Take me out," he said gruffly.

The redhead followed suit and undid his slacks, then pulled his cock out. He pointed to the other and asked her to get on the bed as he lay on his back. "And you, come give Daddy that pretty pussy of yours," he instructed her, throwing her a sly smirk.

I think we've got enough.

I got out of my seat and quietly made my way closer to the French doors.

The senator's hands skimmed over the brunette's thighs, opening her legs wider as she straddled his face. The chandelier's light glinted off the gold ring on his left finger as he brought her down to his face while the redhead swirled her tongue around his cock.

They were all too occupied to see that I'd opened the doors wider and was now leaning a shoulder against the doorframe. My favorite part of suffering through this was about to come and I waited another few seconds just for show.

I have to entertain myself in some way.

"I see you're making good use of the money you owe me."

The girl on the floor spat out his limp dick as he shot up

straight, throwing the other girl away from him and off the bed.

"What the—" He cut himself off when he realized who I was. His face paled and he scrambled off the bed, tucking himself back in his pants. He grabbed the girls' clothes off the floor and threw them at them. "Leave," he ordered.

"But you still have a full hour," one of them whined. She shifted her attention to me. "The more, the merrier," she suggested.

"I'm married."

"That's what they all say," she said, coming closer.

I put a hand out to stop her in her tracks. "I would never disrespect my wife."

It wasn't for their lack of looks that I'd rejected the offer, but it's been two weeks since I saw Sienna for the first time and no one would ever hold a candle to her.

"Leave. Now," Senator Ricci barked, pointing at the door.

"You haven't paid us yet," the redhead interjected.

"You'll be paid for your time," I informed them. "You may go now," I finished, nodding for them to head to the door.

"How—"

"You have my word."

Seeming to finally believe me, they pulled their clothes back on and walked out the door.

I pushed off the doorframe and walked over to him, closing the distance. "Now, where were we?"

"I-I can explain," he tripped over his words, backing away from me.

"There's no need." I tapped my fingers on the front of my suit pocket where a microscopic camera was attached. "I've got everything here."

Shock colored his face. "Please, don't tell my wife."

I gave him a rough laugh. "She deserves better, but that's not why I'm here."

"I-I'll get you your money," he promised, but I knew better.

"We're past that now. I need something else from you."

I took another step in his direction and he stepped back, cornering himself into the wall and giving me the perfect opportunity to pull my gun out.

His hands shot up, his shoulders hunching. "Please don't kill me. I'll give you anything you want."

Using the barrel of my gun, I gave him a small tap on his cheek. He flinched, closing his eyes shut. "Now where would the fun be if I did that?" I taunted.

He opened his eyes when the cold metal left his skin.

I sighed, resting on the edge of the bed, my gun aimed at him. He was trembling and I reveled in it.

"Back to you giving me everything I want," I told him calmly and he lowered his defenses.

"Anything, I swear."

I smirked. "Good." Not wanting to waste any more time, I said, "I need you to give me the time Bianchi is meeting with Barrera next Friday. And I would refrain from lying and telling me you have no idea what I'm talking about. I know you're on their payroll and they're using your offices to meet."

Kai, Valentina, and I had tried everything, but we still couldn't figure out the time of the meeting. We'd combed every email and document shared between Bianchi and Barrera with no luck. So I'd decided to take the old-fashioned route of blackmailing.

He straightened up, his face paling even more. "I can't do that."

"You can and you will. If you refuse, the video I just recorded of you with two girls who are probably the same age as your daughter will be plastered on every media outlet on the island I can find. I don't believe you'd want your wife to find out about your indiscretions or your constituents to learn how you like to spend their money."

"But they'll kill me if they—"

I sighed. "I don't particularly care. And it's only if they find out." I clicked the safety off, aiming the barrel at his head. "Now, be a good boy and give me the information I need or I'll be the one to kill you."

He brought his hands back up in front of his face, shielding himself. As if they would protect him from a bullet.

Pathetic.

"O-okay, I'll tell you. Just please don't shoot me," he begged, warily eyeing the weapon aimed at him.

I pointed the silencer lower and shot the side of his knee. "I'm running out of patience, Senator Ricci."

He screamed in pain and fell to his knees. His hands clasped on the wound as blood seeped out, painting the beige fabric red.

So dramatic. I barely grazed him.

"We're supposed to leave the office before seven p.m.," he whimpered. "That's all I know, I swear." He cried quietly, holding on tightly to his injured knee.

"See, that was easy. If you tell anyone this conversation took place, your little escapade from tonight will find its way to the entire island," I informed him, then got up and exited the room.

"Did you have to shoot him?" Kai asked when I pushed the button for the elevator.

I tucked the gun in my waistband behind my back as I stepped into the cabin. "It was for good measure. Besides, I barely made a dent in him. He was exaggerating his injury. "

He sighed. "You coming home or do you have more business to attend to?"

"This was enough for tonight. I'll see you in a bit."

The door slid open and I stepped off, removing the earpiece and sliding it into one of my inside pockets. I passed the hotel lobby and pushed open the glass doors to the renowned five-star hotel most politicians liked to visit for their secret encounters.

The valet stood with my car already parked up front. I

thanked him and slid him an extra few bills for getting my car on time like I'd requested when I came in.

He nodded. "Always a pleasure, Mr. Brown."

I fell into the driver's seat and threw my car into gear, the tires screeching as I pulled away, the sun setting behind me.

CHAPTER 12

Two weeks had passed since I'd been naked in front of my husband and he'd taken care of me.

He'd been different that night, letting me see a side of him I'd never imagined possible. I thought things would change, that he'd be more approachable, but I was wrong.

Like a switch had gone off, he went back to the Jamal I'd grown accustomed to. He became even more distant and had barely spoken a word to me since then.

I was walking toward the staff lounge after my shift when I heard my name being called out.

"Sienna, wait up," a familiar voice said.

I turned to see Kenna, in scrubs, making her way toward me from the end of the hall. "Kenna?" I asked, surprised to see her here.

I knew the hospital she worked at was still renovating

after the flood since we were still receiving their influx of patients, but I was confused as to what she was doing here.

She finally made her way over and bumped my shoulder as we continued walking. "Hey, beautiful," she greeted me.

"Hi, gorgeous. What are you doing here?"

"I got a page that one of my patients landed in the ER here. She's scheduled for a CABG next week, so I came to check her out myself."

I chuckled, pushing the staff's room door open. "You know we have doctors here, right?"

"No offense to your staff, but I'd rather check her out myself," she said as she straddled the wooden bench in front of the row of lockers.

I shook my head at her and opened my locker. "You're the only doctor I know who will come on their day off, to another hospital, might I add, to check on a patient."

I grabbed my clothes out of my locker and placed them on the bench she was sitting on.

She rolled her eyes at me, her fingers tapping on the side of the seat. "You mean except you."

I let out a small laugh and changed out of my scrubs and into a pair of ribbed leggings and my favorite oversized Formula One sweatshirt. We were in the middle of spring, but it was still so cold outside.

"Are you still coming to the wedding?" she asked, and I groaned internally.

Fuck, I completely forgot about the wedding.

I dropped the hospital scrubs into the hamper and sat next to her. "Absolutely, I am," I confirmed, infusing as much enthusiasm as I could into my voice.

She narrowed her eyes at me. "You forgot, didn't you?"

"Of course not. It's your wedding. How could I forget such an important day in your life?"

"Oh, yeah? So you'll be there Saturday."

This Saturday. Like Saturday in two days.

"Mmhmm," I lied, giving her a forced smile as I mentally went through every resident, trying to figure out who I could switch shifts with since I was working that day.

She flicked me over the side of the head. "Sienna, cut the shit. I know you forgot."

"Okay, I did. I'm sorry," I apologized, my shoulders dropping.

"Lucky for you, my wedding is actually next week, so you have plenty of time to find someone to replace you if you're working next Saturday. Are you... bringing *him*?"

By him, she meant my husband. Well, the other supposed one.

"I'll have to ask him."

"Talking about Mateo, how's being married to him?" she asked, crossing her arms over her chest. "He better be treating you well."

Yeah, I still hadn't told her or Esra about my new marital situation.

My finger mindlessly started tapping against the side of

the bench. "Um, Kenna, about my wedding…" I trailed off, pausing and contemplating whether I should tell her the truth or not.

She glanced down and noticed I was getting more anxious by the minute. She placed her hand over mine, rubbing circles over my knuckles.

I looked up at her and she furrowed her brows at the look on my face.

"Sienna, what's wrong?" she asked, worried.

"I didn't marry Mateo," I blurted out and immediately let out a sigh of relief.

God, telling her felt good. I'd been wanting to talk about everything that had happened with her and Esra, but confessing my father's shortcomings once had already been difficult, so I'd been dreading having to do it again.

Kenna raised her brows. "What do you mean you didn't marry Mateo?"

I unwound my hands from her, fidgeting with my ring.

"Turns out my father had already promised me to someone else," I said, letting out a sardonic laugh.

"Please tell me you're joking."

"I wish I were."

I spend the next few minutes catching her up on everything. With every additional detail I gave her, her frustration grew.

She muttered under her breath before saying, "I know he's your father, but, respectfully, what an as—"

Her pager buzzed, cutting her off. She glanced down at

it before meeting my gaze. "I have to go, but we'll talk more later."

She got up and walked to the door, only to pause on her way out. She whipped around and walked back over to me, then wrapped her arms around me.

I froze for a moment.

Kenna, much like me, wasn't really a hugger, so I didn't know how to feel about her sudden affectionate outburst.

She pulled back almost immediately and laughed softly. "I know we don't do this, but I love you."

"I love you too," I replied, giving her a small smile.

"Okay, I really have to go now," she said, rushing out of the room.

I slid off the bench, grabbed my bag from my locker, and made my way to my car.

I was halfway home when the buzzing that my car usually made grew louder. I cursed under my breath and gripped my steering wheel tighter.

I groaned. "Please, please don't give up on me. Not now." I hoped the car gods would hear my prayer and get me home before it gave up on me.

But I spoke too soon.

The sun was dipping low behind the horizon when black smoke poured out of the hood. I barely had time to pull over when it stuttered to a stop.

No me jodas.

I dropped my head back, running my hands over my face and fighting the urge to laugh at my lack of luck.

Gathering myself, I pushed on the distress signal. After I made sure there were no cars in sight, I climbed out and rounded to the front of my car. I popped the hood and stepped back, letting the steam disperse in the air.

I looked over at the transmission, knowing that was most likely the issue, only to find that it was completely blown.

Of course this would happen to me.

The repairs would cost me a fortune. One I definitely couldn't afford on a resident's salary.

Once I realized that there wasn't any way for me to fix it this time, I mentally went through who I could call to help. Kenna was at work and Esra was out of town for a fashion show. My parents' house was about an hour away in the other direction.

I let out a huffed breath then fished my phone out of my pocket and dialed the last number I wanted to call. Surprisingly, less than twenty minutes later, his car pulled over in front of mine.

He glared at me as soon as I stepped out of my car. "What did you do?"

What the hell is his problem?

Ignoring his attitude, I calmly replied, "My transmission finally gave out on me. It's usually fine, but I guess today wasn't my lucky day."

His brows slammed together. "Wait, you mean to tell me that you've been driving this thing with a bad transmission?"

He did not just call my car 'this thing.' Breathe, Sienna. He's not worth getting worked up over.

"It's not a big d—"

His eyes squinted in frustration, and he closed the distance, cutting me off. "A big deal? *A big deal?* Do you know how dangerous that is?" he asked, towering over me.

My back was now pressed against the front of my car. Irritation clawed at my chest at his tone. I placed my hands over his chest and pushed him back. "I didn't call you to be berated. I called you for help. Now, if you're not going to, you can leave." I groaned. "I'll just call someone else."

I slipped from under him and moved to walk away, but he wrapped his fingers around my wrist and pulled me flush to his chest. He leaned his head down, his lips almost brushing mine. "You will do no such thing. I am your husband and therefore the *only* one you call when you need help," he gritted through his teeth.

Then he let go of me and I stumbled back, my heart hammering in my chest.

Nudging his head toward his car, he said, "Get in the car, Sienna."

"What about my car?"

"Already taken care of." He pulled the passenger door open. "Now get in."

We got home in half the time it usually would have

taken me and the entire ride was spent in a deafening silence. My heart was still pounding from earlier and I could feel his irritation coming off of him in waves.

I should be the one angry. *My* car gave out on me and now I needed to find another way to get to work. Not only that, but I'd lost the only thing that gave me a semblance of freedom. The place I could escape to when I needed a break from the house, and now I didn't even know if I'd get it back.

He parked into his spot and slammed his door shut behind him, then came to my side to open the door for me before he moved toward the front door. I stepped out and followed behind him, listening to him mutter under his breath in French and growing more furious with each step I took.

I've had enough.

"What's your problem?" I huffed out, gripping the strap of my tote bag to rein myself in.

I wasn't one to let frustration take control of my emotions, but he was just *infuriating*. I had complied with this marriage, moved in with him, and agreed to his stupid rules and that's how he acted.

He whipped around. "My problem?"

"Yes, your problem? I had nothing to do with this," I said, gesturing back and forth between us. "*You* made me marry you. I've been nothing but nice and you just…" I frowned and huffed, imitating him.

He coughed up a laugh.

"This isn't funny, I'm serious," I said sternly, but he peered at me like I was joking.

He cocked his head to the side. "It's a little bit funny if you think that's what I look like."

"Well, it is."

He surprised me by letting out an actual laugh. It was short-lived, but it was now ingrained in my brain. I wanted to stay mad, but hearing him laugh for the first time was a sight to see. His eyes wrinkled on the sides and a dimple popped in one of his cheeks.

Rain trickled over my head and I schooled my features back to an irritated expression. "Let's just go inside."

"After you, *wife*."

I frowned. "Don't call me that," I replied, brushing past him.

Once we were inside, he disappeared into his office without another word and I walked over to the kitchen, my stomach growling from the fact that I hadn't eaten since lunch and it was almost 9:00 p.m.

After eating leftovers from last night, I went to bed feeling unsettled. The word wife and the way he'd said it on a constant loop in my head.

CHAPTER 13

I WOKE UP STILL THINKING ABOUT HIM AND I HATED MYSELF for it.

I shouldn't be feeling anything for him except hatred and yet…

Shaking off these absurd feelings, I got out of bed and stepped under a cold shower, hoping it would knock some sense into me.

It didn't work.

Stepping out of the shower, I walked into the closet through the door that connected both rooms and grabbed clothes. Walking back inside my bedroom, I briefly glanced at the clock. It was almost 4:45 a.m., which meant I still had a little time before I had to leave.

It was criminal to be up this early, but after being down a car, I needed to leave the house earlier than I usually would if I wanted to be on time for my shift.

I packed my workbag and changed into my oversized gray Matrix Motorsports sweater, pairing it with loose black cargo pants.

Then I tiptoed down the stairs to avoid waking Jamal and quickly stopped in the kitchen to grab a granola bar for breakfast. It was almost 5:00 a.m. by the time I stepped out of the house and started walking toward the bus stop.

The sun was rising and a slight ocean breeze brushed over me. I wrapped my arms around my body and cursed myself for not wearing a jacket. I usually didn't have to since I was in the confines of my car, but I didn't think of checking the weather before rushing out of the house.

I pulled my phone out of my cargos and checked the time: 5:15 a.m. I only had eight more minutes before the bus would be there and the stop still seemed so far away from where I was.

I picked up my pace, praying I would reach it in time. Arriving late to a shift as a resident wasn't a good look. I had a stellar record, so I wasn't about to start tainting it now.

Sweat slicked my forehead and my breathing was coming out quicker when I heard the sound of an engine.

Fuck.

"Sienna."

The deep, rich voice of my husband brushed against my skin and stopped me in my tracks.

I turned my head and watched him slow his car to

match my pace. I kept walking. "I'm about to be late for work," I threw out behind me.

He pulled to a stop beside me and called my name again. I stepped down off the curb and walked over to his car, leaning over the rolled down passenger window.

"What do you want?" I asked in a hurry, needing to leave before I missed the bus.

Jamal rested his forearm on the steering wheel and turned his body toward me. "Get in. I'll take you."

"It's okay. The bus will be here in two minutes. I'm sure you have better things to do."

Besides, I planned on watching the first practice while I was on the bus since it was a race weekend. I moved to walk away, but the soft click of the door unlocking halted me in my movement.

"I'm not letting you take public transport. Get in."

"Public transportation is perfectly acceptable."

"I said, get in the car, Sienna."

That's when the bus whirred past us. So I got in the car.

"Just to clarify, I'm only getting in because you made me miss the bus and I can't afford to be late if I wait for the next one."

"Mhmm," was the only thing he said before he pulled away from the curb. He reached for his dashboard and a few seconds later, my seat warmed up.

I sank deeper into it, silently grateful for it.

I slid a brief glance in his direction, wanting to say something to fight this suffocating silence that always seemed to accompany our time together but thought better of it.

Instead, I unlocked my phone and pulled up the sports channel like I'd intended to do this morning. I reached for my headphones in my bag and connected them before placing them over my head. I rested my head against the window and watched the practice as I had intended to.

There were about ten minutes left to FP1 when Jamal pulled up in front of the hospital's main doors. I took my headphones off, the practice still playing on my phone, and looked over at him.

"Thank you."

I moved to open the passenger door but forgot that this wasn't a car I was used to. Before I could look for the handle to open it, he reached over, his body pressed against mine, and pulled a lever from inside the door.

He pushed the side up to open it, but once it was, he didn't move.

I peered down at him and held my breath. My cheeks flushed at his proximity and gravitational force urged me to lean further down and brush my lips against his, but he had the sense to pull away.

Something I should've done first.

My body instantly missed the feel of him pressed against me, but I brushed the thought away and simply muttered another thank you.

I stepped out of the car and closed the door behind me. I was barely a few feet away when he rolled the passenger window down and asked, "What time does your shift end?"

I turned around to face him. "Eight p.m. Why?"

"I'll be here."

Before I could say that it wasn't necessary for him to pick me up, he drove off.

When I walked out of Monte Claro later that evening, he was there, just like he said he would. In fact, he drove me and picked me up for every shift since then, no matter the time.

After the fourth day of driving in total silence, I couldn't bear it anymore. I'd usually welcome it after a long day of work, but if I had to spend another minute like this, I'd lose it.

"So," I said tentatively, breaking the quiet stillness we basked in.

He slowly turned his head toward me. "So?"

"What's your favorite color?" I blurted out.

His brows furrowed and he returned his attention to the road. "My favorite color?"

"Are you going to repeat everything I say? Yes, your favorite color."

"Why?"

"We're married, Jamal," I said sternly. "If we're going to make this marriage believable as per your request, we need to know each other. Or at least pretend to."

"And knowing my favorite color is going to convince people we're madly in love with each other?"

"Never mind."

We went back to the familiar silence before he let out a long sigh.

"Do I get something if I agree?"

"If you're a good boy and answer everything I ask," I replied without thinking.

He spoke before I could say something else to mask what I'd just said. "Brown," he revealed. "I'm only answering five questions, and you already asked one. So if we're doing this, ask better questions."

I straightened in my seat and tucked a leg under me, shifting to face him. "That's not fair."

"I never said I was. Take it or leave it."

"Of all the colors, you chose brown," I said, conceding.

"You said you wanted to ask me questions, not judge my answers."

I held my hands up. "Fair enough. Mine's purple, in case you were wondering.

"What do you do for work?" I asked, curious.

Kai had mentioned they worked together with Valentina, but I still wasn't sure what they actually did. Especially since I couldn't understand how that ultimately led my father to 'request his services.'

"Security."

A small huff left my lips. "I'll need more than one-word answers."

He looked back at me. "You didn't stipulate rules, love."

I crossed my arms over my chest. "I thought it was implied."

He let out another sigh. "Fine. I co-own a cyber-security company with Kai."

"You like it?"

"That sounds like a follow-up question. I can answer it, but that'll count toward your total number of questions."

Even when it came to simple questions, he had rules.

I shook my head. "Fine. We can drop that one." I paused for a moment, thinking of another question. "Okay," I finally said. "This is an easy one. What's your last name?"

His demeanor suddenly shifted at my question. "Brown," he said softly, his face turning serious. His expression felt conflicted and I was about to change the subject when he continued, "But my real last name is Aguerd," he confessed. There was now a softness to his features, as if the confession tugged at a buried memory.

I waited a beat and then asked, "Why Brown?"

My question seemed to snap him out of his thoughts and he gave me a quick look before answering. "I took my uncle's last name when my parents died."

"I'm sorry," I said quietly, resting my hand on his forearm.

He glanced at where my hand touched him and his gaze connected briefly with mine before he turned his attention back to the road. He cleared his throat, changing the subject. "What's your next question?"

Deciding to venture into lighter territory, I asked, "Do you prefer receiving or giving gifts?"

His gaze locked with mine once more as he gave me his answer. "I'm more of a giver."

I flushed at the undertone in his response and shifted in my seat.

"You have one more question," he said, as if what he'd just said didn't send my brain into a frenzy of images of how much of a giver he could be.

Shaking my head, I dismantled the countless images forming in my brain and racked my brain for my final question. There were a ton of personal questions I wanted to ask him, but one in particular kept coming to the forefront.

A question that had been plaguing my brain since the first day we'd met.

"Why did you marry me?" I asked quietly, my eyes trying to find his.

He fell silent, but I waited patiently for him to speak. We stayed silent for a long stretch of time, the sound of our breathing filling the space.

"Because I wanted to," he finally admitted, avoiding my gaze.

He turned the engine off, indicating we were here. The drive over to the house usually felt quite long, but this time, I wished it had been longer.

"We're home," he said before stepping out of the car.

I looked out the passenger window and at the house I'd lived in over the last three weeks.

Yes, we are.

Waiting rooms were usually full of people waiting and hoping for good news, but I knew walking in that the news I was about to give would decimate any hope her parents had.

Lily, five years old. She'd been playing outside when a reckless driver drove into her front yard, injuring her in the process.

She was five. Just five. She had her whole life ahead of her. But despite our attempts at resuscitation, she'd suffered too many injuries and internal bleeding to make it back.

The sound of the flatline still echoed into my skull as I walked over to her parents. I'd lost patients before—hell, I lost another two this week alone—but I'd never expected to lose a young patient.

I felt my finger wanting to reach to my thigh, the anxiety creeping into a crescendo, but I smothered it down.

If you let it take over, you won't be able to do your job.

Lily's parents jumped up when they saw me, their faces briefly lit up with hope that suddenly turned into worry when a smile didn't appear on my face.

That worry morphed into an agonizing cry from her mother as soon as the words "I'm sorry" left my lips.

She dropped to her knees and cries of denial erupted into the room. "No, no, no, it's not true. It can't be."

I tried to maintain a stoic expression, shoving the waves of guilt I felt inside for not being able to bring her daughter back, but every sound she made squeezed my lungs tighter until it made it hard to breathe.

Her husband tried to get her up, but she couldn't.

"My baby is gone," she sobbed.

He joined her on the floor and cradled her head into his chest. "I know, baby. I know," he said, trying to comfort her.

I dropped to my haunches in front of her. My hand moved to reach her, but I refrained from it, not knowing if she'd welcome it. "Nothing I can say could make this any easier, but I'm truly so sorry for your loss. If you'd like, I can take you to see her," I offered softly.

Lily's parents eventually both looked at me and nodded.

After we walked into the room, I left them to their grief and filled out the necessary documents they'd need.

Then I firmly put my mask back on and got back to work, ignoring the incessant pressure clawing at my rib cage and the unending sound of the flatline and shuddering cries of grief occupying every inch of my brain.

CHAPTER 14

As soon as I saw her, I knew something was wrong.

"Are you okay?" I asked as she settled into the passenger seat.

"Yeah, I'm fine." She fastened her seat belt, avoiding looking at me.

"Did someone hurt you?" I asked, my mind going into a frenzy at the thought.

"No, I'm fine." Noticing I hadn't moved, she added, "Let's just go home."

Home. I liked that she called my house her home.

"Okay," I replied quietly, not wanting to push her before she was ready to talk about whatever happened. So I pulled away and beelined home.

We'd been parked in our driveaway for the last ten minutes and she still hadn't moved. I reached for a loose strand of her hair that escaped her bun and tucked it behind her ear.

"Sienna," I murmured.

She hummed quietly, still looking in front of her.

My thumb grazed the soft skin on the side of her face and it jolted her out of her thoughts. "We're home, baby."

She blew out a long breath and finally turned her face toward me.

"Let's get you inside," I said, moving to take her bag from her hand, but she clutched it tighter.

"One minute, Jamal," Sienna said ever so softly I'd barely heard her. "I just need one minute," she whispered, her voice breaking at the end.

Her statement made my heart stutter, the way her voice cracked latching itself into the little nook she'd been digging for herself inside my rib cage.

"Okay," I finally said, taking my hand back. I shifted in my seat to face up front.

I glanced at her sideways to see her close her eyes, noticing a tear trailing down her cheek. My heart sank, threatening to crumble at the sight.

Despite not knowing her for a long time, I knew my wife never showed her vulnerability to others. Especially me. I wanted to ask her what was wrong and how I could help, but she'd already told me.

"One minute," I mirrored. Then, without thinking, I reached for her hand and intertwined our fingers together.

I knew touching her was a bad idea because it meant walking through a fire knowing I'd burn myself.

But for a moment, none of that mattered.

Just for a minute.

I'd always made decisions based on rationality, considering every angle and finding ways to mitigate consequences. But right now, the notions of consequences blurred and the instinct to comfort her overtook me.

I wasn't supposed to give in to these *feelings* she was inspiring. And yet, here I was, letting the need to make sure she was okay guide my actions.

Just for a minute.

For one minute, all I wanted to do was sit with her and forget about who I was and who she was and just be *us*.

A man with a woman who upset the balance of everything he'd believed in.

A husband with his wife in a moment where she needed him to just *be* there.

We sat in silence, the seconds trickling by.

The moment felt longer than a minute, but once it was over, she removed her hand from mine and I missed the contact immediately. I should have been thankful that she'd put a halt to my lapse of judgment, but I couldn't ignore the desire to do it again blazing inside me.

Grabbing her bag, she stepped out of the car and I followed her inside the house.

"I'm going to head to bed," she simply said and

climbed the stairs. She still hadn't looked at me since we'd left the car and I didn't like it.

I didn't like the thought of her being sad, so I did the only thing I could think of and headed to the kitchen.

About an hour later, I stood at her door. I kept lying to myself that I was here because it was the right thing to do. But I apparently couldn't stay away.

Especially when I didn't know if she was still unhappy.

Being here was dangerous, but fuck that if my wife wasn't okay.

I finally knocked after standing here for the past five minutes, staring at her door, trying to determine whether I should or shouldn't. She hesitantly cracked her door open and surprise etched her features when she registered it was me on the other side.

She was freshly showered, her wet hair wrapped in a towel. My eyes drank her in.

Beautiful.

I mean, she always was.

She wore an oversized black T-shirt and matching boxers that hugged her body.

Her cheeks flushed when our gazes met and she shifted, hiding herself behind the door. "Yes?"

I took a step toward her, pushing the bowl of *sancocho* between us. "I made you food."

She stared at me, seeming in disbelief. "You made this for me?

"I thought it might make you feel better," I said hesitantly. I figured she might like something comforting, so I thought this recipe might work, but I might have been wrong. I stepped back. "I can go back down and make you something different if you don't like this. Sorry, I should've asked. Let me—"

She placed a hand on my arm, stopping me in my tracks. "No, Jamal. It's perfect." She took the bowl and spoon from my hands. "Thank you."

I scratched the top of my brow, not knowing what to do next. "Okay, I'll leave you to it."

"Stay," she blurted out, taking me by surprise.

"You've had a long day. I don't want to—"

"I want you to."

She stepped to the side and let me in. Then she walked to her closet and came out pulling a large sweatshirt over her head. It had a similar design on the front to the one she wore the first time I drove her to work but in a different color.

She propped herself on the edge of the bed while I stood a few steps in front of the door, not knowing where to appropriately place myself. The only place to sit was her bed, but I didn't want to make her uncomfortable.

With anyone else, I couldn't have cared less, but it was different with her. I was quite a confident man, but for some reason, being around her unsettled me to the point I didn't know what to do with myself.

She patted the space next to her on the bed. "You can

sit," she offered. "If you want," she quickly added when she sensed my hesitation.

I nodded once in response and walked over to the bed, settling next to her but leaving a generous distance between us to avoid any accidental brushing. I didn't think I could handle touching her again without crossing a line.

I leaned against the headboard and watched her stir the contents of the bowl.

"This smells amazing," she said and somehow it filled me with pride.

"I hope it's good." I knew it would be, but it was still my first time making it, so I didn't want to get ahead of myself.

My eyes zoned in on her slightly parted lips as she blew on the spoonful of the stew. Thoughts of her parting her lips in a different situation swarmed my mind, but I quickly shook my head, dispelling them.

Mais qu'est-ce qui ne va pas chez moi.

She took a bite and I waited for a reaction, but she just shrugged her shoulders.

My brows furrowed. "What's wrong?"

"It's okay," she said, but a small smile tugged on her lips before she wiped it away and took another spoonful of the stewed beef and vegetables.

I narrowed my eyes at her. "You're lying."

She threw her head back in laughter and it echoed off the wall, making its way to my ears. The sound was so rich, it unexpectedly filled me with warmth.

She laughed with her whole body, her face lighting up, and I sucked in a sharp breath. I stared at her parted lips, desperate to hear it again. It was just another realization that she'd taken another jab at the wall I'd erected to keep her away.

The notion that I could get used to hearing it more often planted itself in my mind and that was something I shouldn't want to get used to.

"You should see your face," she said, amused.

I crossed my arms. "Nothing's wrong with my face."

"Oh, trust me. I know," she said, still laughing.

Our eyes met and the possibility of her finding me attractive made me flush.

That's a first.

I cleared my throat. "My turn," I let slip without thinking, wanting to dissipate the tension crackling in the air.

She took a bite from a piece of corn and asked, "Your turn for what?"

I'd cornered myself into this, but instead of regretting it, I ran with it. If I was being honest, I'd been wanting to know more about her since she'd asked me to play along two days ago. "You asked me questions. Now it's my turn."

Her eyebrows drew in before her eyes widened in realization. "You're serious."

"Have I ever made a joke?"

"Good point." She climbed farther onto the bed, joining me. She sat back, leaning her back against the headboard.

Great, so much for keeping my distance. "You also only get five, so what do you want to know?"

"Have you always wanted to be a doctor?"

A warm smile lit up her face.

Comment j'adore la voir sourire.

"Yeah, I have. This might sound very cliché, but I've always wanted to help people in some way and for me, the best way was to become a doctor." She grinned as she continued. "I love the unknown the ER brings, the challenge that comes with every day and how I get to always have my brain on when I'm working. There's a thrill to it and although some days are more challenging than others, I wouldn't trade it for anything else."

I loved how animated she became when she talked about her job. It reminded me of my mother and how much she loved creating her art every day. The more time I spent with Sienna, the more I found a resemblance between her character and my mother's.

And it made me miss her terribly.

I moved on to my next question, the one I'd been thinking about since I'd picked her up. "What happened earlier?"

My question took her off guard. "You don't beat around the bush, do you?" She laughed.

I shrugged. "It's not like me to do so."

She stayed quiet for a moment, taking another scoop of the stew into her mouth. I wondered if she would ignore my question when she finally spoke again. "I lost a patient today," she said quietly. "A young girl. She was only five years old."

I wanted to reach for her but thought better of it. "I'm sorry."

"I'm a doctor. It's part of the job."

"Yeah, but—"

"What's your next question?" She interrupted me.

"What's your biggest fear?"

She let out a small laugh, but I could tell my question unsettled her. "Wow, okay. That's not the direction I thought your questions would take when I'd agreed to this."

She averted her gaze.

"Not finding happiness," she admitted, staring at the ceiling. "I have my dream job, live comfortably, and have a family, but I don't think I can say that I'm happy." Her voice fell to a whisper at the end, as if she caught herself revealing more than she'd intended to.

Her confession hurt to hear and it didn't escape me how her voice faltered when she mentioned her family loving her.

"Tell me about your family."

She swallowed roughly. "That's not really a question, Jamal." She fidgeted with her spoon, twirling around the remainder. She let out a deep breath. "I have two sisters, Iris and Akari, and we had an overall good childhood. My dad used to work in finance and my mom was a nurse before she retired when my dad got his new job. But things went a little downhill after his new…" She paused, looking for the appropriate word for her father's entry into the mafia. "Venture. He let it get to his head a little bit. But despite my grievances with him, he's still my father."

"What about your mom?"

She smiled a little, but she seemed sad. "She has the best heart even if sometimes it is to my detriment."

"What do you mean by that?"

"Just that sometimes her decisions led to too much responsibility falling on my shoulders."

"Sometimes the people we love don't realize the pain they're causing us," I said quietly. "In their own way, they think their decisions are what's best for us, but they're often blinded by their need to do the right thing that they can't realize it happens to be the wrong choice."

She stayed quiet for a moment, as if she was mulling over my words. Then, she simply nodded, and cleared her throat. "Okay, you're down to your last question."

Wanting to see her smile again, I asked, "What's one thing on your bucket list?"

She let out a breath. "Finally an easy one." She shifted to face me and tucked her feet under her. "Follow the F1 calendar for a whole year."

"Is that what you were watching in the car last week?"

"Yes." She laughed lightly and I felt the comforting warmth her laugh brought me seep into my chest.

Putain, je suis foutu.

"Why would you want to watch cars race in circles for a whole year?"

The look of outrage on her face amused me.

She flicked me upside the head. "It's not just cars circling around."

I rubbed the back of my head where she'd slapped me. "What?" I asked, surprised by her playfulness. I wanted more of it.

"I will let you know they're high-performance athletes. Besides, it gives me the same thrill as being in the ER. I've never been to a Grand Prix, but I would lo—"

My phone buzzed, cutting her off. I pulled it out of my slacks and looked at the caller.

Kai. Fuck.

I wanted to stay here for hours, her company surprisingly more delightful than I anticipated. However, I knew I couldn't, so reluctantly, I said, "I'm so sorry. I have to go."

"It's okay," she said, her previous smile dimming.

"Have a good night, *wife*," I teased her, but deep down I was starting to love the way the word sounded.

She laughed. "You too, *husband*."

I got up and was about to walk out when she said, "Thank you, Jamal. For everything.

I turned around to face her, her eyes meeting mine. "You're my wife. You never have to thank me for taking care of you," I said sincerely and closed the door behind me.

Jamal

CHAPTER 15

"Any movement?" I asked through my earpiece.

"None," Kai answered first.

"Negative," Valentina mirrored.

"The meeting should be any minute now. I'm surprised no one's here yet."

We'd been waiting in the building for the last two hours, each in our respective locations. Kai and I had entered the building through the front door, passing security under the pretense that we were meeting a client, while Valentina came in through the roof.

The floor where the meeting was taking place was still under construction, so I sat on a wooden box in the back and waited patiently for Barrera and Bianchi to show up.

Kai was currently on the floor below me, watching through his surveillance equipment, while Valentina was stationed on the floor above mine, near the exit staircase if anyone decided to make a run for it.

Valentina and Kai had spent the last three weeks training since we'd planned for him to be by my side, but before we showed up, I'd lied and told him that I needed him to be my eyes and ears instead of another helping hand.

He might have been prepared, but I'd lost too many people to be willing to jeopardize his safety. Besides, Kai didn't have a bad bone in his body. He might have witnessed me torture and kill a few people in the past, but watching and actually taking someone's life were two different things.

One was scarring while the other was life-altering.

"Jamal—" Kai started saying, but his voice cut off, an unending buzzing replacing it.

"Kai, repeat."

No answer.

I tried again, but a single pair of footsteps echoed down the hall.

Something's off.

I got up and grabbed both of my guns out of their holsters, my fingers ready on the triggers. Pushing the tarp hanging from the ceiling out of my way with one of the barrels, I aimed both weapons at the door whoever was here would have to walk through to access the floor.

"Jamal, retreat," I finally heard Valentina shouting in my ear, warning me, the sound of her running down the stairs echoing in my earpiece. "It's a trap."

Before I could register what she'd just said, I watched the door open on someone I hadn't expected to see.

Mateo Barrera.

I cursed under my breath. *C'est quoi ce bordel.*

He let out a dark chuckle, his rusty laugh grating my nerves. "I'm not who you were expecting, now am I?"

"What are you doing here?" I asked him.

"I'm here to take back what's mine."

Before I could answer Mateo, Kai's voice came back into my ear. "Someone fucking jammed our comms. You're about to be outnumbered. There are seven more men coming your way."

The ding of the elevator doors opening on my left rang into the space. Then, bullets exploded as seven armed men stepped out of the elevator.

Ah, les connards.

I ducked my body behind a column and scanned the room. Five of his men stayed on the far left side with their guns blazing, while two were making their way to Mateo, fingers on their triggers.

The exit staircase was on the right, but Mateo and his men were too close for me to make a beeline for it.

"Valentina, we need to create a distraction. Mateo and two of his men are too close to the exit door for me to make it."

"Got it."

The exit door slammed open and Valentina walked

through it, aimlessly firing her machine gun at the ceiling, debris falling everywhere.

Not the distraction I was thinking of, but it'd do.

Peering through the dust clouding the room, I spotted one man struggling to see and fired straight into his neck. He fell to his knees and his hand shot up to stop the bleeding, but instead, he slammed forward on the concrete floor.

One down, four more to go.

I couldn't find half of them, but the other half were ducked behind stacked bricks on palettes.

"The cops are five minutes out," Kai informed us. "I'm parked behind. Hurry."

I looked over at Valentina, watching her dive her body behind a column next to the exit, reloading her gun. I peered over my shoulder to see Mateo running away, one of his men shielding him while the other shot at us on their way out.

Coward.

Bullets ricocheted against the concrete shielding us.

"Quite the entrance." I chuckled.

"Yeah, I thought so too," she replied, giving me a sly grin. "I'll start firing again on three."

I nodded.

"Three," she shouted before shooting from behind the pillar.

One of the men behind the stacked bricks looked over at where Valentina was and I took the opportunity to shoot him in the head. Blood spattered onto his face and he dropped to the floor.

"You guys have to get out now," Kai urged, the distant wail of sirens growing closer. "The authorities are almost here."

I glanced at Valentina and she gave me a nod, showing her understanding.

We both came out of our hiding and fired while running toward the exit. We leapt over the first flight of stairs and continued running down the rest to reach the ground floor.

We had three more floors to go when the door from right above us slammed open. Several shots were fired at us and I turned back to retaliate. At one point, I felt heat sear my side but ignored it and managed to shoot whoever was after us in the shoulder.

He slumped back against the wall and I whipped around as Valentina pushed the ground floor's door open. We rushed over to Kai's car and as soon as we were inside, he slammed on the gas pedal, speeding away from the cops.

A black SUV chased after us, its sirens wailing furiously. Kai abruptly veered the car to the right, jolting Valentina and me in the back seat. The tires shrieked and he entered a small alley, barely an inch to spare on either side.

He floored the gas again and barreled down the path.

I heard the screech of the SUV behind us and looked through the rear windshield to see them trying to get into the alley, but it was too small for them to fit. So they reversed and sped away, most likely trying to catch us on the other side.

"Kai, you have to go faster," I shouted.

"That's what I'm trying to do," he said before pulling a hard left. The cop car was now barreling down on us and Kai raced toward them. "Hold on," he ordered.

We were about to crash when the SUV turned to the side at the last minute to avoid us. Kai drove even faster now and finally lost them. You could still hear the sirens but couldn't see the car following us anymore.

"You almost got us killed." I laughed, the pressure on my side returning.

"Good thing I didn't," Kai teased.

The pressure kept increasing and I pressed a hand to my side, thinking I'd pulled something, when my hand met something warm. I pulled my hand away and rubbed my fingers together, finally figuring out what it was.

Blood.

Fuck.

Valentina looked down and came to the same conclusion. "You're bleeding."

"Accurate conclusion."

Kai looked at me horrified through the rearview mirror. "You're what?"

Ignoring his panic, Valentina said, "Put pressure on it."

"As you can see, I already was," I deadpanned. I shifted in my seat and winced at the searing pain that was slowly growing. "And I'm fine, Kai. It's just a little blood. Concentrate on getting us home. "

It wasn't for another forty-five minutes until Kai parked into our driveaway. He then barged out of the car and helped me out with Valentina.

I kept pressure on my side, but my fingers were going numb. My other arm went around Kai's shoulder while Valentina went ahead to open the door.

I stopped Kai midway to the door and said, "We have to be quiet. I don't want to alarm Sienna."

My wife might not have been oblivious that I wasn't just a security company owner, considering how we'd met, but I didn't want to drag her into this.

Sienna

CHAPTER 16

You're my wife. You'll never have to thank me for taking care of you.

Jamal's words kept replaying in my mind on a constant loop. Last night was different. *Good* different. I discovered another side of him, one without furrowed brows and angry frown lines and it was… nice.

From him making *sancocho* for me to caring enough to ask me questions. He wanted to get to know *me* and I couldn't remember the last time someone other than my best friends had ever wanted to do that.

I'd expected him to leave when I'd asked him to stay, but he not only came in, but he *wanted* to spend time with me.

It was an unsettling thought to realize that I was starting to like my husband when not even three weeks ago, all I'd wanted to do was get rid of him. There was still so much I didn't know about him, but my initial judgment was unfortunately wrong.

To my demise, Kai had been right. Jamal did put up a front to the world, but when you dug deeper, the man underneath was worth knowing.

I just hoped he felt the same.

I shook the thought away and returned my attention to my laptop. It was my day off, but I needed to occupy myself, so I decided to work on my case presentation that I had to present in a few days.

I was almost done when I heard a commotion downstairs. The sound of something crashing on the floor put me on high alert since Jamal had mentioned that he, Kai, and Valentina wouldn't be home until much later tonight.

I looked around the room to find something to protect me, but the only solid thing I could find was a textbook.

That should do, right?

I grabbed it and slowly cracked my door open, listening for sounds. It was quiet for a moment until I heard a groan followed by a "son of a bitch."

I tiptoed down the hall and made it to the top of the stairs, only to find all three of them gathered in the living room, one of the lamps tipped over on the rug.

Kai must have heard me because he looked my way and that's when I saw Jamal. My heart dropped at the sight and I yelled, "What the hell happened?"

I dropped the textbook on the floor and ran down the stairs.

"We have to get him to a hospital," I said breathlessly when I reached them.

Jamal abruptly stood up. "No! No hospitals," he said harshly, but his voice died down at the end as he bent over, his hand clutching his side.

"Jamal, you're hurt. I'm a doctor. We have to—"

"He can't go to a hospital," Valentina chimed in at the same time Jamal said, "You'll stitch me up."

I glowered at them. "I will, but at the hospital."

He glared at me. "No, Sienna. Here," he said sternly, leaving no room for discussion. Before I could say another word, he added, "If you can't do it, I'll have Kai do it."

Kai looked down at him, surprised. "I will?"

Jamal glared at him before wincing again.

"Absolutely not. I'll do it," I said after seeing the horrified look on Kai's face at the thought of having to stitch up my husband.

I helped Kai move Jamal to the couch. He fell back and dropped his head against the backrest, his left hand resting firmly on the left lower side of his abdomen.

I turned around and said, "Kai, go to my room. There's a duffle bag in my closet with a suture kit inside."

He nodded in understanding and left the room in a hurry.

Once he left, my mind whirled with a million thoughts.

Fuck, fuck, fuck. I needed so many other things, but I had to make do with what I had.

Valentina seemed to notice where my attention went. "We have equipment downstairs I can get for you."

I gave her a nod and she left, walking toward Jamal's office.

Kai came back with my kit a few seconds later after Valentina had left.

"I also need a bottle of whatever hard liquor you have here," I told him.

"You want a drink?"

"No, he'll need it," I said, pointing to Jamal.

I stood up and paced back and forth in front of him, running my fingers through my hair. Then I whipped around to face him, pointing an accusing finger at him. "You are impossible, you know that?" I yelled, furious.

What if he had died?

My stomach bottomed out at the thought.

He shifted in his seat, grimacing. "I'm fine. It's just a scratch."

I flicked him over the head. "*Estupido*, scratches don't fucking bleed like that."

"I like her," Valentina muttered to Kai before handing me gauze and a bottle of saline. I'd barely heard her come back into the room.

"Hey, your poor husband's already injured," Jamal replied teasingly, trying to dissipate the tension in the air.

I smacked him over the head again. "This isn't funny." I dropped to my knees in front of him and placed the supplies next to him on the couch. "You're hurt," I said quietly, my fury transforming into fear at what I would find under his shirt.

What if I didn't have the right equipment? What if he was injured beyond what I could see?

He sat up and cradled my cheek with the hand that wasn't holding his side, rubbing his thumb over my cheek. "Sienna, I'm okay."

I looked at him, his gaze locking with mine.

"Leave," he told Kai and Valentina, and they both complied without saying another word.

I moved away from his touch. "Take off your clothes. I need to see the extent of your injury."

He smiled at me. "We haven't even gone on a first date and you're already getting me naked."

"Stop making jokes and take them off." I scowled at him.

This time, he complied. He started with carefully shrugging off his jacket, then swiftly unbuttoned his shirt. Instead of doing the same and taking it off, he left it on.

I tried not to dwell on his bare chest and focused my attention on needing to do my job, which was helping him, not shamelessly ogling my husband. "I need you to take everything off so I can examine you."

"This is just fine."

Thinking that taking off his jacket took too much out of him, I propped myself on one knee and reached for his shoulders to help him remove his shirt, but before I could make contact, his hand whipped up and grabbed my wrist, stopping me. "No. Leave it on."

I raised an eyebrow. "Jamal, I—"

"Sienna, I'm really tired. Just leave it on, *please*," he pleaded.

The way he said please stopped me from pushing him further.

"Okay," I conceded and moved to open the bottle of whiskey Kai had brought me. "Drink this," I suggested, handing it to Jamal, but he refused.

"I'm fine," he said, pushing the bottle away.

"It'll be painful."

"I've suffered worse," he said simply.

His statement took me aback, but now wasn't the most appropriate time for questions.

I pre-opened all the gauze before grabbing a few and soaked them with saline. I pushed his shirt further open and brought them to his side. As I cleaned, it revealed that his injury was only a graze GSW, but the laceration was deep enough to still be bleeding.

I felt him staring at me while I worked on his open wound. "What?"

"You're not going to ask me what happened?"

Once I was done cleaning, I grabbed my suture kit.

"No," I simply said. "You probably wouldn't tell me anyway."

My hands were clammy as I moved to grab the needle with the needle driver, the tissue forceps with my other hand. I'd done this a million times, but for some unknown reason, I felt nervous as I brought the needle to his skin.

"Tell me something about yourself."

"What?" I asked, pausing my movements.

"You seem nervous, so I thought asking you questions would prevent you from butchering me."

I laughed and my nerves dissipated. "I think I already poured enough of my soul out to you last night." Then I pushed the needle into his skin and got to work, stitching in careful strokes.

We stayed in a comfortable silence until I finished.

"All done," I said after finishing off the last suture and protecting it by wrapping a sterilized bandage on top.

I was about to stand when my eyes traveled down his solid chest and zeroed in on the small tattoo on the left side of his ribs, a few inches above his now stitched-up wound.

It was a short sentence in cursive, but I couldn't decipher what it meant since it was in a different language. With each breath he took, the tattoo moved as if it was floating on his skin, the words creating a wave.

It was almost impossible to tear my eyes away.

Without thinking, my hand reached for his waist and my fingers moved to the skin above his bandage, caressing it. Succumbing to the urge, my thumb traced over the length of his tattoo. He inhaled sharply, but it didn't stop me.

I didn't know where I got the courage from, but I let my index finger trace the words, letter by letter.

"What does it say?" I whispered, my eyes still fixed on the tattoo.

"*Jamais autant que moi,*" he replied, the lilt of his French accent sending a shiver running down my spine.

"What does it mean?"

"It's French. It means never as much as me. My mother used to say it to me when I told her I loved her."

"You must miss her."

"Every day."

I traced it again, feeling the need to comfort him. My fingers moved of their own accord, feeling a pull to explore the rest of him. Goose bumps erupted across his skin under my touch.

Silence cloaked us, the room crackling with tension, suffocating the air around us so much that I could almost taste it.

I finally looked up at him and his head angled down, his eyes boring into mine. My eyes fell to his mouth as I moved farther up, but when my hands reached closer to his shoulders, his hand closed over mine, stopping my exploration.

"We should get some sleep," he said, his voice hoarse.

"We should." I pushed myself up using his knee and

stepped between his legs with the intent to help him to his room, but neither of us moved.

His eyes slowly glided down my body, pausing over my chest before he brought them back to my face. A fire erupted over my skin when his eyes locked with mine. His hands were resting on his thighs and grazed the sides of my legs, goose bumps erupting all over my skin.

I wonder if that was on purpose.

"God, you're beautiful," he whispered.

I stilled once his words registered and my heart ached at the compliment.

I felt his fingertips again and that's when I remembered what I was wearing. My usual boy shorts and an oversized T-shirt with nothing underneath. Desire trickled down to my middle and squeezed, calling for more.

He's injured. I can't.

I cleared my throat. "All right, husband. Let's get you to bed before you say anything else you'll regret."

His fingers brushed the back of my thighs. "I'd never regret calling my wife beautiful. I should hate you"—he shook his head—"but I just can't seem to bring myself to."

His gaze caressed my body once again and his hands grabbed the back of my thighs. Then they started trailing up until I blurted out, "Come to a wedding with me tomorrow." Right as the tips of his fingers grazed the hem of my boy shorts.

"What?" he asked, confused by my sudden statement.

"My best friend Kenna is getting married tomorrow and I told her you'd be there."

"You want me to be your date?" he asked, amused.

"Technically, you're my husband," I said, teasing him.

"Guess we'll actually go on that first date," he said, smirking.

I laughed to myself. "Yeah, I guess we are."

Jamal

CHAPTER 17

I couldn't stop thinking about her.

My hands on her body. Hers on mine.

All night I tossed and turned, trying to find some semblance of peace to sleep since we had a wedding to attend the next day.

But nothing worked.

Any ounce of fatigue I felt after getting injured evaporated the moment her fingers were all over me. The little amount of sleep I got was spent dreaming about her, about her tempting lips, but when I decided to lean in and claim them, I woke up.

Alone.

I wanted her, but I was afraid of the moment she'd see my scars.

I'd learned to live with them, accept that they were a part of me, and there was nothing to be ashamed of, but I couldn't help but feel vulnerable at the thought of someone else, of *her* seeing them. No one other than me and Noah had seen them.

Sure, I'd slept with women in the past, but I'd always kept my shirt on. Even Kai, whom I'd known for a long time, had never seen the extent of my burns.

I wanted to show her that part of me, but the simple thought gnawed at me.

What if she looked at me differently?

I pushed the feeling aside and settled further into my seat.

Today was our first date and, surprisingly, I was looking forward to it. I'd never been on a date before and Sienna was technically my wife, but when she'd asked me last night, a foreign warmth had filled my rib cage.

Her asking me to accompany her was most likely just to keep up a front. Or more specifically, it might've been to stop me from crossing a line that, despite wanting to so very badly, I shouldn't cross.

Sienna had asked me to pick up her *asoebi* from the tailor since she had to be at the hospital for a few hours for a meeting. After coming home, I'd showered and changed into one of my black tuxes.

While I waited in the living room for her to finish getting ready, I grabbed my phone to see if Kai had texted me any updates on yesterday's situation. I had an inkling that the senator had sold us out, but I needed confirmation before teaching him a lesson or two about crossing me.

But when I looked at the time, I quickly realized that if we didn't leave in the next few minutes, we wouldn't arrive at the time she needed to be there. I started to call out for Sienna when I peered up from my phone to see her standing at the top of the stairs.

I froze, stopping mid-sentence because the sight of her crumbled any other thoughts to dust aside from one. I caught her eyes, the brown hues meeting mine, and a simple statement carved itself into my chest.

My wife's beauty is unrivaled.

I tried to prevent it, but desire coiled low in my abdomen and my gaze roamed over her body, taking her in.

She was wearing a deep red maxi dress with some sort of ruching details that ran vertically, the fabric skimming her lush curves. The neckline was modest, yet the way it pushed her breasts sent quite non-modest thoughts whirling around my mind.

The shade of lipstick painted across her lips matched her dress perfectly and the sudden urge to lock her in my room and find ways to smear it hit me.

Brown had always been my favorite color, but I might just make an exception and let the red on her lips compel me into making it my new favorite.

She's becoming your favorite. The thought was fleeting, yet it was making itself louder every day I spent in her presence.

Her hair was pin-straight, something I'd rarely seen on her since she tended to keep her hair in its natural curls. It was parted in the middle and the front sections were pulled behind her ears, gold earrings hanging from them.

When I took a closer look, I noticed they were the same ones she wore at our wedding and it tugged at my heart.

She glided down the stairs, revealing a slit at the side that ran to the top of her thigh and when she turned to grab the garment bag from the couch, the low back of her dress nearly brought me to my knees.

I swallowed hard, my hands itching at my sides to strip her out of that dress and worship her for days.

Oh, fuck me.

"Jamal?" she asked.

I shook my head. "What?" My voice was hoarse as I looked down at her.

She raised an eyebrow. "I asked if you were ready to go," she said, amused.

"Oh, yes. I am." I cleared my throat. "Let me take this for you," I said, grabbing the bag from her hand.

We walked out of the house and I let her in the car, placing the garment bag into the back seat. After shutting her door, I walked around and took a deep breath before getting into the driver's seat. Once settled in my seat, I entered the address of the location into the navigation system and peeled out of the driveaway.

My hands gripped the steering wheel, a million thoughts running through my head as we made our way to the venue.

I felt Sienna everywhere.

This is about to be a long night.

Forty-five minutes later, I parked in front of the private estate. I stepped out and rounded the front to open her door. She'd already grabbed the garment bag from the back, so I extended my hand and with her free one, she grabbed it as I helped her climb out.

"Ready?" I asked, shutting the passenger door behind her, my other hand still holding hers.

She looked down at our joined hands before meeting my gaze. She nodded before uttering a strained, "Yup."

Glad to know I'm not the only one affected.

I didn't want to let go of her hand just yet, so I hooked her arm through mine as we strode through the entrance.

It was early in the afternoon, and the sun was shimmering over the top of the trees. It was my first time at the Altobelli Manor, but I'd looked it up before coming to make sure it was secure.

Acres and acres of land surrounded the property, the backyard overlooking vast fields of grapevines. The estate used to be a winery, but the owner had since then turned it into a private venue for events.

"You'll need to smile more today," Sienna taunted me as she looked around the room. "We're supposed to be a happy, newly married couple."

I glared down at her. "I think I smile just the right amount, *wife*," I retorted, forcing a smile.

She flicked her gaze at me, a reprimanding spark in her eyes.

"Well, *husband*, fix it because you look like someone stuck something up your ass."

No one had ever talked to me the way she did and although she was infuriating at times, or should I say most times, it was addicting. I loved riling her up enough to have her spar with me.

Inside, a group of staff in black attire was placing the final touches in the ballroom for what I assumed would be where the reception would take place.

The room was bright, the walls a cream color. Tan cloths covered the tables, the centerpieces a mix of gold candelabras that held white dripping candles and transparent candle holders with small candles inside, greenery and white florals weaved around.

The giant ballroom had an arch in the back that opened up to a vast backyard. From here, I could see rows of chairs lined up, white flowers decorating the beginning of each row.

"You're here!" someone shouted from behind us. Arms wrapped around Sienna's back and she turned around to wrap hers around whoever was hugging her, forcing me to let her go.

I shifted to meet whoever made my wife let go of my hand.

"Hi, beautiful," Sienna said, hugging back who I assumed was the bride based on the countless rollers in her hair and the white robe tied around her body.

The bride then turned her attention to me, her expression changing into a scolding one.

"You must be the husband," she said sternly.

"Yes, I am," I answered, extending my hand. "Jamal."

"Kenna." She shook it but still looked at me suspiciously.

I found myself wanting to make a good impression on her. Sienna didn't seem to have many friends, so I assumed that whoever she chose to be part of her life was important to her. And I wanted them to accept me, despite the circumstances behind Sienna's and my nuptials.

"I have to finish getting ready before the guests arrive in twenty minutes," Kenna said.

"Oh, yes." Sienna glanced at me behind her shoulder, biting on her bottom lip, a worried look on her face. She turned her attention back to her friend. "Where's Shareef?"

"He should be in his room with his friends and his father." Kenna seemed to understand the intention behind my wife's question when she looked at me and added, "You can stay with him until the ceremony starts."

"I don't want to impose," I said hesitantly.

"You're not. I would tell you if you were. Come, let me show you."

I could see why Sienna liked her so much. My hand hovered over my wife's lower back as Kenna guided us across the ballroom to the back where she eventually turned left into a hallway. We walked a little farther down the hall until she halted in front of a wooden door and knocked softly.

"Shareef, it's Kenna. Sienna's husband is here with her, so only open the door when I leave."

"Okay, baby," a male voice replied without further questions.

Kenna looked at me again. "He won't bite, but I can't promise he won't grill you with questions to make sure you're worthy of our Sienna."

I liked knowing Sienna had people protecting her since it seemed her family didn't do much of that.

I simply nodded.

Sienna unexpectedly placed a hand over my chest and leaned on her tiptoes to whisper in my ear. "Will you be okay?" she asked. She leaned back on her heels and peered at me, waiting.

Her proximity made her faint floral perfume waft to my nose and I found myself wanting to infuse myself with it.

I leaned down, my lips brushing against her forehead, kissing it gently. "Yes, I'll be fine."

"Okay," she said quietly before I watched her leave with Kenna. She glanced at me briefly over her shoulder before she rounded the corner, disappearing from my view.

"Is she gone?" the same voice from earlier called out.

"Yes."

The door unlocked and I pushed it open, the hinges creaking inside. I squared my shoulders and stepped inside. The entire room fell silent in a hush at my arrival.

A Black man in slim black trousers and an ivory suit jacket stepped forward, his right hand extended in greeting.

"You must be Jamal. I'm Shareef, Kenna's husband, or future husband if we're being technical. It's nice to meet you."

I shook it. "Nice to meet you too."

He placed a hand over my shoulder, guiding me farther inside. I internally flinched from where his hand was placed, but I ignored it, not wanting to be rude by shrugging him off.

He closed the door behind me and I looked around the room, spotting an older gentleman to the side with four other men who seemed around the same age as the groom.

"This is my dad, my cousins Deen and Gabriel, and that right there is my best man and childhood friend Lucas," he said, introducing me to everyone.

His father was dressed in traditional attire, while his cousins and friend were all dressed in black tuxedos with white shirts and matching bow ties.

After I shook hands with everyone, introducing myself more officially, they went back to their previous conversation and Shareef invited me to take a seat in the back corner while we waited for the remaining time until the ceremony started.

He leaned back, resting a hand on the back of the couch and propping his ankle over his knee. "So," he started, trailing off.

I waited for him to continue his sentence, but he just appraised me up and down.

Knowing I couldn't bring out my lighter to calm my

growing nerves, I wound my fingers together and let my hands rest on my lap as I leaned back on the couch.

"Congratulations," I answered, not knowing what else to say. I hadn't had to talk to new people since I met Kai, so this was uncharted territory.

"Thanks."

I hummed, once again waiting for him to spark a conversation, but he just kept looking at me. I wished Kai were here. He'd definitely know what to say. I'd much rather have Shareef grill me than the suffocating silence surrounding our corner of the room.

Suddenly, a laugh erupted across from us and Shareef joined them. "I'm just messing with you. You should see the look on your face," he said, teasing me.

I let out a breath. "I'm not great at conversing."

"Yeah, I could tell," he answered playfully and I gave him a tight smile, but his next question made me choke on empty air. "How did you and Sienna meet?"

At our wedding.

"Through friends," I lied.

"And you treat her right?"

"I hope I do, but that's a question you'd have to ask her."

"Good answer."

We made idle conversation until someone knocked at the door to let us know the ceremony was about to start.

"Come with me," Shareef said. "You'll sit at the front with my family."

"Oh, I wouldn't want to imp—"

"No arguments. It's my wedding. Besides, you're Sienna's husband and she's family."

I followed him out and he quickly showed me my seat before he left. A few minutes later, chatter erupted and I looked over my shoulder to see guests trickling in toward the ushers that were waiting at the start of the aisle.

My fingers brushed against the cold metal in my pocket, fidgeting with it and imagining that I was flicking it open and closed.

The seats filled up quickly and I turned my attention back to the front once the quartet strung the first chord, a hush overtaking the crowd.

The first people down the aisle were an older couple and they sat on the section opposite me. Then Shareef and his father came down the aisle and something caught in my throat at the thought that I'd never get to have my parents at my wedding.

I shook myself out of it and watched Shareef stand at the head of the aisle, anticipation painting his expression, while his father took a seat in the row right in front of me with the rest of Shareef's family.

Pairs of bridesmaids and groomsmen came in one by one. I locked eyes with Shareef and he winked at me before turning his attention back to whoever was walking up now.

I shifted in my seat to look at who was coming down the aisle, only to find Lucas with my wife on his arm as they walked down the path. A hint of jealousy licked my veins at the sight of another man with my wife, but I reined it in, reminding myself that it was a common occurrence at weddings for men to offer their arms to whoever they were walking down the aisle.

So instead, I focused my attention on Sienna and watched the wide smile on her face as she gave Shareef a nod. He returned her smile as Lucas left her near the altar. Then she turned her body toward the guests and looked around the crowd until her eyes found mine.

I held her gaze and she gave me a warm smile.

It hit me like a tidal wave.

She might have been a means to an end, but the way she smiled at me suddenly made me realize that she wasn't.

She made me feel infinite and I didn't know how to deal with that realization.

My mind was still focused on Barrera, but she was making me recognize that there might be more to this life than my revenge.

No, Jamal, you have to stay focused.

I pulled my eyes away as the crowd stood to watch the bride enter and I followed suit. I was sure Kenna looked beautiful in her dress, but my eyes landed back on my wife.

And throughout the entire ceremony, I found myself unable to stop staring at her.

CHAPTER 18

We'd been here for the last six hours and the festivities were only now winding down. Most people who had been in attendance were still here, but a few had already gone home.

About an hour into the reception, the bridal party, including my wife, had left to prepare for the traditional part of Kenna and Shareef's wedding. Sienna had told me they'd decided to do both in one day instead of having their guests come to the celebration of their union on two occasions.

She'd walked back into the room right after Shareef's family and him had made their entrance, an MC guiding them through every step of the ceremony. She wore a gold *asoebi* that matched the other bridesmaids', a veiled Kenna in the center dressed in a burgundy *aso-oke* that matched Shareef's *agbada and fila*.

I'd watched Sienna dance for the first time and couldn't tear my eyes away. Throughout the entire day, she'd radiated a lightness that I hadn't seen in her before.

I wanted to see her this way all the time.

I'd been sitting in my seat at our table, swirling my glass of scotch that I still hadn't touched as I watched over my wife. She'd changed back into her red dress when Kenna and Shareef changed into their final outfit.

My skin heated all over again and a surge of… need crashed over me. The need to touch her, to taste her. I was so close last night but retreated when she was in my reach.

What-ifs swirled in my mind and I shook my head, trying to rid myself of the consuming thoughts, but kept failing miserably.

I'd been willing her to look my way, but she was immersed in a lively conversation with another man I'd never met before. My fingers tightened over my drink when she laughed at something he'd said.

Again.

Irritation flared in my chest when he put his hand on her forearm and stepped closer.

Doesn't he see the ring on her finger?

Possessiveness rushed through me and before I knew it, I was crossing the ballroom and sliding an arm around her waist. I pulled her into me and pinned the "didn't understand boundaries" man with a hard stare, challenging him and whoever was watching to touch my wife again.

I pressed a kiss to her temple. "Hey, *mon amour*."

I turned to the gentleman who kept touching her, sticking my hand out and rising to my full height. "I don't think we've had the pleasure of meeting. I'm Jamal, Sienna's husband," I said, placing an emphasis on the word husband. It might make me sound like an asshole, but I didn't really care.

He slipped his hand in mine but looked at Sienna when he spoke. "I had no idea you were married."

"Newly married," Sienna explained.

"Happily and in love," I added, squeezing his hand before letting it go. "We were just about to leave, actually." I felt Sienna's glare on the side of my face. She was about to say something when I dropped my lips to her ear, "It's not a suggestion."

Despite her glaring, I could see the goose bumps breaking out across her skin. She slightly pulled away from me and gave whoever she was talking to a tight smile. "It was nice seeing you again, Kyle."

Again? What did she mean, *again*?

I straightened my back up and watched her say goodbye to her friends and their family. Kenna and Shareef were both looking at me as I watched a seething Sienna walk back to me.

I gave them a small smile and waved them goodbye. I wanted to feel bad for having to leave early, but seeing another man's hands on my wife erased any guilt I might have conjured inside of me.

When Sienna made it back to me, I held out my arm

and she took it. Then I led her out of the ballroom and toward the entrance.

I could hear her teeth grit as she worked her clenched jaw back and forth, hesitating on how hard she would scold me for my behavior. "There was no need to act all jealous, Jamal," she snapped at me as we waited for the valet to bring my car around.

I pinned her with a glare. "Why would I be jealous when I know what's mine?"

She looked stunned by my statement and before she could say anything more, the valet parked in front of us.

"Now, get in," I told her as I opened her door. She got in without objecting and I made my way over to the driver's side after.

Sienna still hadn't said a word as I peeled out of the driveway. My fingers gripped the steering wheel as I attempted to fight off the jealousy running through my veins. The visceral reaction I had to that man was probably inappropriate, especially since it was her friend's wedding, but I couldn't stop myself.

What I really had wanted to do was bend her over and show *nice to see you again Kyle* who she really belonged to, show *her* that she was mine.

So I'd say my original reaction was quite reasonable.

We drove the entire way home in complete silence. The only sound heard was her breathing accelerating with every mile closer to the house. I could tell she was furious because it was practically vibrating the entire car.

Finally passing our place's gates, I drove up the driveway and parked in my spot. Then I stepped out and rounded the front to open her door.

She didn't move.

I placed my hand on the roof and slightly leaned down. "Are you getting out?"

"I don't feel like it," she said, looking straight ahead.

"Get out of the car, Sienna," I ordered her.

"No."

I didn't have time for this.

"Don't make me ask you again."

She turned her face toward me and lifted her chin, her gaze clashing with mine. The rare specks of gold in her irises burned bright, her anger evident. She crossed her arms over her chest, pushing her breasts up, and it took everything in me not to steal a glance.

"Is that your favorite phrase or something?"

"Sienna…" I growled.

"If you want me to get out, *make* me."

Whatever infinitesimal patience I had left snapped.

Make me. I'll show her make me.

"Watch me." I leaned in and over her, reaching for her seat belt. I heard her suck in a breath as the sharpness of my suit brushed against her bare chest.

"Wh-what are you doing?"

I didn't answer her. Once her seat belt was loose, I gripped her waist and slung her over my shoulder.

She squeaked in shock and I slammed the passenger

door down. I wrapped my hand around her thighs so she didn't slide down my back and fall to the ground, then walked to the front door.

"Jamal Aguerd, put me the fuck down," she yelled.

It wasn't lost on me that she used my real name, but my irritation toward her brushed it away.

She wiggled to get away from me, but all she did was slide down my back and made her hips bump against my head. I kept ignoring her as I unlocked the door and walked inside the house.

I was planning on taking her to her room to cool off, but she whacked my backside before she—

"Sienna," I growled. "You did *not* just fucking bite me."

"I told you to—"

I slapped her ass, cutting her off. Changing my mind, I veered toward my office instead of taking the stairs to her room. I stormed inside my office and closed the door behind us with my foot.

I turned and kneeled down to drop her to her feet, her back to the door. Then I slowly straightened, her heaving chest scraping against my suit as I stood to my full height.

My gaze met hers and her anger momentarily dissipated before returning in full force. "Did you just *spank* me?" she asked, bewildered.

"You didn't give me a choice," I deadpanned, turning around and walking away from her. I leaned against my desk and gripped the edge to stop myself from doing it again.

I heard her groan. "Why do you make this so difficult? You know, I was actually starting to think you weren't so bad. But every time I think nice things about you, you do this thing where you close up or do something so infuriating it erases all of it."

My frustration boiled over at her constant defiance. At how much I wanted her but couldn't fucking have her.

Fuck. Fuck. Fuck.

What I wouldn't give to be able to pretend for just one brief moment that she could be mine.

What I wouldn't give to be able to be inside her for just one night.

Ugh, who was I kidding. I bet just one taste of her and I'd be addicted.

I shook my head, running a hand over my face before whipping around to face her again. "And you think it's easy for me?" I seethed, taking a step forward.

Her eyes widened as she stepped back.

"You think it's easy for me to live in *my* own house with *you* in it? I can barely fucking get anything done throughout the day," I continued until she backed into the door, her hands pressing against it to steady herself.

"How is that my fault?" she countered, seething.

Her anger simmered down and she swallowed hard as I stalked closer, barely leaving an inch between us. I wanted to engrain myself in every part of her so she would be mine and mine alone.

I placed a hand over her head. A loose strand of her hair fell over her face and I brought my other hand to brush it away from her face, tucking it behind her ear.

"Because you're all I seem to think about and it drives me fucking insane," I confessed, dropping my forehead against hers. "You're infuriating, but I just can't stop. I shouldn't want you, but for some godforsaken reason, I can't stay away. You're a pain in my ass, but I crave you all the fucking time."

My hand lingered on her face as I cupped her jaw, tilting her head back. She stared up at me through her eyelashes. We'd barely touched, yet we were both panting heavily, our heavy breathing filling the enclosed space.

Every second that passed was torture.

I should walk away.

I really should.

My eyes traveled down to her red-painted lips with only one thought.

Oh, et puis merde.

My head angled down. "Sienna?" I whispered, my thumb softly circling her jaw.

She reached out and gripped my arm, her fingers digging into my bicep. "Yes?"

"Remember your kissing rule?"

She hummed.

"It's absolutely necessary for me to kiss you right now."

Her eyes fluttered closed as I leaned down to kiss her, but just as our lips were finally about to connect after weeks of starving for her taste, the blaring ringtone of my phone blasted in my office.

Really?

Of all the time my phone could have rung, it decided to do so now. I was about to ignore it when my phone buzzed repeatedly with incoming text messages before ringing again.

I groaned and slumped against Sienna, resting my fore-head against the wooden door. I grabbed my phone from my pocket and looked at the caller.

Kai.

I knew he wouldn't call me incessantly if it wasn't for a good reason, especially since it was past 10:00 p.m.

I looked at Sienna. *God, I can't believe I have to do this.* "I really have to take this."

She simply nodded and left my office.

CHAPTER 19

MY HEART POUNDED PAINFULLY AGAINST MY RIBS AS I grabbed the edge of the island to steady myself.

What the hell just happened? Or almost happened.

My body was still humming from his proximity.

The blood in my veins had boiled as his gaze had stricken me. My body flushed with warmth as his body covered mine while he whispered against my lips.

But it was his words that had rendered me breathless.

I crave you all the time.

Well, that made two of us. There was no use in denying it anymore.

These past few weeks had been both the best and the worst of my life. From discovering my father's deceits to finding someone who made my body thrum with need.

With each day that passed, I wanted him more. I wanted

to discover what it was like to be pressed against him, his bare body against mine.

I groaned, ridding myself of consuming thoughts, and turned to grab a bottle of water from the fridge, but instead, I ran into something hard. My hand flew up to hold on to whatever I'd run into, only to be met with someone.

"What the—" My words were cut off when I looked up to find Jamal gripping me tight to steady me.

His dark eyes bore into mine.

"Jamal?" I whispered when he didn't say a word.

One minute he was burning my soul with his gaze and the next, he yanked me into a searing kiss. The moment his lips touched mine, time stood still. The only thing that mattered at that moment was the way his mouth moved against mine.

Euphoric. That's how I would describe what kissing him felt like.

We'd kissed at our wedding, but it was nothing compared to this.

I whimpered into his mouth as his taste invaded my senses and he slid his hand to the small of my back, jerking our bodies together. I gripped his forearms tighter and hesitantly flickered my tongue against his lips, asking for more.

He moved so that I was backed against the fridge and caged me in. He rolled his body against mine and I moaned when his erection pressed against me. His hands found my backside and he bit my lower lip before breaking away.

When he finally spoke, his voice was harsh and gravelly. "Go to your room, Sienna," he ordered.

I startled at his words and stared at him confused. "What?"

"You heard me," he simply replied.

His tone wasn't dismissive. It was luring me into uncharted territories that I wanted to explore, so I made my way upstairs. I didn't look back, but I could feel the weight of his stare against my skin with every click of my heels as I walked up.

Once up the stairs, I rounded up the landing and headed for my room. I halted in front of my bedroom door, hesitating for a second. But as his footsteps grew louder, I pushed the door open and stepped inside.

A few seconds later, he came in, tugging on his tie. After untying it, he let it hang loose around his neck and stalked over to where I stood.

"You looked beautiful tonight in that dress, *mon amour*." His voice had turned low and intimate, one I'd never heard before, and it captivated me. "But I bet you look exquisite out of it." He traced a finger up my bare thigh. "Take it off," he said, the command low but firm.

My pulse raced, the beat increasing rapidly against my veins.

Should I tell him I've never done this?

I was nervous, but the way he looked at me strangely made me feel more comfortable than I thought I would be having to strip in front of him.

His finger toyed with the hem of the high slit. "I want to see how much you want me."

Confident much?

"Who said I wanted you?" I said, not able to help myself.

His gaze trailed down my body, sending a shiver running down my spine. His eyes bore into mine again. "Your body just did."

I turned around. "I need help," I said, peering at him over my shoulder before staring ahead.

He swept my hair to the side and trailed a finger down my spine, inhaling deeply. His fingers finally found the zipper to my dress and I looked up, watching his reflection in the window as he slowly pulled it down.

Once he reached the bottom, his gaze caught mine in our reflection. Jamal's deft fingers slid under the material and trailed up until he reached the strap, my skin prickling under his touch.

"Jamal…"

He pushed them over and down my shoulder until my dress quietly pooled at my feet. He hissed as his eyes traveled down the length of my reflection, discovering I was only wearing a white thong and my strappy gold heels.

His hands went to my waist where he squeezed gently and pulled me into him until my back landed flush against his front.

My chest rose and fell with each heavy breath as his right hand came up and his knuckles grazed the outside of my breast ever so slowly. They traveled down until his hand rested on my hip.

I leaned against him when his other hand repeated the same movements.

He tilted his head down, his stubble grazing my cheek. "Absolutely beautiful."

I gasped, my stomach tightening. A shift happened deep inside me, a warmth awakening and heating my blood. I tilted my head back against his shoulder, seeking his mouth.

"What are you doing to me, *mon amour*?" His breath tickled my lips. I didn't know what it meant, but with the little French I knew, the words made me melt further into his touch.

"I could ask you the same question."

He licked the shell of my ear and kissed down my neck, gently nipping at my shoulder. When he kissed his way back to my jaw, I lifted my hands to wrap around his neck, but he stopped me and turned me around to face him.

He dropped my hands between our bodies and placed a kiss on my lips.

His eyes brushed against my skin as they traveled down my body, taking me in. "Lie down," he said hoarsely, lifting his head. "And keep your heels on."

I complied and slowly lowered myself to my sheets. As my back came flush against the mattress, I propped myself on my elbows and watched Jamal lean against the frame of the fireplace, crossing his arms over his chest and his legs at his ankles.

The heat of his gaze sent a chill down my body and he gave me a devastating smile at my body's response.

"I want to see your cunt," he ordered.

My eyes widened at his bluntness. "You want to see my…" I said, shying from the word. I'd never had a man talk to me like that, but I wanted more. Wanted to see how far tonight would go.

"Yes. I want you to remove your thong and prop your legs up with your heels on the bed," he instructed, his cool demeanor not wavering.

I bit my lip and nodded.

Should be easy enough.

I slowly pulled my thong down my legs and let it drop to the floor. Then I brought my legs up and hesitated before parting them.

A low growl reverberated through his chest and filled the room, desire pooling in his eyes as he watched me.

"Sienna." My name came out on a choked groan and he closed his eyes. When he opened them again, he said, "Touch yourself."

"Wh-what?"

I thought he would do it. I must have said it out loud because he replied, "I can see that you're nervous, so before I touch you, I want to watch you make yourself come." His gaze moved away from mine back to between my legs before he asked, "Are you wet?"

You can do it, Sienna. You've done this. Just add a spectator now.

Great, I was having inner monologues with myself. I swallowed against the lump in my throat and pushed two fingers through my folds, rolling my hips involuntarily.

Then I nodded, unable to form the words to tell him.

"Let me see."

Slowly, I withdrew my hand and held my fingers up.

"Good girl. Now put your fingers back between your thighs and don't stop until you come apart."

My entire body was on fire.

When I hesitated for a moment, his gravelly voice soared through the room. "Slowly stroke down the length of your pussy and coat your fingers," he instructed. "I want to memorize every reaction your body has."

I swallowed hard then reached between my thighs again. At first, I only teased my fingertips between my folds, going slow as he asked.

God, this feels good.

Arousal thrummed through my body, pulsing in my clit as I kept playing with it.

"Keep going, love. You have no idea how magnificent you look playing with yourself."

Every stroke sent an intense wave of prickles across my skin. My head fell back and my back arched at the flare sparking low in my core. Rolling my lips between my teeth, I kept rubbing myself, circling my clit.

A low moan escaped my lips and I almost stopped,

feeling self-conscious about touching myself in front of him, but his praise kept me going.

"My wife is *such* a good listener," he rumbled. "Fuck, you must be so wet."

I whimpered at his words. I'd played with myself before but having him watch me, control it, made this unlike anything I'd ever felt before.

"Part your legs a little more so I can see better," he said and when I did, he added, "Now slide them inside and fuck yourself. I want to see your pussy open and swallow them."

Without reservation this time, my fingers glided through my folds and I pushed a finger inside. I gasped, clenching around it. I thrust it deeper and my free hand fumbled to find something to hold on to as my other worked my finger in and out.

I grabbed the sheets and pressed the heel of my hand against my clit.

He muttered something unintelligible under his breath. "God, if only you could see what I see," Jamal rasped. His breathing grew louder, then he said, "Add another finger."

I finally looked up at him again, my hand slowing. "I don't think I can," I said, my voice trembling.

He stalked toward me. "Yes, you can," he said, dropping to his knees. His breath skated across my sensitive skin as he placed a kiss on my inner thigh. His hands gripped my knees and parted them even farther.

Whimpering, I nodded and slid another finger in, rolling my hips to ease it in. My mouth opened as I rocked back and forth, a strain of moans expelling from my lips.

"That's it, Sienna. Keep going. Ride your hand and imagine it's my cock."

Everything in my mind was hazy, but I focused on how consuming his voice and what he was making me do was. I started riding my fingers for him, like my body had a mind of its own and knew exactly what to do.

My legs trembled with each roll of my hips, his breath fanning over my skin as he pressed feather-light kisses across my skin.

"What a beautiful, filthy thing you are," he praised.

"Oh, God," I whimpered, my pants filling the room. I closed my eyes as my body teetered right on the edge, wanting to take a leap and dive over the finish line.

"Does my love enjoy fucking herself in front of me?"

I muttered something that resembled a yes, but I couldn't tell, too lost to the overwhelming sensations.

"I couldn't quite hear that," he said, biting my inner thigh.

"Yes," I shouted.

"Open your pretty eyes, *mon amour*. Make yourself come so we can both watch."

I opened my eyes and the sight of him on his knees watching me, his hands gripping my inner thighs sent me over the edge. Pleasure rippled through me and washed over my body as I cried out his name.

"Beautiful," he murmured.

I floated in the aftermath of my orgasm, barely aware that Jamal had pulled my hand free. He brought my hand to his mouth and closed his lips around them, sucking.

That's the hottest thing I've ever seen.

My cheeks flushed at the sight of his eyes closing and the warmth of his tongue lapping my fingers, forcing more moans out of me.

His eyes opened as he dragged my fingers slowly out of his lips, giving me a devilish smile. "You taste divine."

Still on his knees, Jamal threaded his fingers between mine and guided them up my stomach to palm my breast, his calloused thumb swiping over the top of my nipple.

A breathy hiss left me at the touch, my muscles coiling all over again.

"Your pussy is the most beautiful thing I've ever seen," he groaned against it. "I'll just have one taste," he continued before burying his face in it and taking a slow, long lick through my wetness.

He kept his eyes on me as he took time tasting it, alternating between long licks and short flicks. "You can give me one more," he said to me before his lips wrapped around my clit and sucked.

His grip around my fingers tightened as he continued his ministrations. I bucked against his mouth and my free hand pushed against his head to get him off or closer, I didn't know anymore.

"It feels…" My voice trailed off. "I've never…"

He placed his free hand firmly on my stomach and

pressed down to keep me still. He grinned against me. "Is your husband the first one to fuck you with his mouth?"

My lips parted. "Yes," I whispered.

"Good." His hand on my stomach glided down until a finger slowly teased my entrance. Then he pushed it in, watching me the entire time. His eyes widened. *"Putain.* Sienna, has anyone fucked you before?"

"No," I breathed out, suppressing the urge to bite my lip at how full just one of his fingers felt.

His irises flared, his pupils dilating as he pushed farther. My lips parted and my breath caught in my throat. "Jamal, I—"

"I know," he groaned. He withdrew his finger, only to slide deeper this time.

He repeated the motion until I felt myself stretch further each time until he pressed all the way in, pushing his thick finger inside me.

It had felt good before, but this was...

He curled into a spot that blurred my vision. There was a slight pain, but it slowly turned into an ecstatic feeling.

Our joined hands alternately played with each of my breasts as he rubbed the inside of my pussy. Then he withdrew his finger completely before sliding it again, but this time adding another one.

I felt full and stretched and...

A whirlwind of sensation swarmed over me and my toes curled in my shoes, the heels digging into the mattress.

I rocked against his touch as he placed his mouth over me once again.

"Jamal," I warned him.

"It's okay, baby. Give it to me," he said, capturing my clit in his mouth as his fingers worked inside me.

My response was almost immediate as waves of elation rolled over me, my whimpers and his groans echoing off the walls of my bedroom. My cries grew louder as I writhed under him as he coaxed everything I had left.

This time the pleasure was violent and all-consuming.

Then it slowly faded away and he placed a kiss on my clit as he pulled our hands free. I slumped on the bed, barely able to move. A few moments later, he straightened up, sliding his fingers out of me, and I shuddered at the loss.

"That was—"

"Life-altering," he finished, gently removing my heels.

I stared up at him lazily and my body trickled with a flush when I realized he was still fully clothed, his erection evidently pressing against the fabric of his suit pants.

It somehow made this even hotter.

He briefly walked into the bathroom and emerged with a wet cloth. I struggled into a seated position and reached for him, but he stopped me.

"Next time. Let me just take care of you tonight," he said before adjusting himself and kneeling in front of my bed. He gripped my hips to bring me to the edge of the bed and cleaned me with such gentleness, it warmed my heart.

He then tossed the cloth into the hamper and walked into my closet to grab me clothes to sleep in. After changing into my loungewear, I spontaneously said, "Stay."

A beat passed before a soft smile spread across his face as he exhaled. "Okay."

"You don't want to change?" I asked.

"I'll be okay."

I nodded, then quickly stepped into the bathroom to wash my makeup off and go through my usual routine as he took off his shoes and climbed into my bed.

After I finished applying my products, I looked at myself in the mirror. My hand brushed against my lips and over my skin, relishing what just happened.

Although this started out as a duty, my relationship with Jamal was morphing into something I'd never expected I'd find in life. It wasn't just what transpired between us. It was all the unsaid things that were starting to surface.

When he touched me, my body felt equally alive and relaxed to a degree I'd never experienced before.

When he looked at me, it felt like there was nothing more important that he'd rather have his attention on.

When he kissed me... it was like I was *his*.

And that was all I could think of as I climbed into bed next to him, reveling in the warmth of his body wrapped against mine.

CHAPTER 20

I WAS FUCKED.

Sienna's body was tightly pressed against mine, one of her arms splayed across my front. Having her in my arms felt strangely familiar, despite it being the first time we'd shared the same bed.

Well, when I was aware of it.

Her whimpers of pleasure were the only thing I'd been thinking of for every minute that had passed since she fell asleep. Being with her was setting me off-balance and gave me this overwhelming feeling that left me breathless.

Being with her felt like…

Home.

That paired with this intense need for her fueled my body every time I was near her. I'd only planned to watch, but when she'd parted her knees, I'd almost fallen to mine.

And when she started playing with herself and taking

instructions so well, I couldn't help but want to get a closer look.

I wanted to learn every curve on her body, every sweet spot that would make her scream my name. I wanted to fuck her until our bodies became one. I wanted to be her first in every way possible. And the last man she'd ever be with.

I wanted to make her mine.

Then she'd come apart so beautifully and the thought of getting a taste shot through me like electricity. But one swipe of my tongue across her sweet cunt wasn't enough because as soon as her taste burst across my tongue, it rewired my starving brain to crave that, and only that.

So I was fucked.

But for the first time in a long time, I felt a sense of calm. I may be in over my head. Correction, I was in over my head, but I'd let myself dream of a future while I had her in my arms.

Even though a future with her wasn't a possibility.

I looked down at her next to me. She was asleep on her stomach, hugging one of her pillows under her head. The sheet was down at her waist and the oversized T-shirt she was wearing had ridden up throughout the night, exposing a sliver of her stomach.

What was the point of having words like breathtaking when it didn't even come close to describing the sight of her like this.

My wife was so fucking perfect, it hurt.

My fingers itched to touch her, but I suppressed the incessant urge. I wanted to give in last night when she wanted more, but she'd never been with anyone before and I didn't want her to feel overwhelmed or obligated to do more.

She'd only come into my life a month ago, but in that little time, she'd turned it upside down. I still couldn't grasp exactly how I felt about her, but one thing I knew was that I'd never wanted anything or anyone this badly.

I hadn't planned any of this, and yet I found myself not regretting a single thing.

My phone buzzed in my pocket with a text from Valentina, pulling me out of my thoughts.

Valentina: He's ready for you

Jamal: Be there in 15.

Closing the text on my phone, I took one last look at my wife before swiftly sliding off her bed. Then I passed by my office to grab my keys and walked out the door.

The knife I held to my side was dripping blood from the tip onto the polished concrete floor of the warehouse I used for meetings like these.

I'd bought all the vacant land surrounding our property when we moved in to ensure no one would come near it without my saying so. Most of it was still vacant, but we had this place built for my more discreet meetings.

Senator Ricci was a pitiful sight for the eyes. Strapped to a metal chair with his arms and legs bound with ropes, his head was slumped after my last lesson, blood pooling under his left hand where two of his fingers were missing.

He stirred, muttering whimpers of agony as he slowly emerged out of unconsciousness, for the third time since I showed up.

I leaned forward in my chair that was a few feet in front of Ricci and used the bloodied blade to push his matted brown hair away from his face. "Shall we resume?" I said, cocking an eyebrow at him.

His brain finally caught up to what was happening and he shook his head fervently, weeping and begging for me to stop.

Great, he's crying again.

I tsked. "There's no need for that."

"I had to," he cried out, his face dissolving into misery. "He was going to kill me and come after my family…"

I threw my head back, a sardonic laugh escaping my lips. "And what did you think I was going to do to you when I found out you crossed me for money?"

Men like him were pathetic. They never valued the good life they had and always wanted more, discarding the helping hand they were lent for more.

He swallowed, his gaze flicking to the soiled knife in my hand then back to me. "Please. Please…"

Pitiful.

"You like it?" I taunted before I plunged the knife into his thigh and twisted it sharply.

His screams pierced the air, blood gushing from his wound. Crimson streamed down the chair leg, joining the pool of blood on the floor below.

Pulling the knife out, I sat back in my chair and looked at my work as Ricci struggled to breathe between his incessant sobs. His white T-shirt was splattered and stained, and his black jogging pants were torn, his shoes tossed to the side.

What a dumb decision it was to go for a jog late at night after making the grave mistake of selling me out.

I waited for his whimpers to quiet down before I drove the knife into his other thigh, flesh and bone yielding under the razor-sharp steel. His screeching bounced off the walls, the sound grating my ears.

I usually would have enjoyed seeing him suffer, but my mood worsened every minute I was having to deal with this when I'd rather be with my wife.

I returned my attention to Ricci. His eyes bulged in pain, wheezing gasps leaving his throat as sweat mixed with blood trickled down the sides of his face.

"You made a mistake by sharing our little conversation, Senator Ricci."

He stared at me with his remaining good eye, the other one swollen shut. "It wasn't h—" he started, but his sentence was cut short when my knife slid across his throat, severing both jugulars.

I was done wasting my time listening to his excuses. I didn't kill often, unless you put the ones I cared about in danger. Valentina or Kai could have been killed, and Ricci deserved his final fate.

I turned my attention back to him and watched him struggle with air until his gurgled pleas eventually quieted for good, blood sputtering out of his mouth.

I dropped the knife onto the floor and got out of my seat. After shooting a quick message to Valentina to tell her I was done with my recreation, I quickly wiped my hands with a clean rag and headed for my car that was parked in the adjoining garage of the facility.

It was early morning by the time I got home.

I rolled my neck under the hot water, every muscle in my body wound tight and sore. I threw my head back and ran my hands over my face, taking a deep breath.

My mind whirled with a million thoughts. I was getting closer every day to the answers I'd been looking for, but I couldn't help but dread it at the same time.

All because of her.

She preoccupied my mind more than my need to avenge my parents and I didn't know if it was a good thing or a bad one.

Pushing the thought away, I rinsed myself off and stepped out of the shower and headed for my bedroom. I was about to grab my phone off my bed to check if the cleaning crew had taken care of Ricci's body when I heard a small gasp.

I froze in my tracks when my gaze landed on someone standing at my bedroom door. It took me a second to register that Sienna was here and a cold shiver ran down my spine, realizing that I was completely bare for her to see.

I'd always been careful to hide that part of myself. No one except Noah had seen the countless scar tissues marring my back.

Non... Elle ne peut pas me voir comme ça.

Panic built in my chest like wildfire before turning molten and sinking to the bottom of my stomach.

"Get out of my room," I roared at her.

Her eyebrows furrowed at my sudden outburst. Her hand dropped from the doorknob and she came closer. Her hand reached for me, but I stepped back and out of reach. "Jamal..."

"I said. Get. Out," I repeated, trembling. My short nails dug into my palm by the sheer force of how tightly I was fisting my hands.

I breathed out slowly, attempting to calm myself down, but it wasn't working. I didn't want to do this. I hated having to raise my voice at her, but I wasn't ready for her to *see* me. Wasn't ready to have her look at me differently. So raising my voice and acting cold was the only way I could think of to make her leave.

Her eyes zeroed in on the raised skin that started where

my neck met my right shoulder before our gazes met again. Ignoring my request, she placed a hand on my forearm, but I jerked away from her.

"Don't touch me," I warned her in a broken whisper.

Her hands fell at her side. "Why do you keep insisting on pushing me away?" she asked with a pained expression.

God, I hated this.

"Sienna," I growled as she stepped farther toward me. I stepped back again, trying to figure out how I could hide, but the only thing I had accessible to hide them from her was the towel currently wrapped around my waist.

"Jamal, talk to me."

There was a long silence before I spoke again.

"Sienna," I pleaded, hoping she would stop coming closer. But my wishes were in vain.

"Jamal, what is it?"

My shoulder tensed as she halted right in front of me. I looked over her head, unable to meet her gaze. I opened my mouth to say something, but stubbornly the words refused to come out.

My heart was pounding frantically against my chest, fighting with my lungs, both competing with each other to take over.

Releasing an unsteady breath, I slowly turned around, my back now to her. A feeling of dread solidified in my gut and I looked straight ahead at the wall, trying to focus on anything but the blaring thought ricocheting in my mind.

Elle ne me regardera plus de la même manière.

My heart pounded even faster, so fast I feared it might give out. I wanted to see the expression on her face, but I was afraid to.

The room slowly filled with a suffocating silence.

I waited for her to leave, for a disgusted sound to reach my ears. But instead, her soft fingers tentatively brushed over the raised scars, her touch impossibly light. She ran the tips of her fingers from my lower back and upward until she reached the one that traveled over my shoulder.

I glanced at her over it, watching as she gently explored them, her eyes filled with sorrow as she took in the extent of the damage.

But the look on her face wasn't one of disgust.

Or pity.

She looked at me with…

Tenderness.

"Why…" she trailed off. "Why didn't you tell me?" Her voice was so faint, I'd barely heard her question.

"I didn't want you to see them," I said, my voice straining as the confession slipped out.

Her eyes met mine and her brows furrowed. "Did you think…"

I averted my gaze, closing my eyes as I faced forward again. "I didn't want you to see how damaged I am," I whispered, so low I hoped she hadn't heard me.

I felt her hands leave my skin, but her lips quickly replaced them as she placed a gentle kiss between my shoulder blades.

My body trembled beneath her touch and my eyes burned at the tenderness of her gesture. It registered in a part of my being I never thought could ever be reached.

But she did.

"The only thing I see is proof that you survived." She placed another kiss on my shoulder, tracing a path of featherlight kisses as she rounded my side to stand in front of me.

"Jamal, look at me."

My eyes were still closed because I was afraid to look at her, but when her hands framed my face, her thumbs brushing against my cheeks, urging me to open my eyes, I swallowed back the emotion threatening to bubble out and obliged.

I peered down to see her rising on her tiptoes so that her face would be more leveled to mine. She rested her forehead against mine and I closed my eyes once more.

"You're beautiful, not damaged." She pressed a kiss to the corner of my lips. "And I'm grateful for your scars because they mean you're here with me." Another kiss to the other side. "You'll never have to hide. Especially from me."

My chest squeezed tight at her words. They held so much conviction.

How did I get so lucky?

Everything was silent except for the loud roar of my heartbeat.

"Kiss me," she said softly as she moved one hand from

my face to the back of my neck, bringing our faces closer, while the other rested against my chest.

"I shouldn't," I answered, glancing down to meet her eyes.

Our mouths hovered against each other, only a whisper apart.

She tilted her head, her bottom lip brushing over mine. "Kiss me anyway."

I cradled her face and did exactly that.

CHAPTER 21

His heart pumped faster beneath my touch as his lips met mine.

My heart ached at the idea that he thought I would look at him any differently. He was beautiful. All of him.

Unlike our other kisses, this one wasn't hard or demanding. It was sweet and sent a different type of warmth all over my body.

But it was short-lived when his arm wrapped around my waist and he yanked me flush against him. So close that he almost lifted me off the ground.

The kiss turned ravaging, both of us greedy for more.

His other hand fisted my hair and he deepened the kiss, sliding his tongue between my lips and demanding access. I eagerly gave it to him and moved the hand that was resting against his chest to the back of his neck.

I didn't have much experience, but an innate instinct guided me to match whatever he was doing.

Was I doing this right? I didn't know, but I also didn't care.

Every stroke of his tongue against mine reached farther inside, unfurling the dormant longing I hadn't felt before I met him.

He groaned and slipped his hands under my thighs, hooking my legs around his waist before carrying me to his bed without ever breaking our kiss. His thick erection pressed firmly against my aching core once he sat down, my thighs straddling his waist.

The burning desire I felt for him consumed me and I slightly rocked my hips down.

Oh, that feels good.

So I did it again.

He rested his hands on my hips possessively to halt my movements as he continued to kiss me, but every few moments, he thrust upward, sliding his erection up against me.

His fingers made their way underneath my shirt and my skin tingled with anticipation. His hands moved higher until they were right beneath my bare breasts, making my nipples harden as he brushed the skin there.

My pussy clenched in response and I rocked against him. My lips parted and I moaned his name when his finger brushed over my right nipple. "Jamal."

"Yes, *mon amour*," he said before trailing kisses down my chin toward my neck.

I gently pressed my hands to his chest, stopping him. "I *need* you."

His eyes found mine and my gaze bore into his. Without another word, he lifted my shirt over my head, revealing me to him. He sucked in a sharp breath and his eyes darkened from their usual brown to an almost black as they roamed over me, taking in every inch of my exposed skin.

"Beautiful," he whispered against my skin as he placed a kiss above my breast. Cupping it into his palm, his wet, hot mouth latched over a nipple and he sucked.

"Fuck." I gasped, arching into his touch as he explored my breasts, giving them equal undivided attention.

Gripping. Sucking.

"*Simplement magnifique*," he muttered against my skin before biting down gently on my nipple.

I felt myself grow wetter with each of his ministrations and my thin pair of briefs weren't doing much to hide it. The fire running through me grew stronger with each stroke of his tongue and every time his cock rubbed against my clit.

It felt like hours of torture, his tongue never tiring, until he finally kissed his way back up to take my mouth with those sinful lips again.

"More," I mumbled breathlessly against his lips.

I wanted him everywhere. On me. Against me. Inside of me.

He hummed against my lips before sucking my bottom one between his teeth and nipping at it. A strangled sound broke free out of my throat, a mix between a gasp and a sigh.

"What do you want?" he asked in between kisses. His hands moved back to my hips, gripping them as I moved back and forth against him.

I whimpered against his mouth.

"What does my greedy wife want?"

I pulled back, my hands firmly on his shoulders now. My gaze instantly locked with his. "I want you to fuck me," I said boldly, shocking myself.

And by the expression on his face, shocking him too.

Suddenly embarrassed by my statement, I bit on my bottom lip, working it back and forth with my teeth, and averted my gaze.

I want you to fuck me. Really, Sienna?

One of his hands left my hip and he gripped my chin, forcing me to face him. "No, Sienna. Don't turn away. Look at me."

I slowly looked up and when I met his gaze, his eyes were filled with unfiltered lust.

"You want me to fuck you?" he whispered, softly brushing his lips against mine.

I nodded.

"Words, *mon amour*."

"Yes," I choked out.

Jamal lifted me off his lap and placed me between his spread legs, my knees resting between them. His hands then left my body and he rested his palms behind him against his bed.

I sat on my heels and my hands dropped to my sides, unsure of what he was waiting for. "Umm…" I frowned, confused.

He gave me a small smile. "Don't look so sad," he teased, reaching forward to press a kiss in the middle of my forehead, right above my frown lines. "I'll give you what you want. But first…" He paused, returning to his previous position. "Have you touched a man before?"

I shook my head slowly. "No."

His smile grew bigger. "Good. Unwrap my towel."

I reached for him, trying my hardest to steady my hands before I placed them against his chest. Once I made contact with his burning skin, desire overshadowed my shyness.

I slowly slid them along the planes of his stomach, exploring. Every ridge and valley of his abdomen tightened against my touch as I made my way down his body. His skin was blistering hot, just like I felt mine was.

I paused at the hem, my eyes flickering between his face and his erection clearly straining against the cloth. My fingers brushed lightly against it as they dipped underneath the towel to flick it open.

Puta madre.

My mouth watered at the sight and my tongue darted out to lick at my lower lip.

I'd technically seen some at work before or had a glimpse while watching television shows or movies, but I'd never seen one this close and like *this*.

His penis was thick and the swollen top shone with pre-cum, a smear of it near his hip.

I wonder what it tastes like.

He groaned and I looked up at him. "Sienna, you can't look at me like that."

"Oh, why?"

"Or I won't be able to restrain myself."

I was doing this to him. He was turned on because of me. That fact surged through me and dispelled more of the nervousness I was feeling. I reached down tentatively, brushing my fingers against it, and it twitched at the contact.

I retreated.

"It's okay, you can touch me," he choked out and I nodded.

My heart was beating so loudly against my rib cage, it almost felt like it would jump out of its place. Summoning the courage, I ran a finger up the vein along the underside of his shaft and he hissed through gritted teeth.

I ripped my hand away, but he grabbed it and brought it back.

"No," he panted. "Keep going."

My finger returned, this time exploring his crown and

over the leaking slit at the top. Curious, I brought my index finger to my lips and swiped it against my tongue as I looked at him.

Surprisingly, it didn't taste as bad as I thought. It was warm and salty, not bitter as I imagined.

A soft curse left his lips. "*Ah, putain tu vas me tuer.*"

I wasn't sure what he said, but I lit up from the expression on his face and went back to what I was doing. I stroked down his cock and fondled with his sac, weighing and tentatively squeezing.

The second I did, he choked out my name, squeezing his eyes shut and falling back into his bed, throwing his arm over his face.

I stretched and crawled over to him. "I'm sorry," I said, panicked. "Are you okay? I didn't mean to…"

He peered at me under his arm. "Sienna, it's okay. I just…" He chuckled lightly. "My body is yours to do anything you want, baby. Just be gentle around the tip and the scrotum since they're both more sensitive. You can touch it and play with it, but not too aggressively."

Threading his fingers around mine, he wrapped our hands over his penis and tugged up and down slowly. My skin grew a thousand degrees hotter at the gesture.

"Just like that," he husked.

That's fucking hot.

I slanted my hips sideways, searching for the right angle to relieve some of the aching pressure in my core with my heel.

He let go shortly after, my skin tingling from the loss.

"Okay," I whispered, trying to remember how he seemed to like it.

My hands ran down his ribs, and I wrapped one hand around his base, tugging upward, then down. My hand didn't fully wrap around him and that fact both terrified and excited me.

He lay back down and closed his eyes. Every now and then, he whimpered, flexing his hips into my touch, which only fueled me further.

I experimented with the pace and the tightness, and he let me. Every time I was rewarded with another moan of satisfaction, I became more eager to make him come.

His chest was heaving and pride flared in my chest that I was the cause of it. I kept going more aggressively, watching his swollen tip emerge at the end of my fist over and over again.

His pants grew more ragged and he abruptly sat up, gripping my wrist in his hand. "Enough," he growled, his voice strained.

I opened my mouth to say something, but he shook his head before dropping his forehead to mine. "You didn't do anything wrong," he got out quickly between ragged breaths. "I just don't want to come before you do."

He pressed a small kiss to my lips before grinning against my mouth.

"Besides, I want to come inside of you."

Jamal

CHAPTER 22

AGONY.

Watching her, having her touch me like that had been pure fucking agony. Her curious and eager hands roved all over my skin, and when she touched my cock, it took everything in me not to pin her to my bed and claim her.

The way she'd looked at me had sent electricity skittering all over my skin, my senses buzzing with a deep want for her. I tried my hardest to be patient—not my strongest suit when it comes to her—and let her experiment, but I had to put a stop to it before I came all over her beautiful skin.

Her current shocked expression after I said I wanted to coat her pussy with my cum was quite adorable. I crawled farther into the bed so that I was sitting with my back against the headboard, towel left behind.

I pointed at the remaining barrier between us. "Take it

off and come here," I softly commanded and she did as told.

Getting off the bed, she removed her cotton briefs and crawled over to me, the sight leaving me breathless. My head fell back against the headboard in defeat.

C'est pas pour me vanter, mais je suis le mec le plus veinard de la planète.

Sienna was everything. My wife was smart, witty, and fucking sexy.

My mouth found hers in my next breath as she straddled my waist. I fucked her mouth with my tongue, giving her a small taste of what was coming next. She turned boneless in my arms, her soaking cunt grinding against the underside of my cock without a barrier between us this time.

We both hissed at the sensation, and I swallowed her moans.

I trailed kisses down her neck until my teeth gently nipped at her shoulder. Her groan filled the space around us and I kissed the spot before gripping her waist with both hands.

"Grab the headboard," I finally managed to say.

I slid my body down under her to have her straddle my neck, making her cunt available for me to eat.

She glanced down at me, perplexed. "Why?"

"I need to get you ready and you'll need leverage to ride my face, *mon amour*."

"What do you mean ready? Ready for what?" She

placed her hands on the headboard and I finally got to do what I'd been dreaming of doing ever since I tasted her for the first time last night.

Doing it again.

"To take me," I said and gripped her hips hard to bring her closer to my face. "You're fucking drenched," I groaned, running the tip of my nose along her pussy.

"Jamal," she panted. "I…"

Before she could finish, I leaned forward and licked her once before I buried my face in her pussy and devoured her. She squirmed and gasped at every flick of my tongue.

My body hummed to life at the sound of her pleasure. She was becoming an addiction I never wanted to sober from.

I focused on her clit, sucking and biting every now and then, bringing her closer to the edge. What I wouldn't give to see the expression on her face.

Actually…

I pulled back slightly and she mewled a "no" in protest.

I chuckled. "I'm not stopping. I just wanted to look at your face." I met her hooded gaze as I took one slow lick through her lips.

She quivered and her legs melted around me, bringing her pussy even closer.

I moved away from her clit and speared my tongue into her opening, going as deep as possible.

"I'm gonna…" she whispered, her last words barely audible.

She was so fucking sweet.

Her hands found my hair and her nails dug into my scalp as she rode my face to get herself off. "Right there," she gasped, a string of Spanish curse words following right behind.

Hottest fucking thing I've ever seen.

She moved against me as I focused all my attention on her clit and I could feel her getting closer. I gave her one more swipe of my tongue and she cried out in a jumble of moans, her back arching and bucking against my face.

Her taste exploded against my tongue and her arousal poured out of her, down my throat, and all over my face.

Those delicious sounds combined with hearing my name being repeatedly screamed by those beautiful lips of hers spurred me on until she was finished and utterly limp above me.

I ran my tongue through her cunt one more time and her eyes shut closed.

I waited for her breathing to even out before I moved her down my body until she was back to straddling my waist. Then I kissed her, and she moaned into my mouth as I made her taste herself with my tongue.

I gripped her hips and guided her to roll her hips to coat myself in her.

"That feels so good," she murmured against my lips, rolling her hips to do it again.

"It'll feel even better very soon." I resisted every urge that roared inside me to slam her down my cock and fill her up. Somehow, I pushed the thundering thought aside to reach over for a condom in my nightstand, but she stopped me before I could.

"No," she said before adding, "I have an implant."

My hands drew patterns against her hips, the crown of my cock still nestled against her as I said, "I haven't been with anyone in a long time and the last time I got tested, all my tests came back clear."

"Okay," she said.

"Okay?" I mirrored, waiting to see if she'd change her mind.

"I want to feel everything while you're inside me."

My chest vibrated with a groan at her words. "Are you sure?" I asked. "Because as soon as I'm inside you, you're m—"

She shut me up with a kiss and spread her legs wider. "I already am."

Yes, you are. And I'm yours.

I took myself in my hand and slid my crown back and forth through her folds. I teased her entrance, watching her shiver with every touch.

"You're nice and wet and ready for me, so it shouldn't hurt, but you might feel a pinch," I told her.

She rolled her eyes. "I'm a doctor, Jamal. I'm aware."

I nipped at her bottom lip. "I know you are, Dr. Bruni," I teased. I smeared her arousal down my cock and slid my tip down to her entrance again. Pausing, my eyes found hers, and I held myself steady for her. "I'm at your mercy, baby."

Sienna's hands found my chest and she hesitated for a moment, inhaling a shuddering breath before slowly lowering herself down, just enough to stretch herself open to take me.

When my tip squeezed inside of her, we both let out strangled moans. Her nails dug into my skin as I gripped her ass to prevent myself from thrusting upward. I was barely inside her and the hot need to release scorched my veins.

I loosened my grip on her and moved my hands to rest on her hips, reminding myself that I was letting her take control.

"You need to relax, baby," I murmured, dropping my forehead to hers. "Relax so you can fit me all the way in."

She nodded, her hands coming up to lace around my neck. She took in a weak breath and lifted up before sinking down a little further.

"Good girl."

I glided one hand from her waist and rubbed circles up and down her spine. Her body slowly relaxed under my hands.

"That's it," I encouraged her.

She took in a deeper breath as she slid out. She sank further down this time and I peered down between us. Watching her stretch around my cock, taking me in, was the prettiest thing I'd ever seen.

I trembled at the sight.

"You're shaking," she noted, her tone worried.

I placed a kiss on her lips. "It's because of how beautifully you're taking me."

She whimpered against my lips and rolled her hips, testing before repeating the motion. I slightly pulled back and let myself appreciate the beauty she was as she rode me, slowly finding her rhythm and sinking a bit more each time.

The hesitancy in her movement slowly faded away to let confidence take the rein. "Jamal," she moaned, and I bit back a groan at the feeling of her walls clenching around me.

"*Oh putain*," I cursed, my words coming out raspy as she took another inch, almost there.

She withdrew slowly, and I watched my cock drenched in her. Pausing, her gaze locked with mine for a moment.

Then she sank all the way down and she felt so good, I nearly blacked out.

Sienna

CHAPTER 23

My lips parted, but no words came out.

I rolled my hips once, testing having him completely inside me. Jamal dropped his face into my neck and bit back a groan.

"Yes." I gasped, my eyes fluttering shut as I rolled my hips again.

I felt full. So full.

The pain I initially felt intensified, but with every roll of my hips, his cock stretched me open further and the pain subsided, allowing pleasure to surface and take over.

He buried his hands in my hair and his lips were on me, kissing me reverently. I felt his heart battering against his chest, the beat matching my own.

He opened up his thighs and with his hands on my waist, he helped lift me almost all the way out before slamming me back down.

I cried out and he swallowed it with a kiss. I wrapped my arms around his neck and met each thrust of his tongue, each nip against my bottom lip with my own.

"You feel incredible," he praised, driving his hips upward. He was moving achingly slow as his hips met mine. He tugged on my hair, yanking my head back. He peppered kisses along my jaw, down my neck, where he pulled the skin into his mouth and sucked on it.

"You… You do too, but—"

He angled his hips, cutting my sentence short.

"Yes," I cried out. "More."

And he started to fuck me, somehow driving deeper inside me with each thrust. I kept riding him and his upward thrust became more erratic, fucking me relentlessly.

My body's temperature reached a scorching level and the tension in my core tightened, spiraling higher and higher, waiting patiently to unfurl.

His teeth scraped along my pulse point and my breathing quickened as my orgasm kept climbing.

"You look so good taking my cock, *mon amour*," he husked. "I love the feeling of your tight pussy stretching open for me."

Jamal reached between us and pinched my clit.

"Jamal," I cried out.

"That's it, Sienna," he said, his other hand gripping my side a little tighter to help me ride. "Ride my cock until you come."

Desire fueled me and I rode him faster, an overwhelming feeling taking over.

It was all too much. I'd come on his fingers and on his tongue before but this…

This was pure ecstasy.

Jamal rubbed my clit as I alternated between bouncing on him and rolling my hips, chasing the pleasure that waited right at my fingertips. I felt his cock swell inside me and my walls clenched around him.

"*Fuck*," he groaned. "Your cunt is squeezing me so tight, Sienna. I can feel you dripping down my balls."

"Jamal," I said breathlessly. His words were too much. The picture he was painting was sending jolts of electricity down my spine, intensifying my imminent descent.

He slid a hand up between my heaving breasts and grabbed one, taking a nipple into his mouth. His tongue swirled around before he tugged on it with his teeth.

That's all it took for my orgasm to rip through me like a thunderstorm.

Stars exploded behind my eyes and I cried out his name over and over again as he fucked me hard and fast, squeezing every ounce of my pleasure.

"God, you're something else. Just so beautiful coming around my cock."

He kept driving into me until I fell completely limp in his arms.

Just as I thought it was over, Jamal held me to him and flipped us over so I was on my back. "You did so well, but

I think you can do even better and give me another one," he demanded.

He withdrew his cock and tilted my hips up, positioning himself at my entrance before he slid into my tender core.

"Oh," I whimpered, my hands flying to his neck.

"I want to fill you with my cum. I want to be the only man to ever come in this pussy." His pelvis hit my clit each time he rolled his hips up and into me, another orgasm awakening.

"Yes," I said, but my moans drowned out my response.

Jamal was panting loudly as he drove in and out, his fingers gripping my hips so tightly, they'd most likely leave bruises. And I wasn't opposed to it, to him marking me.

I wanted to carry a reminder of this moment beyond how I was feeling right now, how *he* was making me feel. I was drunk on him and I never wanted to sober up.

"God, I'll never get enough of you." Jamal sealed his mouth over mine and gave me a bruising kiss.

I met him thrust for thrust when his body started trembling. Our eyes met and his charged gaze caused my stomach to tighten. He laid a foot flat on the bed, changing his position and making his cock brush against my most sensitive spot, over and over again.

"I… I…" My vision blurred as my orgasm flared in my core and shot through me.

The noise that came out of me was one I didn't recognize.

Jamal's mouth suddenly slanted over mine as he

succumbed to his own orgasm. I felt warmth spill into me as he continued to thrust for what felt like hours. We were coming together and the blissful feeling catapulted me into another dimension of euphoria.

Wave after wave until his hips slowed. "Just fucking beautiful," he said and placed a gentle kiss to my temple. He dropped his elbows on each side of my head, caging me with his arms. He searched my gaze. "Are you okay?" he asked softly, still inside me.

"I just had the most amazing experience of my life. I think I'm more than okay."

He laughed softly, pressing a kiss to my nose this time. "That makes two of us."

I never thought I'd see this side of my husband.

Sweet, gentle, *caring*. And I liked it. I loved it, actually.

Carefully, he removed himself from inside me and pulled me into his lap, rubbing my back gently and running his fingers through my hair. Our heaving chests eventually slowed and the room grew quieter, a blissful atmosphere enveloping us.

"Let's get you cleaned up," he said with a small smile.

Too spent to walk, Jamal carried me into his bathroom and gently placed me on the counter. Then he ran the shower warm before helping me step inside. He stood right behind me and wrapped his arms around my waist as the water trickled down on us.

I sighed in contentment, relishing in the moment. I was… happy. And I don't think I'd felt that in a long time.

I never craved someone's company, never wanted to share my life with someone, but the more time I spent with him, the more I could see myself wanting that with him.

And that thought scared me more than anything else.

Jamal held me for a long time before we finally showered as we intended to in the first place. He spent his time delicately washing my body, giving particular attention between my legs.

We eventually came out and changed into new clothes. I was slipping into one of his shirts and a pair of sweatpants that he'd given me, rolling the hem twice to avoid it dragging on the floor since he was significantly taller than me.

I turned around when I heard him come out of his closet. He'd changed into a pair of dark navy flannel bottoms and a white long-sleeved shirt that clung snugly against his broad frame.

I bit against a smile, containing a chuckle.

"What's wrong?" he asked, one brow arching up.

"Nothing, you just look…" My eyes roamed over his body, taking him in. "Very relaxed."

His brows furrowed. "I'm always relaxed."

I let out a laugh. "If you say so."

He walked over to me and pressed his lips to mine. "Come on, smart-ass. Let's get you some food."

We left his room and headed for the kitchen. As I reached the bottom of the stairs, he unexpectedly gave my right cheek a slap.

I whipped around. "Jamal," I warned in a hushed tone, laughing.

He gave me a smile, his eyes lighting up, but his expression sobered up when he looked behind me. I turned around, only to find Kai and Valentina standing in the kitchen, a surprised look on both of their faces. Valentina's cup was paused midway to her mouth while Kai was biting into a fluffy pastry.

My body warmed, a flush creeping up my neck as they both looked back and forth between Jamal and me, a knowing expression replacing their previous surprise.

Fuck, did they... hear us? Hear me screaming.

I rolled my lips between my teeth and cleared my throat as I stepped into the kitchen, Jamal right behind me. "Um, hi."

"Hi," they said simultaneously before fixing their gazes on Jamal.

His front brushed against my back as his hand rested on my waist and pressed a kiss against my wet hair. "Quit staring," he directed at them.

"We're not," Kai said, amused. "We've just been waiting for your famous Sunday feast."

Jamal shook his head and walked over to grab two mugs from the cupboard. He filled them with coffee before returning to me and placing one in front of me.

"Thank you," I murmured, giving him a small smile before he left my side and reached for the fridge to grab a variety of ingredients.

I braced my arms on the island, warm cup in my hands as I stood opposite to where Kai and Valentina were also standing. My attention snagged on Jamal as he carefully rolled up his sleeves before washing his hands.

God, he looked good.

I watched him cut vegetables and the simple gesture of his biceps straining against the fabric of his shirt, his deft fingers holding the ingredient, sent warmth blooming into my core, memories of his hands all over my body flooding my brain.

A few seconds passed by when I realized I was forgetting something. I blinked, coming out of my thoughts. "Wait, did you say Sunday?" I asked no one in particular.

I didn't have work today since it was my weekend off nor was it a race day. So what was I forgetting? I wasn't a forgetful person, but the sex definitely jumbled my mind a little.

"He did, why?" Jamal replied, arching a brow.

Fuck.

My eyes flickered to the clock on the stove and I let out a long sigh. I was supposed to meet Esra for brunch today. And I was late.

I straightened up. "I have to leave."

Jamal stopped whisking and turned to me, a bowl in hand. "Why?"

"I just remembered I have a brunch date with Esra."

His brows creased at the news and he looked... sad.

Guilt of leaving him right after what transpired between us overtook me, but I couldn't bail on Esra.

I walked over to the sink and dumped the remaining coffee in the sink, then quickly rinsed out my mug before putting it in the dishwasher. I placed a hand on his lower back as I brushed past him and muttered a sorry on my way out of the kitchen.

I mumbled a goodbye to Kai and Valentina and rushed upstairs. In a hurry, I quickly changed into a pair of sage green straight-leg cargos, an oversized white T-shirt, and threw on a large hoodie that was a few shades darker than my pants.

I then brushed my wet hair into a slicked back low bun and slung my purse over my shoulder, then threw in my wallet and my phone after shooting Esra a quick text that I was on my way.

Not really, but she didn't have to know that.

I walked out of the house in a hurry, only to stand still in the middle of our driveway.

"Dammit!"

I stepped back into the house. All three of them were still in the kitchen, talking and laughing, but they immediately directed their gazes at me when the front door closed behind me.

Jamal was already halfway to me before I even said a word. "What's wrong?" he asked, drawing closer.

"Umm, I forgot my car's still out of commission," I said, smiling tightly.

"You can take mine," he proposed, but there was no way I was driving *that*.

"You'd let me drive your car? That thing costs too much for me to drive it." There's a reason why I always kept mine.

"First off, it's not a *thing*. Besides, it's just a car. Let me get you the keys."

I shook my head and placed a hand on his forearm, stopping him. "It's okay. I'll just call a taxi." It was sweet that he trusted me with his car, but I wouldn't even know how to drive it. And too much risk of crashing it.

"Then I'll take you," he countered, but I didn't want to interfere with their routine.

I was about to tell him he didn't need to when Valentina chimed in. "I'll drop her off. I have some business to attend to in the city anyway."

"On a Sunday?" Kai asked.

She simply rolled her eyes at him and downed the rest of her coffee. She placed it in the sink and brushed past me and Jamal. "Let's go."

I stood on the balls of my feet and pressed a kiss to Jamal's jaw. My cheeks instantly burned bright at the realization of what I'd done, but before I could overthink it, I whipped around and followed Valentina out.

CHAPTER 24

I RELUCTANTLY HEADED BACK INTO THE KITCHEN.

Realistically, I knew it was more logical for Valentina to take her because if I did, I'd just spend however long she spent with her friend waiting outside for her to be done.

But I couldn't hide the fact that I was disappointed to not spend more time with her today. We both worked quite often and with her schedule, we hadn't had the chance to see each other as often as I'd like.

The only time we did was in my car when I drove her to and back from work. And that would soon change since the garage where Kai had taken her car when it broke down was almost done with the repairs.

I'd considered buying her a brand-new one because hers was quite frankly not something I liked her driving, but I knew she wouldn't want that. She had a strange attachment to that old piece of metal and I didn't want to take that away from her.

I stood in front of the stove and poured the mixture of egg, vegetables, and spices into the pan. I then turned the heat on under a new pan and placed slices of turkey bacon into it.

The room was awfully quiet, the silence suffocating as I felt Kai's gaze burning the back of my skull with a million questions. I frowned, peering at him over my shoulder to find him now perched at the kitchen island, sipping on his coffee.

"Can I help you with something?" I asked him.

He stayed quiet for a moment, studying my face before he finally said what I knew he'd been itching to ask since I walked in not too long ago with Sienna.

"Anything you want to tell me?"

"What do you mean?" I deflected.

He gave me a look that said *don't play me for a fool.* "Jamal, she was wearing your clothes."

Oh. I'd forgotten about that.

I returned my attention back to the pans. I folded the eggs with a spatula in one and flipped the bacon with tongs in the other to buy myself some time.

"So?" he prompted.

I had no idea how to answer. On one hand, I wanted to scream at the top of my lungs that Sienna was mine. That whenever she was around, I couldn't think straight.

That she was all I could think about.

That I wanted her. Needed her. That I…

That I was falling for my wife.

That final realization hit the hardest. I couldn't hide it or pretend I didn't anymore. I'd never loved anyone or been in love. Sure, I had occasional casual hookups while in college, but my heart was never in it.

But now…

I slid the cooked bacon onto a paper towel covered plate and placed the omelet in another one. After heating up some bread in the air fryer, I placed everything onto the island.

"I have all day," he added, putting his elbow on the island and patting the seat right next to him.

I groaned and sat down, hoping he'd let it go, but it didn't take long before he spoke again.

"You like her," he stated, not missing a beat. He sounded amused, his low chuckle filling the kitchen.

I watched him from the corner of my eye and his grin widened the longer I stayed silent. I broke a piece of bread and scooped some of the omelet up with it then brought it to my mouth.

I could deny it and change the subject, but what was the point? So I swallowed and turned to face him, taking a deep inhale. "How did you know?"

Kai laughed. "It's pretty obvious. *And* I haven't seen you smile like this in…" He paused, as if he were sifting through all his memories starting from the day we met. "Ever, actually."

Kai was a pain in my ass most of the time, but he *was* right. Again.

Although at first I had found Sienna to be infuriating, I knew now that I only thought that because of what she'd stirred inside me the moment I'd laid eyes on her.

"I smile," I started, but when he pinned me with a glare, I added, "Sometimes."

"*Heavy* on the sometimes," he deadpanned before placing a bite of his own into his mouth.

We ate in silence for a few minutes before he spoke again.

"Have you told her?" he asked softly.

I knew exactly what he was talking about and the answer to his question was, I hadn't. I'd opened up to her about losing my parents, even told her my real name, but I never told her more than the fact that they'd died. So many things were still a mystery to me and I didn't see the point in dragging her into it.

She's already dragged into it, my brain chimed in, but I ignored it.

So I shook my head in response.

"Is she worth it?"

"Yes," I answered immediately, not needing to think about it.

She's more than worth it.

"Then can I give you a piece of advice?" He continued before I could decline. "I know you want revenge for your parents, but don't let it get in the way of you finding happiness. And from what I see, she makes your grumpy self happy."

I swallowed the lump in my throat and scooped another bite with bread, cutting a piece of bacon and adding it to it.

Not wanting to dive into this any further, I changed the subject. "Anything new on the Barrera front?"

Kai's face fell and I knew it only meant bad news. Which seemed to be the only kind we'd been getting since I started all of this.

"We've been hitting a wall for the last week," he explained. "Nothing Valentina throws at his systems works. Every time she finds a new lead, it comes to a dead end or she discovers something we already knew."

"What do you mean?"

"Anything before your parents' deaths is a dead end because the money trail keeps cutting short and we can't trace it to its original sender," he added.

Frustration clawed at my chest because we'd been at this for the last four years and still nothing. The only way to get to the end of this seemed to be getting Barrera alone to get the information out of him, but his security was ironclad.

I'd tried on several occasions in the past, but whenever I got too close, we got burned. Add his son to the mix and it made everything more complicated than it already was.

A few months after I learned about the true nature of my parents' deaths, I'd found who had lit the flame that blazed what I once knew. He'd become my first kill. But my raging anger had taken the best of me and I'd killed him before I got the chance to ask who'd hired him.

My attention went back to Kai and my eyes roamed over his face. I could tell he wanted to tell me something but was debating on whether or not he should.

"What is it?" I asked, worried.

"It's probably nothing," he said, brushing off whatever he wanted to say.

"Tell me anyway."

"I don't want to get your hopes up, but Valentina thinks she found a pattern in some of the real estate contracts Barrera signed while your father was investigating him, but she needs a bit more time to figure out what it all means."

"What did she find?"

"She thinks the electronic files contain crypto keys and that could have been how the communication was established with whoever set the fire since those contracts are accessible to the public. If we're able to decrypt the keys—"

"We'll find the source," I finished for him.

"Exactly. We'll get him," Kai reassured me, placing a hand on my shoulder.

I sure hope so.

We caught each other up on work and finished eating. Once we were done, Kai got up and brought the dirty dishes to the sink. Since I cooked, he was on cleaning duty.

"Since we talked about my love life, what's new with yours?" I asked, spinning my chair to face him.

"Why the sudden interest?" Kai asked without looking at me.

"Well, you *did* ask about mine."

He finished loading the plates into the dishwasher before turning to face me. He leaned into the border of the sink and crossed his arms over his chest.

"Fair enough, but there's nothing new on that front," he said, but his face gave him away.

I narrowed my eyes. "You forget I know you. If you're hiding something, then it must be good," I said, teasing him.

Kai usually loved to talk, especially about himself, and tended to overshare, so to see him so quiet and deflecting only made me want to dig more because that meant someone was making him feel off-balance.

Since he wasn't giving in, I added, "Who is it?"

He let out a long sigh, conceding. "There is someone, but it will never go anywhere."

I gave him a look. Kai could get anyone he wanted. "Why not?" I asked.

"She doesn't feel the same way," he confessed, his shoulders dropping.

My brows furrowed. "She told you that?"

"No, she didn't but—"

"Well, if she hasn't told you, then you can't know," I said before he finished his thought.

"Trust me, she doesn't need to tell me. And it would complicate things."

Complicate things. I wondered who this person was for him to say this. I wanted to push him about it more, but he cut me off before I could ask another question.

"I have some work to get done in preparation for this week. I'll see you later," he said before leaving the kitchen and heading toward his and Valentina's wing.

Guess I'll have to dig further another time.

I grabbed my laptop from my office and headed for my bedroom, deciding to get ahead of this week since I had the rest of the day free.

I stepped into my room and my eyes immediately caught on the rumpled sheets on my bed. The sight flooded my mind with flashbacks of Sienna's gorgeous body on top of mine.

Not to mention the screams of pleasure she made still echoing inside my brain.

I groaned and changed the sheets, throwing the others into the washing machine before I settled on top of my bed.

While I waited for my computer to power up, I grabbed my phone to text Valentina.

Jamal: Did you drop her off safely?

Valentina: You're turning soft.

Jamal: Answer the question, Valentina

Valentina: She's inside, safe and sound.

I opened my conversation thread with Sienna and sent her a message this time.

Jamal: Got there okay?

I only waited a few seconds before she answered.

Sienna: Just walked inside Fiori.

Jamal: Good.

Sienna: Was there anything else you wanted?

Jamal: You.

I groaned, berating myself for that answer.
You. What kind of lame answer is that?
I *was* turning soft.

Sienna: That's a good answer.

I wanted to keep texting her but didn't want to keep her from her time with her friend. So I placed my phone back onto my nightstand and forced myself to concentrate on my work.

It only partially worked.

CHAPTER 25

I walked into Fiori and shoved my phone into my purse, trying to hide the smile on my face. I never expected my husband to check if I got here, let alone for him to be so… sweet.

And I couldn't hide the fact that I liked it.

I shot a quick glance over my shoulder to see if Valentina was still here, only to find her already gone.

We'd spent the thirty-minute drive over here in complete silence. Not that I'd expected any small talk from Valentina, but I thought she'd ask about me and Jamal after this morning.

I guessed I should be grateful for the lack of probing from her end. Unlike the interrogation I was about to be subjected to when—not if—Esra found out.

She always seemed to read me like an open book.

Speaking of which.

I spotted Esra sitting at our regular booth, her brows knitted together as she furiously typed on her phone.

"I'm here!" I said, rushing over to her.

She looked up from her phone and her previous serious expression morphed into a gleeful one. "Hey, beautiful," she greeted me, getting out of her seat to hug me.

I wrapped my arms around her. "I'm so sorry for being late. I lost track of time," I explained, hoping she wouldn't ask why.

"It's okay. I was dealing with a work emergency, so I barely noticed," she shared before pulling back, giving me a small smile.

Esra sat back down and I slid into the booth next to her, giving her my bag to place next to hers on the other side.

"Same emergency that kept you from Kenna's wedding?" I asked.

She winced, nodding.

The makeup artist had been putting the final touches to Kenna's makeup when my phone rang. I'd picked up, surprised to see Esra's name flashing on the screen. She'd called right before the ceremony started, apologizing profusely because her new boss had asked her to amend the entirety of their upcoming fall/winter line.

She'd been working on the collection since last December, but a media tycoon who seemed to love making her life harder had recently acquired her company.

Esra had explained that the asshole—her words, not mine—had unexpectedly shown up right before she had to leave and had critiqued every single piece from their upcoming line.

Since they were only two weeks away before her team was meant to send the collection into production for it to come on time for their fashion show set in a few months, she'd have to spend the next few days working overtime to meet the deadline.

Esra already spent most of her days at work, but he seemed to be wanting to make her spend even more time there since he took over.

"I still can't believe the asshole is making me alter every single piece. The only reason I'm not at the atelier right now is because his royal pain in the ass is having a celebratory party for becoming CEO." She let out an exasperated sigh, brushing a stray curl out of her eye. "Anyways, enough about me. How's married life?"

"Oh, you know." I paused, looking for non-incriminating words. "Marriage," I finished.

Great, Sienna. Just great.

I grabbed the menu lying on top of the table and looked over it. I didn't need to since we came here often and I always ordered the same thing—their specialty loaded Mediterranean omelette and an espresso—but I needed to keep myself busy before I gave myself away.

Pretty sure you already did, my mind mocked me.

Esra reached over and lowered the menu I was using to shield myself. My eyes met hers and I gave her a small smile.

"You're glowing," she remarked, her green eyes sparkling with curiosity.

Fuck. She knows.

"What?" I choked, my heart speeding up. Heat crept up my neck and I shifted in my seat, pretending to get more comfortable. I cleared my throat. "No, I'm not," I added, shaking my head at the same time.

"You are. Your face." She paused, looking for the right words. "You're more relaxed." Her eyes widened in realization. "You had sex," she said, loud enough for the people around our table to hear.

I whipped my hand out, placing it over her mouth to stop her from announcing to the entire restaurant that I got laid. "Esra," I condemned.

Triumph glowed in her eyes. "I knew it," she said, the words muffled under my palm. She wrapped her hand around my wrist, signaling she would watch her volume.

I took my hand off and she opened her mouth to speak, but before she could, our server came up to our table.

"Hi, I'm Alessandra," she introduced herself. "Can I get you anything?"

We greeted her in return and placed our orders before handing Alessandra our menus. Looking up, we both gave her a small smile before she walked away. Our server wasn't even fully out of earshot before Esra finally looked back at me and the questions started coming in.

"Oh, I'm *so* happy for you!" She clasped her hands together. "Was it good? Was *he* good?" she whispered. Or at least, tried to because the couple at the table in front of us gave us judgmental looks.

I sighed, rubbing an exasperated hand over my face. "Esra."

"What?" she said, holding up her hands. "It was your first time. I want to make sure Jamal took care of—"

Her sentence was cut short when Alessandra came over with our food. She placed our respective plates in front of us before briefly leaving our table and coming back with our coffees.

"Enjoy," she said to us before walking away.

I grabbed my fork and cut a piece of my omelet. I brought the piece to my mouth, hoping to buy myself some time.

It wasn't that I didn't want to tell her, but that I didn't know what to say. Yes, Jamal and I had sex. Yes, I'd lost my virginity. But it was so much more.

I wasn't supposed to care about him. He'd forced me into this union, threatened my family if I didn't, and turned my life upside down.

I hadn't given myself the chance to think about the changing nature of our relationship. But with time, Jamal's mask had fallen away, revealing more and more of who he was, and…

I shook myself out of my thoughts and finally looked at Esra again, only to find her on her phone. Before I got to ask her what she was doing, her phone lit up with an incoming video chat call from our newly wedded friend.

"*Esra.*"

She simply shrugged and answered, Kenna's face filling the screen. Esra scooted closer and held her phone between us so we could both be on the screen.

"You had *sex*?" Kenna asked without preamble.

I groaned. "Hi, Kenna."

"Let's skip the formalities." Kenna shifted and I caught a glimpse of her white nightgown. She reached out of the frame and put on her glasses. Making herself comfortable, she sat up in her bed and said, "Tell us everything."

I was sweating.

"Aren't you supposed to be enjoying time with your new husband?" I said, deflecting.

"Oh, he doesn't mind. Don't you, Shareef?" She tilted the camera to the side, showing a glimpse of her husband half-asleep. He gave a noncommittal wave and mumbled something resembling a "no" before she brought the camera back on her.

"So did he make it good for you?" Kenna continued.

I let out another sigh.

"It was fine," I downplayed.

Both Kenna and Esra spoke at the same time.

Esra turned to look at me, her brows furrowed. "Fine?"

"Just fine?" Kenna added, shocked. "I thought that looking like *that*, it would at least be good, not 'fine.'"

I leaned back against the vinyl booth, throwing my head back, and closed my eyes. "Ugh." I sat back up straight.

"Okay, it was amazing. Actually, it was better than amazing. It was…"

"*Oh*, he has a magical dick," Esra quipped, her eyes glittering with laughter.

I pinned Esra with a glare. "Esra."

"*Esra*," she mimicked me. "Stop saying my name like that. I'm just telling the truth. You should see the look on your face," she noted, amused. "He must have rocked your world."

Shaking my head, I huffed out a laugh. He had indeed.

Kenna's expression turned serious. "So now what?" Kenna asked the same question I'd been asking myself since this morning.

"Buzzkill," Esra said, rolling her eyes.

"Well, someone has to ask the question," Kenna replied, defending her stance.

"I don't know," I answered truthfully, averting my gaze.

"Do you…" Kenna trailed off.

I took a deep breath, knowing exactly what she was asking.

There was no point in lying. "Yeah, I think I do," I answered honestly, my voice almost a whisper.

Kenna gave me a small smile.

"But I can't… I shouldn't," I added, reaching for my now cold espresso to sip on it.

I was falling in love with my husband and if I was being honest with myself, I'd been falling for Jamal for a while now.

"Why?" they both asked.

I glanced back and forth between them. "I…" I tried to find the words but couldn't think of anything. "Nothing."

"I think, aside from your very obvious feelings, you need to ask yourself if you want this, if you can see this working out," Kenna said, a soft expression on her face.

She was right. I knew she was right. My reservations weren't just if *I* wanted this.

Did *he* want this?

I'm here to collect what's mine.

The words echoed in my mind, reminding me of how Jamal and I had met.

Our relationship was built on a transactional foundation. This all started as a business transaction. I was collateral damage, a debt collected, and I couldn't help but wonder if that's all my husband saw me as.

A payment.

A blaring ringtone interrupted my thoughts. Esra's phone flashed with an incoming call, Kenna's face replaced by the name "asshole" showing up on the screen.

Esra's face contorted in exasperation and she let the call go to voicemail, but her phone rang again the second after. This time she declined it.

"Everything okay?" Kenna asked.

"Yes, everything's fine," Esra replied, a tight smile on her face.

Her phone rang again with another call, followed by an incoming text that said, "Answer."

She let out a frustrated sigh.

"I'm sorry. I have to take this or he won't stop calling," Esra said, apologizing.

We quickly said our goodbyes to Kenna and Esra finally answered.

Concern sprouted in my chest as I watched her listen to whatever her boss was telling her on the phone without saying a word. I couldn't exactly hear what he was saying, but his harsh tone was loud enough for me to hear through the phone.

She simply muttered a disgruntled "okay" before hanging up on him. Then she looked over at me and my uneasiness about her situation grew. Esra rarely looked rattled, if ever, so whatever he'd told her must've really pissed her off.

Her shoulders slumped. "I'm so sorry to bail on you, but there's an emergency at work and I have to go."

"It's okay, go." I placed a hand on her thigh, hoping to reassure her. She grabbed her purse and reached for her wallet, but I stopped her. "I've got you. Text me when you get there."

She downed her black coffee and wrapped her croissant in a napkin before dropping a kiss on my cheek.

"Love you," she said before sliding out of the booth from the other side.

As soon as she stepped out of Fiori, I opened my phone to continue reading some of the research I was going through for my presentation that was due next week at work while I finished eating.

Once I was done, I settled the bill and texted Valentina that I was ready to go whenever she was, returning to my reading as I waited for her response. A few minutes later, my phone pinged with a reply from her, notifying me that she was outside.

That was fast.

I got up and grabbed my things from the bench, saying a quick thank you to Alessandra before making my way outside. Once inside the car, the deafening silence was back and I was left alone with my thoughts.

With Kenna's words replaying in my mind.

CHAPTER 26

I PLACED MY SCRUBS INTO THE HAMPER AND WAS MAKING my way back to my locker when the door to the staff locker room cracked open.

Leena stood at the threshold. "Oh, good, you're still here," she stated, relieved.

"Is everything okay, Leena?" I asked, worried there was something wrong with one of my patients.

I'd done one last check before I ended my shift and everyone seemed stable, but this was the ER, so occasionally things changed quickly. I knew she'd just started her shift, so she might have noticed something I'd missed.

"No, Dr. Bruni. Everyone's okay," she said, giving me a wide smile. "I just wanted to wish you a happy birthday before you left for the day."

Oh. I'd been working with Leena since I started my residency and it shouldn't be a surprise that she remembered what today was, but I was so used to people forgetting that it caught me off guard.

It was always funny to me how someone who I'd only been working with remembered more than my own family had.

"Thank you, Leena," I replied, giving her a grateful smile.

"All right, I'll let you go before someone else keeps you from doing so," she said, letting out a small chuckle.

I huffed out a laugh because she was right. If I stayed any longer, a nurse, a student, or another resident would stop me to ask a question. Not that I minded, but it had been a long day and I was ready to go home.

"Have a good night," I said.

"You as well, Dr. Bruni," she answered before leaving and closing the door behind her.

I plucked my phone off the top shelf in my locker and checked it one more time to see if I'd gotten any messages. My hope that this year would be different died a quick death when the only texts I found were from my group chat with Kenna and Esra.

You shouldn't be surprised, my mind mocked me.

After quickly answering Kenna's and Esra's birthday wishes, I grabbed my bag from the bench and closed my locker behind me, then headed out.

I hadn't seen either of them since the weekend of Kenna's wedding two weeks ago. Esra had been swamped with the collection and Kenna went back to North Western the following week of her wedding, the repairs from the flood finally over.

I walked out the employee exit and walked through the parking lot behind the hospital, heading for my car.

Initially when Jamal had said he was taking care of it, I'd thought he would get it towed and scrapped since he'd often complained about the atrocious state of my car.

Instead, he'd surprised me a few days ago after picking me up from work with a revamped version of what my little compact SUV once was.

He'd not only fixed the transmission, but he'd also had the shop give my car a facelift, updated the A/C so it would actually work and added seat warmers so I wouldn't be cold on the drive to the hospital when the temperature dropped in the winters.

When I'd complained that I couldn't afford all these repairs, he'd simply pinned me with a glare and told me that he would never be comfortable letting his wife drive around in a car like that.

Although I *was* happy to have her back, the fact still left me with a bittersweet feeling. I might not have initially enjoyed Jamal driving me everywhere, but I'd grown to look forward to our time together every day.

Our quiet rides had turned into moments where I'd learned a little more about him every time and I'd miss them.

Another thing Jamal did over the last two weeks, aside from giving me the best orgasms, was move me into his bedroom. He claimed that his wife should be sleeping in his bed, not her own.

It didn't take much convincing.

I drove through town, making a quick stop at the grocery store before heading home. Once parked in our driveway, I turned off the ignition and adjusted my seat back.

Then I reached over to the passenger seat and grabbed the items I'd gotten at the grocery store from my tote bag.

After pulling a candle out of the packaging, I lifted the lid of the box holding a single chocolate cupcake. The sweet scent immediately hit my nose and my stomach growled, reminding me I'd barely eaten today.

I plunged the candle in the middle of the cupcake when my phone rang. I glanced down at it and saw my mother's name flashing on the screen. I placed the dessert on the dashboard and picked up my phone from the cup holder.

A small spark of hope reignited in my chest. I hesitated for a moment before I took a deep breath and finally answered. "*Hola, mami*," I greeted her.

"I need your help with something," she said immediately, dousing the previous glimmer.

Of course that's why she's calling.

I let out a deep sigh. "What is it?"

"Poor Akari is struggling a little in her mathematics class and needs a private tutor to make sure she doesn't fail it. If she does, she'll have to repeat the year. You know how it is with your dad so…" She trailed off.

I knew my mother well enough that she wouldn't outright ask me for what she needed. She always waited for me to offer it so she wouldn't feel guilty about what she was asking me afterward.

I was well aware of her tactics and I should say no, but she was my mother and I wouldn't let my sister be punished because my parents couldn't do their job as parents.

"How much?" I asked, not wanting to prolong this conversation any longer.

"Just five hundred dollars," she said, like that was nothing. "But I'll pay you back as soon as I get paid," she quickly added.

I knew I'd never see that money again. I held in my exasperation and reluctantly said, "I'll send you a transfer in a little bit. Anything else?"

"No, thank you, *mija*. I don't know what we would do without you."

"Yeah, good night, *mami*."

She hung up the phone without saying goodbye. Or wishing me a happy birthday.

Tears pricked at my eyes, but I looked up, willing them to go away.

You're okay, Sienna, I told myself. *Crying won't help.*

My body shook with the bitter laugh I'd been holding back. This wasn't funny, it was sad really, but what was I supposed to do?

My parents had given me a good upbringing. They had

never laid their hands on me or starved me. They just forgot I existed unless I was useful to them.

I pushed my disappointment aside, adding it to the endless pile that I'd been shoving away in the back of my mind over the years, and reached for the cupcake again after tossing my phone into my purse.

I pulled a small box of matchsticks out of the side of the driver's door and lit one. The small flame burned bright in the dark confines of my car, and I brought it closer to the wick and held it there until it caught on.

I leaned forward, closed my eyes, then blew out the flame.

Happy birthday, Sienna.

I sat back, pulled out the used candle, and ate the cupcake. After I was done, I grabbed my things and headed inside. Once I opened the door, I unfortunately heard chatter coming from the kitchen.

Just my luck.

I was ready for bed and didn't have the energy to face anyone else tonight. I just wanted to have the rest of the evening to myself. I eventually took a deep breath and looked up, but my lungs squeezed tight once my eyes landed on what was happening in the kitchen.

My eyes widened.

How did he know?

I blinked, thinking my eyes were playing tricks on me, but when I opened them again, the image in front of me was still the same.

Standing in the middle of the kitchen was Jamal and Kai. Even Valentina was there. The space was decorated with floating purple balloons that were fully covering the ceiling. A *happy birthday* banner was hanging in front of the island and there was even a large bouquet of white and purple carnations on top of the counter.

My gaze jumped back and forth between all of them.

"Surprise," they said in unison.

My chest tightened even more.

To most, this didn't seem like much. But to me. To me this was everything.

Years of suppressed feelings came crashing down on me and tears freely trickled down my cheeks.

Jamal was standing in front of me instantly, his hands rubbing up and down my arms. "Sienna, what's wrong? I'm so sorry. I just thought…" His shoulders slumped.

"I—" My voice cracked. I couldn't find the right words to describe how I was feeling. I glanced up at him and finally managed to say, "This is the nicest thing anyone has ever done for me."

He let out a breath of relief. A glimmer filled his eyes and he wrapped his arm around my shoulders, bringing me flush to his side before placing a soft kiss on the top of my head.

"Come here," he said as we strolled over to the kitchen.

He left my side for a moment and reached for the refrigerator, then pulled out a white box from inside of it.

He set the cardboard box on the island and looked at me, apprehension filling his irises.

"Open it," he said.

I brushed a finger under my eyes, wiping the streaks there and forcing myself to stop this madness. I wasn't even someone who really cried, so this was a very unusual reaction for me.

I nervously reached out and tugged on the purple ribbon that was tied in a perfect bow. When I pulled the lid off and looked inside, warmth radiated through my chest. I bit my lip, trying and failing to contain my smile.

"Sorry if it's too much purple. You said it was your favorite color, so I—"

I glanced back at him. "It's perfect," I said before he finished his sentence. I placed a hand over his bicep and stood on my tiptoes to give him a gentle kiss on his cheek before I could convince myself otherwise. "Thank you," I said quietly before landing back on my heels.

I looked back at the cake. It was a one-tier round semi-naked chocolate cake with a mix of white and dark purple buttercream decorating it. The words "Happy Birthday, Sienna" were written on top in white frosting.

"You'll have to thank whoever made this cake because it's seriously beautiful. Almost too beautiful to eat," I teased, trying to fend off the emotions clawing at my throat.

I kept my eyes down, my gaze roaming over the confection.

I'd never had a surprise birthday, let alone a cake made

especially for me. Sure, as a kid, my parents bought the generic cake on that day and we ate it together, but once they had Iris and Akari, the focus shifted to them and I was quickly forgotten.

Nowadays, it was either a birthday call days later or none at all.

"You can thank him yourself," Kai said, pulling me out of my thoughts.

I glanced up at him. "What do you mean?" I asked, my brows furrowing.

Kai nudged his head toward Jamal and I turned my attention to my husband, only to find him blushing.

"You made this?"

He shrugged. "It's nothing," he said nonchalantly, turning to a drawer behind us and pulling a lighter and candles out.

"I didn't know you could bake," I said, watching him stick a few candles sparsely.

Jamal cooked every day for us, but I'd never seen him bake, let alone make a cake like this.

"He learned for your birthday," Kai answered in his place and Jamal glared at him, mouthing for him to shut up.

I just fell for him a little more.

Jamal lit all the candles as he and Kai proceeded to sing me happy birthday in English, Spanish, and Jamal even sang it in French.

Valentina simply stood to the side, her arms crossed over her chest as she leaned against the counter. She didn't join them, but for her to be here was more than I could ask for.

I focused my attention back on the singers and my heart erupted at the sight of them singing off-key. For me.

Once they were done, I closed my eyes for the second time tonight and exhaled a deep breath. I usually didn't wish for anything, but this time, this time surrounded by people other than myself, I wished for one thing.

Happiness.

I'd spent my whole life living for others, making sure everyone else was happy, but it was time for me to think of myself and make sure *I* was happy.

A small smile tugged at my lips and I blew out the candles. When I opened my eyes, the stream of white smoke billowed in front of my face. Unable to help myself, I dipped my finger into the frosting between two layers and brought it to my mouth, sucking it off.

Damn, this is actually good.

I heard Jamal groan and I looked up at him, watching his jaw clench, his eyes laser-focused on my lips. My eyes glimmered with mischief, knowing exactly where his mind went.

He cleared his throat. "I have something for you," he said, reaching for his back pocket and handing me a white envelope.

My cheeks flushed as I took it from him. "You didn't have to get me anything." I almost wanted to give it back but stopped myself from doing so. I wasn't used to receiving gifts, so I didn't know how to react.

I opened the envelope and pulled out what was inside. A pang hit my chest once I registered what the pieces of paper were for. "Jamal…" I trailed off, glancing up at him. My eyes fell again on the tickets in my hands, my fingers brushing over the words as I read them over and over again. "No, you didn't…"

He'd gotten me Paddock passes for the British Grand Prix.

Excitement swarmed every inch of my body at the thought of seeing something I'd loved for as long as I could remember up close. But my face instantly fell when I realized it was this weekend.

I was working.

My gaze moved back to Jamal and I opened my mouth to tell him, but he spoke before I could.

"Before you say you can't go, I already called your residency supervisor and asked to give you the rest of the week off. He owed me a favor, so it didn't take much convincing," he said with a small smile. "I hope you don't mind," he rushed out.

I wrapped my arms around his middle and hugged him, placing my head over his erratically beating heart. I swallowed past the tight fist my emotions had around my throat and managed to say, "Thank you," against his shirt, my voice hoarse.

He hesitated for a moment, his arms by his side. Then

he wrapped his arms around me and pulled me tighter, his hand mindlessly rubbing circles over my back.

I pulled back and leaned up to kiss him. I was about to pull back when he cupped my face with his other hand and deepened the kiss.

I loved how natural being in his arms had become, how peaceful I felt being with him. I'd never had that before.

I'd forgotten we had company until someone in the room cleared their throat and we both pulled away.

"How about some cake?" Kai said, his cheeks flushed.

Jamal dropped a soft kiss on my forehead before grabbing a knife from another drawer and handing it to me. I cut each of us a piece and we all stood around the island, eating.

Kai asked me a plethora of questions about Formula One, from my favorite team to how I got into it, while Jamal watched our interaction, an amused look on his face and his hand resting on my thigh.

Surprisingly, Valentina stayed around. She hadn't joined the conversation, but I didn't expect anything different from her. But what *was* different was how every once in a while, she looked over at Kai with a different expression on her face, like she was torn about something when it came to him.

I'd seen him sporting the same expression before, but this was the first time I'd seen it on her.

And she was doing it now.

She must have felt my gaze on her because our eyes

locked before she averted them quickly, a blush creeping over her face.

Never thought I'd see the day Valentina blushed.

It was almost ten when Valentina got up. "I have some work to do," she said, brushing past Kai to set her plate on the counter next to the sink.

"Yeah, I should go, too," Kai echoed, grabbing another piece of cut cake from the box to take with him.

Once they were both gone, I placed my hands over Jamal's and turned the stool I was sitting on to face his side.

"How did you know?" I asked, curious since I'd never told him.

He swallowed his previous bite of cake and said, "Know what?" Swiveling his chair, he brought mine closer to him and placed my knees between his now parted legs.

"I never told you about my birthday."

He just shrugged and placed a kiss on my mouth before saying, "You're my wife. Why wouldn't I know?"

CHAPTER 27

I STOOD AND DROPPED A SOFT KISS ON TOP OF HER HEAD this time.

Our gazes caught and lingered. My mind wandered back to the look on her face when she realized this was all for her.

A pang ricocheted in my chest at the thought that this was the nicest thing someone had ever done for her. She deserved to be celebrated and I couldn't believe no one had wanted to do that for her before.

I'd been strangely nervous when she opened the envelope to find the Grand Prix tickets inside, but seeing her face light up the way it did was more than worth it.

Falling for her would be my downfall, but I'd take the plunge any day if it meant being with her.

"Need some help?" Sienna offered, pulling me out of my thoughts.

I hadn't realized that I started cleaning up. I glanced at her. "A birthday girl shouldn't be on cleanup duty."

I closed the lid on the cake box and placed it back into the refrigerator along with the orange juice container. I promise it wasn't my idea. Kai had a strange inclination to combine orange juice with pretty much everything. It was fine on certain occasions, but I would never be able to see the appeal of mixing orange juice and cake.

I grabbed Sienna's and my dirty dishes and set the plates and cutlery next to Valentina's. Then I turned and opened the dishwasher. As I loaded everything into it, Sienna came up behind me and wrapped her arms around my middle.

A smile tugged at my lips.

I liked how comfortable she felt now to touch me whenever she wanted. We'd been intimate multiple times over the last two weeks, especially ever since she started sleeping in my bed.

But moments like these were the ones I reveled in the most.

I'd never had this kind of intimacy with anyone and I had the overwhelming sense that this, *us*, was exactly where I was meant to be. I knew I shouldn't live comfortably in the idea that this could be it because not only was there still so much I was hiding from her, but I still had a goal to achieve.

What if you let it go, a deep part of my subconscious tried to break free.

Shaking my head to dispel the idea, I finished cleaning out the sink. I'd switched the water to a colder temperature to wash my hands when Sienna's hand reached forward.

I originally thought she wanted to wash her hands as well, but instead, she grabbed the pull-out sprayer, angled it upward, and pushed the button to switch the setting.

Ice-cold water hit me in the chest, soaking through my long-sleeved white shirt. Nervous laughter spilled from her lips and she immediately released it, stepping away from me.

I dropped my chin down, assessing the damage she'd done.

I was drenched.

I looked up at her and she had her hands resting above her mouth. "I'm sorry, it was too tempting not to do it," she said in between fits of laughter.

I narrowed my eyes at her. "You think that's funny?" I grabbed the faucet and aimed it toward her.

Her eyes widened. "You wouldn't," she warned.

"It's only fair if I even the score."

Looking her straight in the eyes, I pulled the trigger. The water splashed all over her front, soaking her top. She looked down at the extent of my handiwork before pinning me with a glare.

I huffed out a laugh at the outraged expression on her face. She was cute when she got mad.

"Jamal…"

I shrugged my shoulders. "I guess, I'm sorry too," I

said, although I really wasn't because the view was quite spectacular.

My eyes roamed over her.

Her shirt molded her body, making her breasts even more mouthwatering, and all I could think of was running my tongue along every divot of her skin, drawing in the little sounds she made in response to my touch.

"You just declared a war," she told me before she quickly closed the distance between us and extended her hand toward the faucet behind me. But I wrapped an arm around her waist quicker and hauled her into me before she could reach it.

She let out a yelp, squirming under my grip. Her ass rubbed against my groin and I suddenly became hyper aware of how much of our bodies was touching.

I tightened my grip, my voice dipping low. "Don't start one when you can't win, *mon amour*."

"Jamal," she breathed out, chuckling.

My hands landed on her hips and I spun her around to face me. Then I walked her backward a few steps until she was trapped between me and the edge of the island.

She squealed when I placed her on top of the counter. I nudged her legs apart, fitting myself between them. Cupping her chin with my thumb and forefinger, I tilted her face up to mine. "You've got a little something on your face," I said, peering down at her.

She had a small smear of purple frosting at the corner of her mouth.

Before she could reply, I trailed my nose down the side of her face and snaked my tongue out, licking it. She whimpered and her fingers gripped at my nape.

The divine sound was my undoing.

My hands traveled down her body and I pulled her to the edge until there was no space between us. My hips involuntarily grinded into hers, my cock creating friction against her center.

Then I kissed her.

The hint of chocolate mixed with her own taste flooded my senses and I tipped her head back further. I groaned and deepened our kiss. Our tongues tangled and I grew even hungrier for her.

I could never tire of this.

Every time I kissed her felt like the first time all over again. Nothing else existed except this. The feel of her soft lips against mine. The breathy moans she let out whenever our lips parted for even just a fraction of a second.

The feel of her hands on my skin.

Every day, Sienna wrapped me in her orbit and I never wanted to unravel.

I finally came up for air and rested my forehead against hers, our chests heaving. Our soft inhales and exhales the only sounds in the room.

"You're dangerous for me, you know that?" I murmured between the small space separating our lips.

She peered up at me, her breaths shallow. "And you're dangerous for me."

"I have another gift for you," I said while yanking up the fabric of her maxi skirt. My fingertips hooked onto the side of her panties, slowly dragging them down her legs.

My palms smoothed up her bare legs until I reached the apex of her thighs.

Her warm brown eyes landed on mine, her pupils dilated with desire. "Really," she said, amused.

Her breathing grew more shallow as I dragged a finger down her pussy, letting it linger at her entrance.

"Such a perfect pussy," I growled, my finger dipping inside of her. "Perfectly ready for my taking." I stroked her inner wall, curling my finger to apply pressure exactly where she liked it.

"Jamal," she said in a breathy whisper. Her back arched into me as she grinded down on my hand.

Her hands slid down my back and slipped beneath the fabric of my linen pants and boxers, her fingertips skimming over the skin of my backside.

She greedily gripped my ass and brought me closer. "More," she cried out and I kissed her, swallowing it.

I continued teasing her as I lowered my mouth to her ear, my breath gliding across her skin. "As much as I love having my fingers inside your sweet little cunt and how I'd like you to come all over my hand, I have a better idea."

I reluctantly removed my finger from her pussy and stepped back. A dark flush colored her cheeks and the sight was satisfying.

My chest rumbled with pride that *I* did that.

She whimpered from the loss. "No…"

I dropped to my knees.

She peered down at me. Her throat flexed with a swallow as her previous haze slowly dissipated. "Should we go upstairs? I mean, what if Kai or Valentina come back here and they catch us?" she asked, biting her bottom lip in worry.

I skimmed my nose across her perfect pussy and a shiver rippled through her. I peered at her from above the hem of her skirt to see her biting that bottom lip again.

"Let them," I said, hovering my lips over her pussy. She shivered and moved to close her thighs, but I stopped her, my palms landing on her inner thighs and squeezing.

In other circumstances, I wouldn't mind letting her suffocate me, but I wanted to be able to see her pretty face when she came. She always looked so exquisite when pleasure crashed over her.

"Keep these pretty thighs open for me," I ordered, pushing her farther open before putting my mouth on her cunt.

Sienna moaned my name like a prayer as I dragged my tongue down between her lips to taste her.

God, my name always sounds better when she says it like that.

I suctioned my lips firmly around her clit and groaned against her pussy as I alternated between licking and sucking.

I don't think I could ever tire of this.

"Jamal," she moaned again, her voice strained. Her hand wrapped around the back of my head, pushing my face harder into her. "I-I'm going to come."

I knew she was holding back, afraid that Kai or Valentina would walk back in or worse, that they could hear her. Technically, they could come back, but I knew they wouldn't. Besides, our wings were separated by a soundproof door, so it would be very unlikely that they'd hear the beautiful sounds she made.

I slowed my strokes up and down her cunt as my eyes flitted to her face, only to find her watching me. "No need to be quiet, *mon amour*," I murmured against her pussy. "Let me hear you."

I slid my tongue down and penetrated her opening. She clenched around it as I fucked her with it and I reveled in every sound she made. It was like music to my ears.

"Yes," she cried out. "Right… right there."

I kept my eyes on her as I slid my tongue back out and dragged it upward toward her clit again, knowing she was about to tumble over the edge.

She rolled her hips against my mouth and her grip on my head tightened. It was the sexiest thing to see her chase her pleasure. When I felt she was ready, my teeth clamped down on her clit.

Her eyes fluttered shut and a strangled sound escaped her as her climax washed over her.

It doesn't get any better than this.

"Fuck," I growled against her as I licked her through her orgasm.

"Jamal," she whimpered. "Too sensitive." She tried to pull away from my tongue, but I gripped her hips, keeping her cunt on my face, and dragged my tongue through her lips one more time.

"Jamal." She gasped and squirmed under my touch.

I finally let her go and stood, standing above her, traces of her pleasure covering my face. I licked my lips and her lips were on mine the next instant. My tongue tangled with hers and she kissed me like she wanted to be consumed.

My lips left her to find her neck and I sucked on the soft skin there, aiming to mark her. I wanted to mark her all over her body to show the world that she was mine.

Her hands found the button on my slacks and she popped it open, then dropped the zipper. Her hand reached inside my boxers and her palm wrapped around my cock, squeezing gently.

My hips involuntarily thrust into her hand, begging for relief.

My mouth kissed up her neck, moving to her lips as she stroked me and I was close to losing it.

I mean, who wouldn't with a wife like that?

"Sienna," I groaned against her mouth.

"I want to taste you too," she murmured as she pushed my pants and boxers down. She moved to hop off the counter, but I gripped her hips, keeping her in place.

"I'll teach you later," I said, making a mental note of it. "I need to be inside of you when I come."

I wrapped my hand over the one she still had around my cock and dragged the tip over her clit before pausing at her entrance.

Then I thrust home.

CHAPTER 28

After landing in London on Wednesday afternoon, Jamal and I had driven over to a small town situated near Silverstone.

It took us forever to get to our destination from the airport because of the dense traffic on the highway and because it was Jamal's first time driving here.

It was quite the sight to see him so flustered while driving. His usual confidence slowly withered with every honk he'd gotten for either driving too slow or going over the lines.

He'd tried to hide it, but with over two hours of nothing else to do, watching him quickly became more entertaining than watching endless roads drowning with cars.

Jamal seemed to have relaxed, getting the hang of driving on the wrong side of the road until someone behind him honked. The car sped past us, but not before the driver flipped us off.

Jamal's grip on the steering wheel tightened and his previously relaxed posture went rigid. My face twitched as I tried to stifle the laugh threatening to escape.

I managed to hold it for a few seconds before I erupted into a fit of laughter.

"Ha. Ha. Ha. Very funny. I'm glad this is amusing for you," Jamal said, a scowl on his face.

"I'm sorry," I said, trying to contain my laughter. "It's just… you should see yourself right now. I've never seen you so stressed."

"I'm not stressed," he stated, his scowl deepening.

Reaching into my hoodie's front pocket, I then pulled out my phone and snapped a picture as we exited the highway.

Jamal's gaze averted to me. "Sienna, what are you doing?"

I snapped another picture.

We stopped at a red light and Jamal quickly reached over and grabbed my phone out of my hands.

"Hey!" I said, attempting to snatch it back from him.

He kept it out of my reach and looked up to see the picture I'd taken of him.

"Give it back," I said as I pushed down the strap of my seat belt and stretched to snag it from his grip. "Jamal." I chuckled. "Promise, I won't—"

He locked my phone and turned his head, then

placed a kiss on my lips to shut me up. His hand snaked around my head and he pulled me closer by the neck. When he released me, I felt a little dizzy, his kiss blurring the reason why I was halfway out of my seat.

I heard the click of a camera and realized he'd taken a picture on his phone.

"For keepsake," he stated before putting his phone back on the dashboard and giving mine back. "You looked too beautiful not to immortalize."

"You're impossible," I said, shaking my head and stifling the smile that wanted to burst all over my face.

The light turned green and I settled back into my seat, adjusting my seat belt.

The sun was setting when Jamal drove up a sweeping gravel driveway.

When he said he'd rented a small cottage, I'd pictured a *small* cozy house tucked somewhere in the countryside of the south of England. Not the gigantic manor that erupted in front of us.

The only thing I'd gotten right was the location. The English-style country house stood in the middle of two acres of land that we had all to ourselves, lush greenery surrounding it.

I would like to say I was shocked, but I was married to him after all and even if it hadn't been for long, I knew my husband didn't do anything simply.

I laughed under my breath.

"What's so funny?" Jamal questioned as he parked in front of the residence and turned the engine off.

I aimed a skeptical look his way, cocking a brow. "Jamal, you said we were staying in a small cottage."

"This *is* small," he replied.

I chuckled, shaking my head. "If you call *this*"—I gestured to the mansion in front of us—"small, then I'd be curious to know what you call something that's *actually* small," I teased him.

He reached over and gripped my chin, then placed a kiss on my lips. "Smart-ass."

He got out of the car and grabbed both of our suitcases and my backpack from the trunk, then walked back over to my side as I stepped out. I closed the passenger door behind me and followed behind him.

He left our bags on the porch and reached into the small mailbox attached to the side of the doors and grabbed a pair of keys from inside.

When we stepped through the double doors, a large living room with floor-to-ceiling windows greeted us. The house was surprisingly cold, so Jamal went to the back and grabbed a few logs to start a fire after placing our luggage at the bottom of the staircase.

While he did that, I explored the rest of the house.

There were so many rooms I lost count. It wasn't until a few more rooms later that I eventually found the bedroom where we'd be sleeping.

It was filled with blue and cream tones, a French

Nightingale wallpaper decorating the walls. I walked past the large mattress, my fingers skimming over the luxurious sheets, and stepped out onto the small balcony attached to the far right of the master bedroom.

The view was breathtaking. Luscious green trees. A garden beneath with thriving flower beds. I could even make out a small lake nestled between the trees afar before it expanded into rolling hills on the other side, moonlight reflecting on the moving surface from the faint gusts of wind.

I rested my elbows on the concrete balustrade, taking everything in.

I couldn't believe I was here, in London, only hours away from my first ever Grand Prix. I'd always dreamed of attending one but never had the time or the money.

I'd loved F1 for as long as I could remember. It was one of the only things my father and I had in common and although I hadn't found it in me yet to forgive him for what he did, I couldn't help the bittersweet feeling that overtook me that he wasn't here with me.

The sound of luggage being dragged up the stairs shook me out of my thoughts. I glanced over my shoulder as Jamal entered the room and placed our luggage next to the bed before joining me on the balcony.

"Baby, it's cold out here." He placed his hands on either side of me, enveloping me in his warmth.

I turned to face him and his hands grabbed my waist as I rested my back against the banister. "Good thing you're here now," I said teasingly, tucking my hands in the back pockets of his pants and bringing his body closer.

"Thank you again, for all of this," I said breathlessly.

"You never have to thank me for doing things for you." He leaned down and pressed a kiss to my lips. "I like making you happy."

He remained quiet for a moment, watching me intently. A foreign look painted his irises.

"What is it?" I asked.

He ran the pad of his thumb along my lower lip. "You're beautiful, Sienna."

He tipped my chin up with his index finger and placed his lips over mine. Our kiss was slow and sensual, sending sparks buzzing across my skin.

We'd kissed many times, but this felt different.

It was filled with a plethora of unsaid things that I think neither of us was ready to say, but the way his lips moved over mine told me all I needed to know.

I bit down on his lower lip and he groaned into my mouth.

"Mine," he rasped, bringing his forehead to mine.

"Same goes for you," I said through a smile.

He pressed a gentle kiss over my lips before dragging me back inside since the wind had picked up.

"I could use a shower," I said, placing my carry-on on the ground and rummaging through it for clothes to change into. I placed the pieces on top of the bed and moved toward the en suite bathroom.

I stopped under the doorway and took off my clothes in a pile next to me. I propped my hands on each side of the doorframe, completely naked.

I'd always loved my body, but over the last few weeks, I'd grown more comfortable in being naked in front of him. I always associated being completely bare in front of anyone with being in a position of vulnerability until Jamal spent endless hours worshiping my body.

His hungry eyes roamed over me, taking in every inch of my skin.

I cocked my head to the side. "Care to join me?"

He didn't need to be told twice. He abandoned his search for whatever he was looking for in his suitcase and strode toward me with determination.

Overwhelmed didn't cover how I felt right now. The venue was way more crowded and the Paddock was even worse. Media, photographers, celebrities, and drivers were walking up and down the pit lane as they got ready for the race today.

Jamal had gotten us garage access for Matrix Motorsports, my favorite team, and seeing everything up close felt quite surreal.

We'd spent the last two days watching the main events, Practice and Qualifying, as well as exploring the track. We'd watched them from both the Paddock club and various Grandstands so that I'd get to see different views of the circuit.

Jamal had even planned a part of our weekend for me to sit in a car, which had always been one of my biggest dreams.

When I was younger, I'd entertained the idea of becoming a driver, but I'd always wanted to be a doctor, so committing to racing was impossible to do if I wanted to achieve it.

My gaze roamed over the busy garage and landed on Isaiah King, one of their drivers and the current world champion. He was standing to the side with his race engineers, most likely discussing their strategy for today.

Jamal and I were standing to the side with one of the team's reps, who was explaining to us who everyone in the garage was and how today would go.

"How long have you been a fan of F1?" the rep, Stella, asked my husband, batting her eyelashes at him. She'd been flirting with him since we'd gotten here, but I just ignored her, or at least tried to.

Since she escorted us from the entrance this morning, she'd been making eyes at my husband and tried to touch him any chance she got—not that Jamal let her, but that's beside the point.

I wasn't a jealous person by nature, but I didn't like her trying to get what was mine.

You would think that the rings on *both* of our fingers would have given her a hint that Jamal was taken, but that didn't seem to faze her. It only seemed to make her try even harder.

Jamal must have sensed my growing jealousy because he wrapped an arm around my waist and pulled me flush to his side. "Actually, my beautiful wife is the big fan."

I glanced up at him and he gave me one of his rare smiles.

"Oh." Stella raised a brow, averting her gaze to me and acknowledging me for the first time since we got here. "I would have never guessed."

Ugh, she's one of those.

I hated when people assumed that women couldn't like motorsports. That and when men started drilling you with technical questions when they learned you did.

I kept myself from rolling my eyes and gave her a tight smile instead. "Yup, I'm the fan," I said, trying to infuse my tone with enthusiasm instead of the bitterness I felt toward her.

She uttered a fake laugh before returning to her explanations. I tuned her out when I felt a shift in the room. A few crew members' heads snapped toward the garage entrance and I followed their lead to see who had stepped inside.

My eyes landed on her and I held back a squeal of excitement.

Cynara Cruz. Last year's Champion in Formula Three. And the first female driver to ever join Matrix's Junior Team.

I'd been following her career since her karting days and to see her now wearing my favorite team's colors was incredible. Not only was she one of my favorites, if she performed at the Academy this year, she could very well be the first female F1 driver.

What I wouldn't give to be able to witness that one day.

She was talking with an older Asian woman that I recognized was Matrix's communications manager, which meant she most likely just came back from some interviews.

Cynara gathered her long brown curly hair on top of her head and secured it with a claw clip before fanning herself.

Compared to the last two rainy days, the sun was beaming today. We couldn't feel it in the garage, but I wouldn't want to be outside under the searing temperatures.

Her hazel eyes drifted over to where Isaiah was standing and he immediately turned around. A palpable tension filled the room when their gazes locked, but she quickly looked away, making her way to the back of the garage.

Isaiah then returned his attention back to whatever data his race engineer was showing on the screen.

Interesting.

My attention was pulled back when I heard Stella excusing herself because she had to take care of some things before the race started. We were given headsets and taken to the side of the garage where small TVs were lined up to watch the race.

Matrix's crew and the other team's crew were on track, waiting for the drivers to show up with their cars to set them up in their respective positions throughout the grid as the pit lane closed.

After the national anthem, each team's crew left the circuit to head back into their respective garages. Once the track was cleared, the cars drove around the track once and were now back from their formation lap, waiting for the lights to go out.

After the green flag was waved, one by one, the five lights above the start/finish line flashed before shutting off at the same time. The cars squealed as they sped past the grid and my nerves skyrocketed as the cars bunched together to overtake.

As they rounded the first corner, Jayden Thorn, Matrix's other driver, locked up and made contact with Nathaniel, a driver from one of the other teams, knocking himself out of the race.

Loud groans reverberated into the garage from Jayden's crew as we witnessed his car spin around and out of the track. A yellow flag banner appeared on the screen while they brought Jayden's car back into the pits.

Nathaniel was able to keep racing after a quick front wing change to replace the damaged one, but Jayden had to retire, a disappointing early ending to his home race.

Jayden's team had tried to work on his car to see if the damages were salvageable, but unfortunately, there were too many to allow him to rejoin the race.

Frustration waved off Jayden as he exited his car, but my eyes remained glued to the TV, my attention focused on the race.

Isaiah's car was leading by a great margin, like he had been for most of the season. He'd been undefeated for the last five races and I hoped I could see him break a record today by winning his sixth consecutive race, especially since this was also his home race.

Jamal was behind me and I rested my back against his front as I attentively watched the action on the track.

We could hear Isaiah and his engineer communicating as they relayed information on the car back and forth every once in a while. Isaiah eventually rounded the last corner of his final lap and crossed the finish line ahead by ten seconds.

I fisted my hands in excitement, trying to contain myself from letting out a squeal of delight at seeing one of my favorite drivers break a record. I looked up at Jamal, expecting him to be watching the screen, but his eyes were trained on me, the hint of a smile tugging at his lips.

It meant a lot that he would stay with me and be willing to experience this together even if it wasn't necessarily something he loved.

Once all the cars crossed the finish line, I spun around to face him, placing my palms over his chest. "He won."

His eyes sparkled with amusement. "He did, *mon amour*."

I grabbed his hand and brought him outside, weaving us

through the crowd of people to wait for each of the three top drivers to place their cars in front of their respective signs.

Once they were done with their post-race interviews, they walked back inside and we waited under the balcony where the podiums were for the ceremony to start.

My cheeks hurt from smiling at the end of the celebration.

Jamal's mouth found mine and pure contentment washed over me.

"I propose we go back home"—he trailed off, lowering his head even more to nuzzle it in my neck—"and have a celebration of our own."

I grabbed onto the lapels of his suit and shifted onto the balls of my feet. "I like that idea very much," I whispered before pressing a kiss to his lips. "But first, can we walk the track again before we leave?" I asked, giving him a sweet smile.

Nodding, he grinned at me and the sight titled me off axis.

I'd never forget today.

Sienna

CHAPTER 29

I WENT STRAIGHT BACK TO WORK AFTER OUR WEEKEND IN London.

It had been by far one of the best weekends of my life, the best *birthday* I'd ever experienced. Although I would have loved to stay longer, not that Jamal hadn't tried to convince me to do so, I would lie if I said I hadn't missed work.

I finished typing my notes and saved it under Mrs. Potter's lengthy file. She had a habit of coming to the ER for any minor inconvenience, but I didn't mind. She'd lost her husband a few months ago and had no one else.

I could tell she came here to have some company, so I indulged her.

No one should feel alone and if spending a few minutes with her once in a while when she visited made her life better, then we would happily do it. The staff and residents had even agreed to rotate who saw her every time she came in so that she wouldn't think we were onto her.

After locking my profile, I got up, grabbed my water bottle from the station, and headed to the locker room after my twelve-hour shift.

I'd changed my schedule this month so I could work fewer days during the month. I'd still spend a lot of time here, but I selfishly wanted more free time to spend with my husband.

Tonight had been a quiet night—I hadn't said that during my shift in case I triggered the curse and the emergency room became flooded with patients—and I was glad to go home.

I never cared about working long hours, but when I barely had any patients, the time seemed to drag on longer than it should have.

After changing into my clothes, I sat on the bench in front of the row of lockers where mine was and pulled my phone out of my bag, then dialed my younger sister's number.

I felt bad for not doing it before, especially after my mother called to ask me for money for her tutoring classes, but that phone call had left me rattled and then Jamal and I had immediately left for England.

I'd sent her and Iris, my youngest sister, a message before my flight and pictures of my trip, asking if they'd wanted anything. Akari had asked for the UK version of her favorite book while Iris simply had wanted a red telephone booth keychain.

I'd planned on giving it to them when I went back home, but I didn't know when that would be since I hadn't gone back since my wedding. Although I wanted to see my sisters, I wasn't yet ready to face my father.

Akari picked up after the first ring, immediately switching our phone call into a video one. She was at her desk in her room, her headphones on and a pen in her hand.

"Hey, Kiki," I greeted her, propping my back against the wall behind me.

"Hi, Nana," she answered. When she was a baby, Akari couldn't pronounce my full name, only repeating the last syllable, so the nickname stuck since then.

"*¿Qué lo que, cómo va todo?*" I asked, letting her decide what she wanted to talk about.

My instinct was to ask her about school and how things were going with her new tutor, but I didn't want to pressure her, especially since I seemed to have caught her in the middle of studying.

"Not much, just busy with school," she said, her tone sounding a little defeated. She averted her gaze from the camera, twirling her pen between her fingers.

"Wanna talk about it?" I prompted.

"Not really…" She trailed off, but I knew she wanted to get it off her chest.

"Well, I'll be here when you want to, okay?"

"I started with Sloane, my tutor, last week and it's been

really helpful," she started, finally looking at me. "It's just *mamá* has been on my ass—"

"Language, Akari," I reprimanded her. My mother probably deserved it, but regardless.

"Sorry. *Mamá* has been on me every day about it and why my grades weren't already up. I tried to explain to her that it would take some time, but she wouldn't hear it."

That doesn't surprise me.

"I'll talk to her," I promise and my sister's body immediately relaxed.

"Thank you, Nana. Anyways," she said, her eyes glimmering. "I wanna hear about your trip and what it's like to be married. *¡Dímelo cantando!*"

I spent the next few minutes summarizing our trip and gave her a brief overview of what married life was like. I was open with both my sisters because I wanted them to be comfortable sharing anything with me, but there were a few things they didn't have to know.

Iris joined us as well after I'd asked Akari to call her over and we chatted about anything and everything.

My parents might have burdened me with taking care of their children and it was tough at times, but I wouldn't have it any other way. I had the chance to have sisters and *have* a relationship with them. I would never trade that.

It was 10:00 p.m. by the time we hung up and I left the hospital. I sent a quick message to Jamal, letting him know that I'd lost track of time talking to my sisters after my shift and was on my way home.

Home. Because that's what it became over the last months.

I didn't dread going to the place where I lived. I now actually looked forward to it, looked forward to having someone be there when I got home or be the person there for when Jamal got home.

I looked forward to spending the night in bed with someone I loved sleeping next to.

I hadn't had the chance to tell him yet, not because I was afraid to, but because I wanted it to be at the right time.

I made my way to the parking lot, rummaging through my tote bag to get my keys out. I finally found them, tucked between the pages of my clinical notebook, and fished them out.

I pressed the button to unlock the doors and opened the driver's side, then threw my bag into the passenger seat. I was about to get inside when hands came up behind me, clamping tightly over my mouth.

"Do not make a sound," a voice warned me.

My keys slipped from my fingers and I tried to fight off my attacker by slamming my fist against his hands and trying to kick his shins.

But I suddenly felt a sharp sting on the side of my leg.

I bent my neck to see what hit me, only to see whoever was behind me depressing the plunger of a large syringe into my upper thigh.

Son of a bitch.

He removed the needle from my muscle and tossed the

empty syringe to the side. I didn't know what he injected me with, but I knew I still had a little bit of time before it kicked in.

I jammed my head backward with every ounce of strength I had.

"Motherfucker," he barked. I wiggled against him, but he banded his forearm over my front, pinning me against his chest. "Stop moving, you bitch."

I heard the screech of tires behind us, then my body was thrown in the back of a black van, three other bulky men already waiting inside.

"Let me go," I screamed.

"Shut up," he spat out angrily, slapping me across the face.

My head reared back by the force of it, ricocheting against the hard floor of the van. They made a quick move to bind my hands together with zip ties, then moved to do the same to my feet.

I was getting desperate to get free and managed to kick one of the masked men before they finished tying my feet, but it was all in vain. The energy I'd spent combined with whatever sedative my attacker had given me surged through my body, submerging each of my limbs into a dormant state.

Someone loomed over my body and gripped my arms, reaching for my left hand. Then they ripped my wedding ring off my finger and dangled it in front of my face.

"You won't be needing this anymore," the man sneered,

tossing it behind him like a coin before closing the back door of the car.

The engine roared back to life and I was jolted across when the driver sped out of the parking lot. I fought against my restraints, but my consciousness began to fade.

"Let… let me… let me go…"

The person who'd attacked me finally removed their mask, but half of their face was hidden in the shadows. I blinked my eyes repeatedly, trying to fend off my loss of consciousness, but only enough to discern who was on top of me.

My eyes widened when the picture of the culprit finally unraveled before me. Right before the haze on the edge of my vision took over, my gaze locked with the one I was supposed to vow my life to a couple months ago.

My ex-fiancé.

Mateo Barrera.

The last thing I remembered was a flash of Jamal's grin right before we'd left the track last weekend before my eyes rolled back, giving in to the darkness.

My head was pounding as I slowly rose out of consciousness. My eyes peeled open slowly and I wrestled with a blurred vision. My mind was still foggy, but I fought against the haze holding the last few hours locked in.

Slowly, scattered memories of how I got here began to surface.

Mierda.

I stirred and tried to stretch my body, only to realize that my hands were tied behind my back and my lips were stretched open by a damp gag in my mouth.

My legs were still bound together, but this time with rope instead of zip ties. It was the same for my hands, the coarse fabric rubbing against my wrists and ankles.

I looked down to find the chair I was sitting on screwed into the ground on each leg. Panic flooded my chest, but I tried to ignore it, knowing that fear wouldn't help me out of whatever situation I was in.

I blinked again, my eyes steadily becoming accustomed to the dim lighting until the rest of the room finally came into focus.

Drawing in a deep breath, I forced myself to concentrate and quickly scanned my surroundings.

We were in some sort of warehouse since it was filled with pallets of boxes in the back and dozens of steel barrels with warning signs on them, indicating they contained potentially flammable liquids.

A run-down green two-seater couch was a little on the far left of where I was sitting, debris and empty amber glass bottles scattered everywhere.

A few feet away from me, two men with their backs to me were hunched over a folding table talking, but I couldn't quite make out what they were saying.

The one on the right had long blond hair that was tied in a loose bun while the other had dark hair, buzzed short. Both of them were wearing long-sleeved black shirts and dark jeans.

Out of my periphery, over to the left, I could see my piece-of-shit ex-fiancé pacing, talking to someone on the phone. He seemed agitated, gesturing as he spoke to whoever was on the other end of the line.

He finally hung up the phone and made his way over to who I assumed were his men. They both turned to face him.

I immediately closed my eyes, pretending I was still unconscious before I entered his field of vision. My ears perked up to listen to their conversation.

"What did Boss say, sir?" the blond-haired one asked.

"Who cares about what my father has to say," Mateo gritted out. "Keep an eye on her." I felt his gaze burning my skin. "I want to know when she wakes up."

"Yes, sir," both of them said.

The sound of his footsteps grew quieter as he walked away.

Jamal would come to help. Or at least, I really hoped he did.

Jamal

CHAPTER 30

IT WAS ALMOST 11:00 P.M. WHEN I FINALLY GOT HOME. I'D picked up food for all of us on the way since I was too tired to cook anything and knowing Sienna, Kai, and Valentina, they'd probably barely eaten today.

My stomach growled, reminding me that I hadn't either.

I grabbed the takeout bags from the Dominican restaurant that was near the office out of the passenger seat and headed inside. As I unlocked the door, I couldn't help the calming feeling that coming home had become.

I'd lived with Kai and Valentina for a few years now, and yet, I'd never had this sense of happiness greet me at the thought of entering my house. Yes, Kai kept me company most of the time, Valentina occasionally joining us, but having a wife, *my* wife to share life with was…

Nice.

For years, loneliness and anger had been my only

companions. All I'd wanted was to exact revenge on who'd robbed me of a childhood and a life with the love of my parents.

Meeting Sienna (although by force) skewed the only trajectory I'd come to know and she'd unknowingly changed my life for the better.

And if I wanted a future with her, I had to tell her everything and show her that everything between us was real, despite how it all started.

Tonight. I will do it tonight.

I unlocked the front door and stepped inside, then locked the door behind me. I took off my shoes and moved to the kitchen, where I dropped the bags filled with bowls of *locrio de pollo*, a large salad, and a box of *maduras* onto the island.

There was an unusual stillness around the house. Kai and Valentina were still at the office, working on decrypting the last key that would allow us to find the information we needed, but I thought Sienna would be here already.

"Sienna," I called out, but no one answered.

Unease curled around my middle and I rushed upstairs to look in our room. Silence swallowed me whole as I opened our bedroom, only to find it empty, completely untouched from when I left it this morning.

I headed for her old bedroom and gently pushed it open, finding it in the same state as ours. Empty.

She's supposed to be home already.

I ran downstairs and went from room to room, even through Kai and Valentina's wing, with the same undesired revelation. Sienna was nowhere to be found.

I hurried back to the living area and paused in my steps. *Was her car even out front?*

I quickly unlocked the front door and looked outside, only to find our driveway empty, except for my car and Kai's since he'd driven to work with Valentina. I then realized that her car had never been there in the first place.

I cursed myself for not paying closer attention because it wasn't like me to not notice these things. I had been too focused on getting inside our home, on getting to her, that I hadn't registered whether or not she was here.

My racing heart slowed for a moment, realizing that my panic had been unfounded. She might just be running late and forgot to text me. I walked back inside and pulled my phone out of my suit pocket, checking if I had any missed texts or calls from her.

There were no new ones since she'd texted me around 10:00 p.m., letting me know that she was on her way, so she should have been home by now, unless…

My heart picked up pace, battering against my rib cage as my mind sifted through thousands of horrible scenarios. I dialed her number, the ringing seeming like an endless tone. Her voicemail greeted me.

You've reached Sienna. I can't answer, so please leave a message and I'll call you as soon as I—

I hung up and redialed her number before the message ended.

Pick up, baby. Please.

My heart dropped, panic clogging every pore of my body, and my throat tightened under a vice grip when she didn't.

Merde.

I headed to my office and threw the door to the basement open. I stirred our devices open and promptly called Kai. He answered on the first ring and I placed my phone on top of the desk, putting him on speaker.

"Wh—"

"I can't find Sienna," I said, cutting him off.

"Hold on, what do you mean you can't find her?"

"Kai, I don't know where my wife is," I bit out.

"She's not home?" he asked.

Impatience and anger slowly replaced the suffocating panic overwhelming my lungs. "She clearly isn't or I wouldn't be calling you. She texted me an hour ago saying she was coming home, but there's no one here and she isn't answering her phone."

"Did you track her?"

"That's what I'm doing."

My stomach twisted, dread zipping up my spine as I waited the few seconds it took for the program to pinpoint her location.

Wait.

"She's at the hospital," I hesitantly relayed to Kai.

"She might have been pulled for an emergency," Kai proposed, most likely trying to soothe my worries, but it wasn't working.

Maybe that was true, but she would have texted me. I know she would have.

"Jamal?"

"Something's not right," I told him, my intuition nagging my gut that something about this felt off. "Meet me there," I ordered before hanging up. Then I locked the computers, picked up my phone, and went upstairs.

After grabbing my keys, I rushed out of the house and into my car.

The temperature had changed and droplets of rain were now drumming lightly against my car windows as I raced down our driveway and toward Monte Claro Hospital.

I pulled into the parking lot thirty minutes later, finding Valentina leaned against her car. I parked right next to hers and jumped out of the driver's seat, then rushed over to her.

I was about to ask where Kai was when he walked out of the employees' exit, an anxious look on his face.

"I just checked at the front desk of the emergency and they said she left as soon as her shift ended," he explained and it only stirred further the deep fear that had rooted in my gut.

My warning instincts from earlier rang louder this time. Sienna wasn't working and she wasn't here either, despite the tracker in her phone indicating that she should be.

I ran my hands over my head frustratingly. "Fuck, fuck, *fuck*!"

I drew my phone out of my pocket, opened the app where I still had the location of her tracker, and followed the red dot, Valentina and Kai trailing close behind.

The signal flashed stronger as I got closer to the back of the parking lot and my eyes landed on her car, but still no sign of her. My mouth went dry as I made my way over, praying I wouldn't find her body lying somewhere.

I kept walking toward her car when I stepped on an object, a crunching sound resounding in the late night.

My stomach bottomed out as I looked at the ground, finding Sienna's phone under my foot. I crouched down and my hand shook as I picked it up, finding the screen fissured at the bottom.

A picture of us from last weekend glinted underneath the cracked screen with several notifications of my missed calls.

"What is it?" Kai asked, looking over my shoulder.

"Sienna's phone," I answered, looking up at him.

My breathing became ragged and I turned on the flashlight on my phone. I loomed it over the cement until a glint reflected off the ground. I stood and walked over there, only to find a ring tossed next to her car.

I bent over and grabbed it, the cold metal burning my palm. Fury raced through my veins like a tidal wave that someone had taken *my* wife.

I turned around and headed for the hospital in a hurry.

"What are you doing?" Kai asked, worry lacing his words. "Jamal, hold on."

I didn't deign to answer him and rounded the corner to enter Monte Claro from the emergency entrance. I didn't know whether or not Kai and Valentina had followed, but at this point I didn't care.

All I cared about was finding Sienna.

I veered toward the hallway on the right, following the signs for the security office. A nurse at the sign-in desk stood up abruptly from behind the plexiglass, but I didn't acknowledge him.

I only heard the whispers of someone behind apologizing for my behavior as I kept walking, running up the stairs and closing the distance to the security's office. I knocked on the door, with only one thought in mind.

I can't lose her.

I'd never listened to my heart because I'd always believed it could play tricks on me, which led me to constantly choose logic.

So I always listened to my head, but I'd learned over the last few weeks that your head could also be fooled.

But my soul, my soul was telling me, *had been* telling me, that she was it for me.

I'd never believed in meeting *the one* because it always seemed like a foolish concept in my head. How could one person in a world filled with seven billion of them be the person that was meant perfectly for you?

I hadn't understood what it meant to find that person until I met Sienna.

And in this moment, I hated myself for never telling her I loved her.

Because now…

Now, it might be too late.

"If anything happened to her…" I whispered.

I'd never forgive myself.

I knocked again and someone shouted "coming" before they opened the door. The bald security guy was mid-chew when he glanced up, finding me glaring at him. He had an unfinished sandwich hanging in his other hand, yellow sauce smeared on the corner of his mouth.

"I need to view your security footage covering the back employee parking lot from the last two hours," I said, my voice tight with furry.

"Sir, you can't be h—"

"It wasn't a question," I snapped, walking into the room as I forced him to step to the side to let me in.

"I wouldn't push him if I were you," I heard Kai say as I headed for the large screens.

The security guard came up beside me and placed his half-eaten sub on his desk. He wiped his hand over his navy blue pants before settling back into his seat and pulling up the files.

My heart pounded furiously as I watched the scene play out on the screen.

Sienna had left the hospital from the employees' back door at 10:05 p.m. and walked toward her car with her head bowed, rummaging through her bag until she found her keys.

The lights of her car flashed as she approached, but someone dressed in all black came up behind her. I stared at the figure locking her body into a tight grip and the urge to rewind time and be there to kill him ignited in my body.

I watched Sienna trying to fight him off, but his right hand suddenly lifted in the air and aimed for her thigh, most likely meaning he'd drugged her.

Despite that, she kept wiggling in his grasp, but the fucker wouldn't budge. My pulse roared with rage when a black van with blacked out windows came into view and she was thrown in it.

"My God," the security guard started, "we need to call the police." He reached over for the phone on his desk, but my hand snapped to stop him.

"No."

"But we have to report th—"

I removed my gun from the holster under my jacket and pressed the metal over his temple. "I said no. Rewind the tape."

He swallowed hard and did as he was told.

I watched the infuriating video again to see if I would notice anything different, any indicator of who would take her. "Stop," I ordered the security guard.

During one of her attempts to set herself free, Sienna had shoved her head back and shifted the mask her attacker was wearing. After he threw her inside and turned around to close the back doors, I caught a small glimpse of his profile.

That son of a bitch.

"We'll get her back," Kai said, placing a hand on my shoulder in an attempt to reassure me.

I should have been there. I should have protected her.

This was all my fucking fault.

If I hadn't stampeded into her life, none of this would have happened. I was the only reason she was in this position.

I vowed to myself that I would find her again.

Even if it meant burning their entire empire down.

CHAPTER 31

IT MUST HAVE BEEN TWO OR THREE DAYS SINCE I HAD BEEN taken hostage. I tried keeping count of how many hours I'd been here, counting to sixty then starting again, but the numbers blurred after a certain time and I'd lost track.

I would have taken into account how many times the sun had risen, but it seemed that I'd been kept in the back of the warehouse since no natural light was cast where I was still tied to the chair.

The only thing I had noticed about this place was blasts coming from boats every once in a while, which could only mean that we were near Sardenya's port.

I hadn't eaten or drunk anything since they'd kidnapped me and it wasn't from their lack of trying, but I wouldn't take anything from them. The potential of being drugged through meals dawned upon me the first time they offered me food and I wanted to stay as alert as I could be.

Although, with the lack of nutrients, my body was weakening by the passing hour. I'd stayed awake for long periods of time before, but the lack of sleep combined with the physical and mental exhaustion was getting to me.

I'd nodded off a few times, but it was never for more than a few minutes at a time.

On top of it, my entire body throbbed from not being able to move for so many hours and the strain my limbs were under from being stretched to accommodate the bindings that were still attached to my wrists and legs.

The only reprieve I'd gotten was from the damp, stinking rag that had been in my mouth when I first woke up. I'd spent most of my time here looking around, searching for a way out, but so far, nothing had come of it.

Mateo's men switched watching duty periodically. The bald guy and the one with red hair were assigned at what seemed like the morning while the blond and dark-haired duo took over in the afternoon before spending half the night watching over me.

I'd tried looking for an opportunity to escape, but my hands and legs were bound so tight to the metal chair, I could barely move an inch. The only time my limbs were moved was when I had to use the restroom—the small rusty bucket next to my chair—and even then, they were the ones moving me around to use it.

I would have been embarrassed, but it was either let them watch or sit in soiled clothes for however long they held me captive. The former was a much better option.

Aside from a few bruises and a killer headache, they'd mostly left me alone. Which I guessed was a good thing. I'd rather be ignored than have them pay too much attention to me.

However, that didn't prevent them from throwing dirty jokes about what they'd do to me and my, and I quote, "fuckable body."

But apart from that, I was deemed off-limits, which I assumed was a command from Mateo.

Speaking of, I hadn't seen or heard of him since the night I'd gotten kidnapped.

The sound of footsteps pounded against the concrete floor and Mateo materialized in front of me a few moments later.

Guess I spoke too soon.

Our gazes met and my stomach lurched at the sight. "You're awake," he noted.

"What a clever observation," I snarked.

He walked over and stopped in front of me, stretching his fingers to caress the side of my face. "Missed me, princess?"

"Don't *fucking* touch me," I hissed, jerking away from his slimy touch.

Mateo grinned and his lips parted, but his phone rang, stopping whatever he was about to say. He took it out and brought it to his ear, listening to the person on the other end for a while.

"Hello to you too, Jamal."

My heart rate increased in speed at the mention of my husband's name.

"She's a little tied up at the moment," he said, then looked over at me, chuckling.

"You should hear how pathetic you sound," he mocked Jamal. "Relax," he drawled. "She's right here." Mateo pulled the phone away from his ear and pressed a button on the screen, putting Jamal on speaker.

"Son of a bitch, if you *dare* fucking touch her," Jamal said.

Mateo tsked at him and held the phone next to my ear. "Say hi to your pitiful husband, Sienna," Mateo ordered me, amused.

"Sienna, *mon amour…*" I could hear the anguish in his voice and it broke my heart knowing that he might blame himself for this, but I didn't.

Mateo's ego had gotten bruised when Jamal interrupted our wedding and this was his feeble way of retaliating.

"Jamal, baby, I'm okay," I said, hoping to give him some reprieve from the thoughts I knew were swirling in his brain. I looked up, my disgusted gaze locking with Mateo's. "Just come kill this *cabrón*," I hissed.

Mateo snatched the phone away and struck me across the face before walking back to the long table and leaning at the edge of it. Heat spread across my face, but I ignored it, spitting the blood pooling in my mouth on the floor, my eyes never leaving Mateo's.

He laughed again and shook his head at whatever threat

Jamal most likely aimed at him. "Poor little Jamal," he said, cocking his head to the side as his eyes roamed all over my frame, hoping I would bow in fear at his tactics and failing. "How poetic that *Daddy dearest* had his go with your parents and now I get to have my turn."

Then, after his last strike, Mateo ended the call.

My heart sank at his words and tears of anger clouded my vision.

This fucker.

Barrera killed my husband's parents.

My body burned with rage at the news and I clenched my fists behind my back, the rope chafing my skin from the tension. "You son of a bitch," I yelled.

He slowly walked toward me, smirking. "Don't flatter me, Sienna." His smile darkened as he leaned in close, leaving barely an inch separating our faces. He gripped my face, squeezing my cheeks together. "*Oh*, how much fun we'll have together now that you're mine."

I spat in his face. "I'll never be yours."

His smile faltered and the last thing I saw before darkness overtook my vision was the sight of his fist lifting before crashing against the side of my face.

I woke up, choking on a pungent smell. I tried to breathe through it, but it was burning its way to my lungs. That's when I realized what it was.

Gasoline.

My eyes watered as I tried opening them and the empty contents of my stomach threatened to rise. I closed my eyes to help with the burning and shook my head before opening them again.

My vision remained blurry, but I could now make out a figure standing in front of me through watering eyes.

A man, by the build of him, was wearing an all black outfit. My eyes traveled over him until they locked on the red gasoline container he was holding. And he was dousing the liquid everywhere.

I froze and watched in horror as he surrounded *me* with it.

The fumes were fogging up my brain, pulling me to sleep, but I fought against it, blinking repeatedly. The man's image was finally brought into full focus from the previous blurred one.

"Mateo?" I forced out, my voice hoarse. "Wh-what are you doing?"

His head shot up, but he kept pouring, the reservoir seeming never-ending.

"If *I* can't have you, then neither can he," he said, his voice sending a chill over my body. He severed eye contact and went back to pouring the gasoline until he fully emptied the canister.

The smell drowned my lungs, but I fought against the cough bubbling up in my throat. "Mateo," I said softly, trying to deescalate the situation I was facing. "You don't have to do this."

"Shut up."

"*Mateo*, look at me."

"No," he shouted before throwing the container to the side and moving to retrieve something from the table behind him.

He turned to face me and I looked down at his right hand, my gaze latching onto what he was holding between his fingers. He still hadn't looked at me, his eyes fixed on the object.

Panic rose in my gut at the sight of the lighter, but I pushed it down, focusing on the task in front of me. I had to stay calm and do my best not to ignite his anger further.

I said his name again, hoping this time he would look my way. And he did.

"Shut up, you bitch," he barked. "Stop fucking talking."

I ignored him and spoke again. "If you do this, you'll also hurt yourself."

Mateo's mouth twisted in a smirk. "I'm not the one tied up to a chair."

He flicked the wheel, a spark igniting. Then he lifted it between us, and my throat jumped.

"We can talk about this…" I tried one more time, a frustrated tear streaming down my cheek as my head dropped.

"Mateo… *Ach hadchi?*" A foreign deep voice said, anger infused in their tone.

My head shot up, my eyes swinging to where Omar Barrera stood in a perfectly tailored dark gray suit. His jaw tightened as he maintained his gaze locked on his son.

That wasn't who I was hoping would show up, but a tendril of hope weaved its way through my middle that he would make his son see reason.

Surprise colored Mateo's features and he looked over at his dad. "I can explain."

He moved forward, but his footsteps halted when he noticed the puddle of gas on the floor. "Do you know how humiliating this will be if it comes out?" he spat out, his anger permeating the air.

"But, Father—"

He assessed his son with what looked like pity. "No, you have done enough. I cannot believe you are making me deal with this. I already had an incompetent son and now you are proving to be another one," he said in disgust. "Let's go. Now," he urged in a low voice. He turned around and started walking back toward the exit I assumed was somewhere behind me, expecting his son to follow.

Mateo stood frozen, watching his father's figure moving away when the previous shame that he projected cracked at the words his father spewed. "No!" he yelled.

Barrera whipped around, fury emanating off his body. "*Ach gelti?*"

"I. Said. No." Mateo punctuated every word with an escalating rage.

I turned my attention back to Mateo, only to find him

branding the dooming silver object again. I watched as he flicked the ignition, with determination this time, and I braced for the inevitable.

He dropped the flame into the puddle in front of him and it raged to life in a matter of seconds. The flames were immediate and I watched in panic as they hopped from pool to pool.

Barrera was long gone while Mateo was still watching, horrified at how fast the fire was eating away at the room, surrounding us.

"No," he roared. "Fuck!"

I fought against my restraints while the fire roared brighter and hotter as it chipped at the distance separating us.

The scene unfolding in front of my eyes was nothing short of hell.

"Help," I cried out as loud as I could, hoping someone, anyone would hear me, knowing Mateo wouldn't come to my rescue. But my cry vanished with the sound of the fire, its flames billowing up and filling the room quickly.

I tried to breathe against the burning air, against the crushing fear that was threatening to overtake me as I rocked back and forth in my chair. I tugged my wrists to the side, hoping the rope would snap.

"Help," I yelled again, but despair wrapped around my middle, squeezing when only crackling wood and blinding smoke answered back.

I took a difficult deep breath and mustered any ounce of

strength my body had left and slammed against the back of my chair. After a few tries, it fell to the floor and my face slammed against the concrete.

My head pounded in pain from the contact, darkness threatening to cloud my vision. I tried to fight it, but the blinding headache and the blood trickling down my face made it hard to believe that I would get out of here alive.

My stomach sank at the thought that I wished I had told Jamal that I loved him at least once. Because as I watched Mateo back away from the flames approaching him and abruptly turn, running through the barrels and attempting to flee from the growing blaze, I knew I'd never see my husband again.

My vision faded and I heard a large explosion ring in the air.

CHAPTER 32

THIRTY MINUTES EARLIER

I STOOD FROZEN, MY LIMBS ANCHORED BY THE WEIGHT OF my guilt. I'd only heard her voice for a few seconds, but it was enough to solidify the dread in my gut that had been cementing there for the last three days.

She sounded horrible and all I wanted was to reach into the phone to comfort her, to tell her that I would come for her.

The fear of losing her was ferociously burning inside me every second she wasn't in my arms and I wanted to tear my own heart out just to soothe it from the constant aching it was under.

Click.

"Mateo?" I shouted at the silence.

Oh, le putain de bâtard.

He hung up on me.

It dawned on me that I'd finally gotten the answer I'd been desperately searching for, but the only thing my mind could focus on was getting my wife back.

My fingers gripped my phone so tightly as I moved it away from my ear that it groaned from the pressure.

I took a deep breath, trying to stay calm so that I could have a clear mind to find Sienna, but my blood pulsed with anger. The need to scour the earth to find Mateo and murder him ever so slowly was stronger than ever.

I growled and slammed my fisted hands against the hard surface of my desk, making it rattle.

I tried taking another deep breath to compose myself, but I struggled to breathe. The vice grip I'd felt around my lungs ever since her disappearance hadn't given me any second of respite.

I'd never felt this hopeless. And I hated it. Hated that I had no idea what was happening to my wife. What they were doing or had done to her in the last sixty-eight hours she'd been gone.

And I was the reason for it.

Sienna had been missing for almost three days with no indication of where she could be and I'd felt like my heart had been ripped out every second of it.

I was losing it.

Literally.

I'd barely eaten or slept. Every time I closed my eyes, all I could see were replays of that security tape and Sienna being taken. So I stayed awake, the only thing fueling my body being sheer will and desperation.

I'd spent day and night rummaging through every known Barrera building with no luck. The only thing I'd left behind was a trail of ashes stating that I wanted my wife back and I would burn anyone who stood in my way.

Barrera was yielding, yet he wasn't the one I wanted. Mateo was, but his son wouldn't give out his location. I'd even incessantly called and sent Mateo messages, but I hadn't gotten a response.

Until today.

And when he did, the small glimpse I'd gotten of Sienna's voice was only a temporary balm to my despair until fury eviscerated the blood in my veins.

She'd been taken from me and it was all my fucking fault.

I kept reminding myself to keep it together, but bile rose in the back of my throat at the thought of them hurting her.

I'd thought my parents' deaths were the worst things that could have happened to me, but Sienna's abduction was even worse.

I missed my wife. I just wanted her back in my arms. All I wanted was for her to please be alive. I just needed her back and I hoped she knew I loved her even though I'd failed to tell her.

It was her day off today and she was fast asleep in our

bed, her knees tucked into her chest and her hands sand-wiched between her thighs.

I reached for the fallen curls of her loose high ponytail and pushed them back away from her face.

I studied her face, entranced by her beauty. The arch of her strong brows. The defined curvature of her cheekbones. The small beauty mark on top of her perfectly soft lips.

Her mouth was slightly parted and a smile curved my lips when I heard her soft snoring. She was adorably cute.

Adorably cute and all mine.

Sienna was a pleasant gift in my life and she made me feel like a kid inside, infusing in my soul a happiness I hadn't experienced in a long time. Or probably ever.

I couldn't wait to unwrap all of her layers and discover more about her.

My thumb softly traced her cheekbone when her eyes fluttered open.

"How long have you been staring at me?" she muttered.

Since the moment I laid eyes on you.

"After you started snoring so loud, you woke me up."

Her eyes widened. "Jamal Aguerd, I do not snore."

I chuckled, brushing a small kiss on the tip of her nose. "I don't mind it."

She shook her head and closed her eyes.

A few seconds later, her eyes flew open again. "What?" she asked as I still stared at her.

My heart expanded in my rib cage and the words "I

love you" bloomed on their way out, but they got stuck in *my throat.*

So instead, I kissed her.

"I found her," Kai announced, drawing my attention to him as he barged into my office where I'd been holed up for the last three days, working on finding her.

I hadn't been able to bring myself to step into our bedroom since then. The simple thought of seeing her clothes with mine in our closet, her scent all over our bed sheets, even the small touches she'd left in our bedroom made my stomach twist.

So I'd stayed here.

Every few hours, Kai came to check in on me. Even Valentina had popped in once or twice, but they never stayed for too long.

Every plate of food Kai brought in was left untouched. The blankets for me to sleep on were still folded on one of the chairs in front of my desk where he'd placed them the first night my Sienna was taken.

The only time I'd left my office was to use the guest bathroom around the corner and shower. But I'd made Kai bring me clothes from upstairs because I just couldn't bring myself to go up there.

"You found her?" I asked, unsure if I'd heard him correctly.

"I found her," he confirmed.

I'd never moved faster in my life.

By the time he finished rattling off the address, I had

grabbed my keys and my gun before darting to my car. As I sped down the highway, going well over the speed limit, Sienna's words reverberated in my skull.

Just come kill this son of a bitch.

That was exactly what I planned to do.

I was halfway to Sardenya's industrial port when a small sedan abruptly appeared in front of me, adding to the fury already coursing through my veins.

I slammed on the horn of my convertible at how infuriatingly slow whoever was fucking driving in front of me was going. The driver was impeding the left lane and instead of fucking moving out of the way, he stubbornly stayed.

I gripped the leather of my steering wheel tighter as I inched closer, barely a millimeter separating my front bumper from his rear. We'd barely driven a mile when I realized he hadn't gotten the message.

Enfoiré.

A car on my right prevented me from being able to use that lane to pass him, so I whirled my car into the service lane. I pressed on the gas pedal and my car surged forward.

My car almost brushed against the concrete barrier separating both sides of the highway as I sped past him, flipping him off, and finally overtook him.

Driving recklessly wasn't normally in my nature, unless

absolutely necessary, but I couldn't have cared less if I got hit or even hit someone. My mind was focused on one thing only.

Getting to my wife.

I crossed the bridge that separated the city and the port and finally veered off the highway. I blew right through a red light, flooring the accelerator as the sun dipped below the horizon.

My heart raced as I swerved into a dark alleyway that opened to the main road leading to the port.

I was somewhat familiar with the grounds since I'd come here occasionally in the past to either make business deals or settle the debts of those who couldn't fulfill their end of the bargain—*cliché, I know*—but it would have never occurred to me that I'd have to come here to save my wife.

I didn't know which warehouse Sienna was in, but I'd search every single one of them until I found her.

I turned into the main entrance and noticed the iron swing gate ahead closed shut. I changed gears and shot down the road, crashing through the mesh and sending it flying over the roof of my McLaren.

I rounded a corner to where the warehouses were when I spotted a black town car parked a little farther away, the engine still running. An older man was hurriedly walking out of a brown brick, old-looking port warehouse as I came up.

Bringing my car to an abrupt stop, my body jerked

forward, and the tires squealed. I killed the engine, grabbed my gun, and burst out of my convertible.

I branded my gun up when I discovered who it was. "Where the fuck is my wife?" I demanded calmly, aiming the gun right where his heart was.

Faint notes of an acrid smell permeated the air and I glanced around until my gaze landed on tendrils of smoke billowing into the night sky from the warehouse he'd just come out of.

Sienna...

My heart jumped in my throat and a biting paralysis washed over me.

I faced Barrera again and our gazes locked. A thousand unspoken words swarmed the space between us.

Four years of unanswered questions. Four years of frustrating dead ends. Four years of built-up anger waiting to be spilled into retribution.

But all of that washed away when one question screamed the loudest.

Love or revenge?

The last few years of my life had been dedicated to seeking justice for what had happened to my parents. The answer to that question had been the *only* thing of importance.

Revenge had been the only thing on my mind.

But none of that mattered anymore because now there was only one choice.

Love.

So I let the man who robbed me of my parents get into the back seat of his car and watched him speed away.

I spun around and broke into a sprint with my gun in hand. My free hand reached for the door when the windows of the warehouse exploded and I was blown backward into the air.

The impact of my back slamming against the hard concrete ground knocked the wind out of my lungs. My head whipped back, my skull reverberating from the contact with the floor.

An incessant ringing filled my hearing as the sky above me trickled with ashes.

The smell of metal and burning flesh filled my nose and I was transported back to twenty years ago. The paralyzing memory overtook my senses.

Wa Mama... Baba... Finkoum?

Panic began to set in, anchoring me to the ground, but the image of my wife, of my Sienna, shattered it in an instant. My eyes fell shut and my body screamed for me to stay put, but I was running out of time.

I forced my eyelids open to find a hot and sticky world rushing in, a cloudy haze blanketing my vision. I rolled to my side, my back groaning in agony.

I have to find her. I have to get to her, I repeatedly told myself as I pushed myself up. But once I was on my feet, I realized that the task of getting her out wasn't going to be so simple.

My limbs were unsteady as I walked inside, the suffocating air making it difficult to breathe. My head spun and after taking a few steps forward, I found myself on my hands and knees.

I tried to breathe and let it pass, but the smoke over-powering the air made it difficult.

You can't save your wife if you're dead, Jamal, my conscience screamed. *Get up.*

The desperate need to find Sienna summoned every strength I had and I got up again. The dizziness hadn't subsided, but I didn't care. I *would* get her out of here even if it meant sacrificing myself.

I could hear the faint sound of sirens wailing in the background. They would be here any minute now and I needed to find Sienna before they came.

"Sienna!" I screamed, walking around scattered debris and keeping low to avoid the dense smoke. I kept yelling her name, hoping she'd show any signs of life, but the more I looked around, the more I felt a sense of doom that I wouldn't find her.

I shoved the sentiment away and continued my search, moving to the back of the crumbling warehouse until…

Terror buckled my knees at the sight in front of me.

A form tangled with a chair lying utterly still, fire closing in on her.

No…

Distress surged through me, extinguishing any fear of the blazing wall separating us, and fueled my steps toward her. I went around it, finding a small pathway that wasn't ignited, and rushed over to her.

I crouched next to her and made quick work to untie her wrists and ankles, freeing them. Once I got them loose, I kicked the chair off her and scooped her in my arms.

Then, with my back to the flames, I beelined for the exit. I heard the sound of something collapsing, a loud thud resonating in the air, but I didn't look back to see what it was.

I had one goal and it was to get us out of here.

I ran so quickly, with all my might, but the journey to the outdoors itself felt like a blur. One minute, the scorching heat was licking my heels and the next, cool air washed over us.

Blaring sirens wailed closer as I fell to my knees, coughing incessantly. My lips crushed against her forehead and I waited to hear Sienna do the same, but when I finally glanced down at her face, she was still unconscious.

"Sienna," I said, gently tapping the side of her face, hoping it would do the trick.

Nothing.

A strangled sound bubbled out of my throat as I shook her body, trying to wake her. "Sienna, baby, wake up." I kept trying, but nothing was working. "*Mon amour*, please. You have to open those beautiful eyes for me, okay?"

Grief welled up inside me when I felt for her pulse and found nothing.

"No!" I roared, placing her on the floor. "Don't you die on me, Sienna Aguerd. Don't you fucking dare!"

I started doing CPR as shades of flashing blues and reds crowded me. My chest pounded and my breaths came in spurts as I cracked her chest with each descent.

"I love you, dammit. You can't leave me before I get to tell you."

I couldn't breathe from the pain that was ripping me in two at seeing the love of my life not waking up.

Muffled shouts rang around me, but all I could focus on was how I could breathe life back into her body, how I could bring her back to me because I would be damned if I didn't get a chance at a fucking future with her.

Suddenly, there was a presence at my back and a force tried to pull me away, yelling unintelligible words, but I tugged my shoulders forward, continuing my compressions.

"Do not touch me again," I growled, the sound vibrating in my chest. "I have to save her."

"Then, *let* us," whoever was behind me said and it pierced through the fog that had taken my brain when I discovered Sienna had no pulse.

My chest compressions progressively slowed and I reluctantly let them pull me away.

Then they immediately got to work, but all of it was a blur.

"Come with me and we'll get you checked out," the person next to me said, brushing my arm to direct me somewhere else.

I shook my head, warmth trickling down my face. That's when I realized I was crying. "You have to save her. She… she can't die."

"They're doing everything they can," the professional tried to reassure me, but it wasn't working. I didn't need them to do everything they could. I needed them to give me my wife back.

I felt frozen in time, every second feeling everlasting until someone shouted, "We got a pulse."

A relief like I'd never felt before washed over every single atom of my being, the breath I'd been holding in finally releasing.

They transferred her onto a stretcher and rolled her toward the ambulance that was parked right next to my car.

I rushed over, but someone tried to stop me. "I'm her husband, so you better get your hands off me or I will break them," I growled in warning, leaving no room for them to argue against.

I climbed in with one of the paramedics at the back of the ambulance while the other jumped into the driver's seat.

As the paramedic closed the door, I finally looked back at the scene we'd just walked out of. I watched the walls collapse inward and the roof caved in as they rushed us to the hospital.

CHAPTER 33

I WAS SLUMPED AGAINST A WALL IN AN EMPTY HOSPITAL hallway, covered in soot, waiting for an update on my wife.

I'd paced every inch of the unit before I finally grew tired and settled in the spot I was currently in. The staff had asked me to move to the waiting room, but I threatened to sue if they didn't let me stay closer to my wife.

I wanted to be within immediate reach if she ever needed me.

All I could do during that time was play with her ring, which felt like a leaden weight in between my fingers.

Please let her be okay.

It'd been two hours. Two hours since I'd held her. Two hours since she'd died in my arms. And these last two hours had been the longest of my life, every second stretching into endless more.

Her vitals were all over the place when they wheeled

her into the emergency room and started working on her, but since then, I hadn't received any updates.

Countless healthcare workers had passed in front of me, but none were from my wife's medical team. I wanted to march in there and demand answers but refrained, choosing logic over emotion and knowing I would get updates when they had them.

My phone had been ringing constantly since we'd come in, but I let every call go to voicemail, not ready to talk to anyone.

I hadn't stepped foot in a hospital since I was discharged from one twenty years ago. I never thought I'd be back here, covered in the guilt of being the reason the woman I loved was here, waiting to see if she was alive.

Despite the noises, everything around me felt too quiet, but my thoughts were the loudest noise of all.

Leaning forward, I buried my face in my hands.

I did this. I did this. I *did this.*

"Jamal," a deep, familiar voice said and I raised my head to see my uncle walking down the hallway toward me.

My eyes widened, surprised to see him. "Noah? What are you doing here?" I asked when he made it to where I was sitting.

He lowered himself down next to me. "My nephew needed me. Why wouldn't I be here?"

I looked away. "You didn't have to come."

"I wanted to," he said immediately. His hand cupped

the back of my head, the way he always did when I was a kid when he wanted to let me know he was there for me.

I glanced back at him, giving him a small nod in acknowledgment.

"Any news?"

Letting out an anguished sigh, I ran a hand over my head. "None since we walked in."

"How long has it been?"

One hour, fifty-seven minutes and thirty-three seconds.

I rubbed a hand over my heart. "Almost two hours."

Silence fell between us as I kept counting the passing minutes, tallying them to my previous count.

"What happened?" he asked after a few moments.

I knew he would ask, but I didn't have an answer. How could I explain to the man who had raised me that my wife was in the hospital because of me? Because of my need for revenge for the death of my parents.

Because of what he'd kept from me.

I would have been angry at him for lying to me all these years, but I had no energy left in me. Besides, I knew deep down that he wouldn't keep something from me out of self-ishness.

He'd only do it to protect me.

"There was a fire and she…" I paused, emotions welling up in my throat, choking the words I wanted to say. "It was my fault and Sienna got wrapped into it."

"I don't understand."

I glanced his way to find his face twisted in confusion, his brows furrowed.

I swallowed the lump in my throat. "I know."

One of his brows lifted. "Know what?"

"I know what really happened to my parents," I finally confessed.

He blinked and shook his head, still seeming confused about where my confession would lead.

I closed my eyes briefly before I scanned his features as I told him what I'd discovered he'd kept from me. "I know the fire wasn't an accident," I continued and his face fell, visible distress painted all over it. "I know that you kept the truth from me to protect me, but you should have told me. You should have told me the truth about Barrera."

He winced and averted his gaze. He stayed quiet, and I thought he'd change subjects like he always did in the past when I asked about them.

But this time I knew the truth.

He let out a deep sigh and brought his knees up, resting his forearms on them. He wrung his hands together and finally spoke, "Your father and I worked on an important case that involved bringing down a very dangerous man. He's a difficult criminal to catch and when we got too close, he wanted to make sure that whatever lead your father had was buried with him." His throat jumped with a swallow. "I didn't want to tell you because you were too young and you'd just lost the two most important people in your life. I didn't want you to foster hate for a man who isn't worth your time."

That's too late, isn't it.

He finally looked at me again. "It's my job to protect you and it's been the greatest gift life could have given me, but I should have told you and I'm sorry I didn't do it sooner."

"I had him, you know. He was right there…" I trailed off. I didn't regret letting him go because Sienna was the only person of importance at the time, but I still couldn't help but think about all the what-ifs.

"He's not worth it, trust me."

Something about Noah's statement sent my subconscious whirling with more questions, but I ignored it, my mind reeling back to why I was at the hospital in the first place.

I rested my head against the wall behind me. "She has to make it."

"She sounds like a fighter," he said, wrapping his arm around my shoulders and bringing me in closer to him. "She'll make it."

Tears stung the back of my eyes. She would, she *had* to.

"Mr. Brown?"

I stiffened at the sight of the doctor stepping out of the room Sienna was in. Her expression was unreadable as she approached me and fear gripped my lungs.

My breathing halted as I launched to my feet. "Please,"

my voice cracked. I cleared my throat and spoke again. "Tell me it's good news. Tell me my wife is okay."

She gave me a soft smile, but it did nothing to reassure me. Her smile could mean two things. Either Sienna was okay and I would get my wife back. Or it could simply be to help soften the stabbing blow a devastating news would bring.

"I'm Dr. Alaoui, the physician that's in charge of your wife. She's stable now, but we're keeping her for observation. She's extremely lucky you got there when you did and—"

I closed my eyes, a sudden rush of relief sweeping over me. I didn't hear anything else she said. The only words I could focus on were that she was okay.

It was all that mattered.

I met the doctor's eyes. "When can I see her?"

"She's resting right now, but you can go in whenever you're ready."

She'd barely finished her sentence and I was already making my way to Sienna. I paused when I reached her hospital room, steeling myself to go in.

What if she doesn't want me here?

I heard footsteps behind me and turned to find Noah had followed me.

"Is there anything I can get you before I leave?"

I shook my head.

"She'll be okay, Jamal," he started, clamping a hand

over my shoulder and squeezing. "Call me when she wakes up, okay?"

"I will," I replied, placing my opposite palm over his hand.

After he left, I braced myself and pushed the door open. I walked into the room and my throat immediately closed up at the sight of her lying in the bed.

She was hooked to a myriad of machines and an IV was connected to her arm. She was asleep, her curly hair fanned across her pillow. Her dark long lashes were resting against her bruised face, black soot streaks still marking her face.

I moved to her bedside and grabbed her hand, then brought it to my mouth and pressed a soft kiss on top of it.

My eyes zeroed in on the slow rise and fall of her chest, and it infused my lungs with the air they had been deprived of since I'd found out her heart had stopped beating.

I hesitantly left her side, grabbed a small cloth from the stack on the bedside table, and headed to the bathroom to wet it. Once out, I went back to her side and gently sat on the edge of her bed.

I brushed some of her hair out of the way and lightly dabbed her face clean, careful around the large bruise.

The steady sound of her heart monitor beeping in the background and the soft sounds of her breathing gave me comfort that she was really here.

That her heart was beating this time.

I watched her unconscious body through a clouded vision and all I thought was that I should have told her. I should have done a better job of protecting her. It killed me. Seeing her like this and knowing I was responsible for it broke something in me.

I transferred to the chair next to her bed and brought it closer, never letting her hand go, the steady pulse there reassuring.

A collection of accusing words echoed in my skull incessantly, letting one thought come to the forefront.

Elle mérite mieux que moi.

I forced her to marry me and fell head over heels in love with her, more than I ever thought possible. She was the only one for me and I had to tell her. Even if she would never hear it.

I'd waited too long to say it and I couldn't waste another moment.

"I love you," I said in a barely audible whisper. I closed my eyes and buried my face against her knuckles. "I love you so fucking much."

But I had to set her free despite how gut-wrenching the simple thought was.

CHAPTER 34

NOAH

FUCK.

Sienna

CHAPTER 35

I woke up to the soft beep and whir of machines.

My heavy eyes opened to a blurry sight of a dimly lit room and my chest felt sore. I brought my hand up to rub against it, only to find cords curled around my arm and the feel of electrodes poking through the stiff fabric I was wearing.

I blinked to rid myself of the hazy sight and followed the cords' trajectory until my eyes landed on an infusion pump and a cardiac monitor.

What the hell...

Disoriented, I scanned my surroundings further, only to realize that I was lying in a hospital bed. My mouth felt extremely dry and I tried to swallow to lubricate it but ended up wincing at the movement.

Slowly, images of what had happened barreled into my memory.

Parking lot. Mateo. Unending days. Fire.

Suddenly, my other senses awakened. I was warm and felt something hard pressed against me. That same something stirred against me and I peered down.

My heart halted when I saw who it was.

Jamal.

He was slumped face down on my lap, the lower half of his body in a high back chair beside my bed. One of his arms was tucked beneath his chest, the other outstretched above his head, clasping my hand in his.

I closed my eyes, trying to keep the tears at bay.

He came for me.

I didn't think I would ever see him again. Or anyone for that matter.

A faint smile of relief tugged at my lips. My husband was here with me and by the looks of it, it seemed he hadn't left my side since however long I'd been here.

The last thing I remembered was being on the hard floor of the warehouse Mateo had brought me to, scorching warmth licking my face as I watched Mateo run away and...

The explosion.

Is he dead?

I hoped he was because if that wasn't the case, knowing my husband, he wouldn't be alive for much longer.

Extending my free arm, I ran a hand over his hair as I took him in. He looked exhausted and my heart twisted in my chest. I smoothed my palm down the side of his face and over his scruffy beard.

Being able to feel him, to touch him brought me so much comfort. I was flooded with emotion. I felt a tear escape and before I knew it, I was crying. Like a dam had broken and I couldn't hold them back anymore.

I didn't remember the last time I actually cried. I was always the type of person to put my emotions aside, telling myself that I'd deal with them later, but now everything came crashing back like a tidal wave.

"You're okay, *mon amour*," a soft voice said. I felt a shift in the bed I was lying in. "I've got you," Jamal whispered, curling his arms around my body. "I'm right here."

I snuggled into him and closed my eyes, burying my face into his shirt.

"You found me," I choked out.

He kissed my forehead. "I never would have stopped looking for you, Sienna." Then he tilted my head away from his shirt and pressed a gentle kiss on each of my closed eyelids, like he was trying to kiss my tears away. "Never."

I opened my eyes and looked up at him. He cupped my wet cheek and brushed his thumb over it, wiping the streaks away. "There'll never be enough words to express how sorry I am for failing you."

Failing me? Does he think I blame him for what happened to me?

I tipped my head up and with the little energy I had, my

lips gently touched his. Pulling away, my eyes were back on his. "You did not fail me. What Mateo did was on him, not you. Got it?"

He gave me a small smile, but it didn't reach his eyes. "How are you feeling?" he asked, shifting the conversation.

"My limbs are sore and my chest hurts a little, but other than that, I think I'm okay."

Something changed in his expression when I mentioned that my chest hurt.

"What is it?" I asked, worried.

His fingers trailed down my arm and hovered around my pulse, his fingertips brushing against my pulse. "Your heart stopped beating for two minutes before they were able to bring you back. You were dead in my arms for two —" His words cut off, tears falling down his cheeks.

I cupped his cheek. "Hey, I'm here." I took his hand and placed it over my beating heart. "I'm right here." My lips trembled as I said the words.

His forehead dropped to mine.

Say it.

I took a shuddering breath and finally said the words I'd been holding onto for far too long. "I love you," I whispered in the air we shared.

I was in love with a man who had forced me to marry him and I would do it all over again if it meant this was the ending. I'd always believed that true love wasn't in the cards for me, but Jamal showed me it was.

He pulled back and his eyes widened. He stood so still,

I couldn't tell if he was even breathing. But I'd finally confessed it. So I repeated it.

"I love you."

His gaze burned into mine and I held my breath, anticipation bubbling in my veins. His fingers reached up to tuck my hair behind my ear, but instead of reciprocating my words, he tipped my face up to his and kissed me.

I couldn't help but feel the hint of sadness that washed over me, but I pushed it aside and opened my mouth to let him in. His hand reached the back of my head and he pulled me closer.

Our kiss was slow, our heads moving in sync with each other, our tongues tangling gently together. He hadn't said it back, but I could feel the unspoken words through his kiss.

I just hoped I wasn't wrong.

It'd been two weeks since I'd been discharged and the relief I'd felt when they announced it was one of the sweetest.

Now, don't get me wrong, I loved being at the hospital. It was one of my favorite places to be, but I *hated* being there as a patient. After the third day of sitting in a bed, doing nothing, I felt like I was losing my mind with boredom.

The only distraction I'd gotten had been when Kai and

Valentina would visit. Valentina only sat in the corner of my room, typing away on her laptop, but Kai made sure I got some entertainment while stuck in a hospital room.

They'd wanted to keep me under observation a little longer, but I'd informed them that I was ready to leave and even felt well enough to return to work. They'd been opposed to it at first, but since I was a doctor too, they'd trusted my opinion and given me the green light after my cardiac and blood tests came back normal.

I'd called my sisters as soon as I was lucid enough to have a conversation, not wanting them to worry more than they already were. Iris had cried a little when she saw my face during our video chat, but I continuously reassured her that I was fine.

Jamal had called my parents when we walked into the hospital and they'd asked to come and visit, but he'd asked them to wait until he got my permission once I woke up.

I'd told him that I wasn't ready to face either of them, especially my father. Besides, if my mother visited, I'd spend the whole time she was here taking care of her and quieting her cries.

And I just didn't have the energy for it, so Jamal had called them back and told them it would be better if they waited for me to reach out.

I didn't know when I *would* be ready, but for once, I had a choice.

Esra and Kenna had shown up the next day after Jamal had called them to tell them I was in the hospital. They'd showered me with food and for some unknown reasons socks, courtesy of Esra. I appreciated the gesture, but who needed ten pairs of new socks while at the hospital? But that was Esra for you.

I'd initially wanted to keep what had happened to me a secret for their own safety, but it was for the same reasons that I'd told them. They'd found a body amidst the remains of the warehouse, but because of the explosion, it took them longer than expected to identify the body.

We both knew who it was, but we didn't want to explain to the authorities or the fire marshal what had actually happened.

All they knew was that Jamal and I were visiting the warehouse for a potential business venture of his when we found ourselves stuck in the fire. They hadn't asked more questions, especially when their superiors called to tell them to let it go.

Guess it helped when your husband had connections.

Speaking of which, in the time I'd been back home, Jamal hadn't left my side. Literally.

But despite being together so often, he felt distant. He kept our conversations short and barely touched me unless it was absolutely necessary. When I'd asked what was wrong, he gave me the same excuse every time.

"You're still recovering."

I'd tried to object, but he just kept shutting me down. His behavior didn't help with the small doubt that had sprouted the night I'd told him I loved him.

What if he doesn't feel the same?

Today was my first day back at work and I'd never been more grateful for a busy ER to keep my mind off things. I was leaving a patient's room when one of the nurses, Isabella, intercepted me on my way to another patient.

"Someone's here for you," she informed me. "They're in the waiting room."

My brows furrowed. I wasn't expecting anyone and if it was Jamal, the front desk would have told Isabella that it was my husband. Besides, he would have just called me if he was coming to see me.

"Do you know who it is?" I asked, wracking my mind to figure out who it might be.

"It was some older gentleman in a suit, but he didn't mention his name. Just said that it was important."

That's weird.

I thanked Isabella and headed out of the unit, passing the automatic sliding doors to the waiting room. I scanned the area until my eyes landed on the only person who looked out of place.

He was standing alone in a corner, away from other patients, holding a briefcase with both hands in front of him. I walked over to him, anxiety tightening my nerves.

Tap.

Tap. Tap. Tap.

My drumming increased until I stood in front of the stranger.

"Dr. Bruni?" he asked, pushing his wire-framed glasses up his nose and extending his right hand to me.

"Yes?" I answered hesitantly, taking his hand in mine and shaking it.

He let go of my hand and cracked his briefcase open, then retrieved a stack of papers from it that he handed to me.

Taking it from him, I started scanning the words printed on it and my heart sank.

My brows drew together. "What's this?" My voice came out like a whisper.

"I'm Jason Ellie, your husband's lawyer," he said, finally introducing himself. "Mr. Brown sent me to give you this," he continued, but I still didn't understand.

Shocked by what I was reading, my eyes flew up to Jamal's supposed lawyer. "I—" I didn't have words for what I was holding.

"I'm sorry," Jason simply said before leaving me standing still in the middle of a waiting room.

My mind went into overdrive while my eyes went back to the papers as I flipped through them. My brain tried to make sense of the ink on those pieces of paper, but everything appeared like a jumbled mess in front of me.

I couldn't move, couldn't breathe.

But the hurt I felt slowly morphed into anger.

What the fuck is this?

My grip tightened against the papers and I fisted them as I walked back into the emergency room, heading straight to my attending's office. I knocked on the door twice before turning the knob and walking in.

"Sienna," Dr. Wu said and I heard her typing slow. "Is everything okay?"

I looked over at where she was sitting at her desk, her fingers paused above her keyboard. "I was wondering if I could leave early?" I asked, needing to get to the bottom of this.

Her eyes filled with worry as she got up and hurriedly walked over to me. Her hands grabbed my forearms. "Are you feeling unwell? I knew you should have taken a few more days before coming back."

I shook my head. "No, I feel okay. An emergency came up at home and I have to leave," I explained, hoping she would believe me.

"Of course. I'll have Dr. Adamos cover for you."

"Thank you," I replied quietly before leaving her office, closing the door behind me and heading for the staff locker room.

The journey back to the house felt like a blur and when I parked in the driveway, my eyes landed on the crumpled papers strewn across the passenger seat.

I grabbed the divorce papers and headed inside.

Jamal

CHAPTER 36

I was working on a client's contract when I heard the front door slam open. Puzzled, I looked at the time on my computer.

It couldn't be Kai and Valentina because they were already here since they'd decided to work from home today, unless one of them decided to go out.

As for Sienna, it was too early for her to be here and *I* was supposed to pick her up after her shift was done, which was only in five hours.

I got my answer the moment my wife stormed into my office, fury emanating off of her.

Not your wife, my mind mocked me, reminding me of what I'd sent her this morning with my lawyer. At least, she wouldn't be for much longer.

She marched over to me and threw a stack of papers on

my desk. They scattered all over the wooden surface. "What is this?" she asked, seething.

I never wanted to do this, but every time I closed my eyes, the sight of her unconscious, with no pulse, flooded my thoughts.

When I met her gaze, it was filled with heat, but not from anger. She was hurt and it made all of this even worse than it already was.

"Divorce papers," I said calmly, but internally I was anything but calm. My heart twisted so tight, I could barely breathe, barely felt anything in my body given how much having to do this hurt.

But it was for the best. It might have been unfair of me to make that decision for her, but I wouldn't let her get hurt. Not again. Not after she died in my arms.

If the paramedics hadn't shown up when they did, I could have lost her forever.

I wouldn't have her put in another situation like this one simply because she was my wife. It was my job to protect her and I'd already failed once. I wouldn't have that again.

She got closer, her finger jamming on top of the stack of papers. "You want a divorce?" she croaked out, her hand slightly trembling.

I tried to maintain her gaze, to appear convincing, but it was too hard, so I looked away. "Yes," I forced the word out. I swallowed against the lump in my throat. "It's for the best."

"Look at me," she ordered. When I didn't, she repeated herself, "I said, look at me. If you're going to divorce me, I want you to look me in the eyes."

So I did look at her.

"Is it the best for me or for *you*?" she asked, her eyes brimming with tears.

Barely able to speak through the persistent tightness in my throat, I said, "It's the right thing to do."

Saying those words, which were far from the truth, ripped my heart open and shattered the muscle into pieces. I loved her more than I thought could ever be possible, but I'd suffer a miserable life if it meant she would be safe.

She took a step back and crossed her arms above her chest. "I see."

Using the opportunity, I grabbed one of the pens on my desk and offered it to her. She just stared at me like I'd grown another head.

"You want me to sign this now?"

"Why wait?"

"Why wait?" she echoed, and I could feel my heart ripping more by the second she prolonged this. She just had to sign and then it would be over, right? The pain would stop and I'd know I made the right decision.

Right?

She'll eventually understand, I tried to convince myself, but it wasn't working. I didn't know if anything would ever work at convincing me that she wasn't the best thing that had ever happened to me.

That *will* ever happen to me.

She hadn't moved, hadn't taken the pen from me or picked up the papers either.

I glanced at her and tried my best to keep my emotions at bay. "Please, Sienna. Just sign the papers."

"No."

My brows snapped together. "What do you mean no?"

"It means no."

"Sienna—"

"No, I'm not signing the papers."

My brows drew in tighter as I grew frustrated. Not at her because she didn't do anything wrong. I was the one putting us in this situation.

But why couldn't she see that this was for the best? Why was she making this harder than it already was?

"Why?" I asked.

She shrugged. "I'm not signing."

I took a shuddering breath and stood from my seat. "Please just sign the papers," I said, my low voice barely above a whisper.

No longer able to face her, I headed for the door to leave the room, but she grabbed my arm and I turned to face her.

"Is it because I said I loved you?"

Of course it wasn't. It was because *I* loved her that I was doing this.

A tear rolled down her face when I didn't answer. She

let go of my arm, bringing her hand up to her cheek and furiously wiping it away.

Fuck.

I wanted to reach for her and comfort her, but it would defeat the purpose of pushing her away. So instead, I fisted my hands at my sides to stop myself from doing so and said, "No, that has nothing to do with it."

"Then what is it? Either it's because you don't care about me or maybe you just don't love me. That must be it," she said, huffing out a sardonic laugh.

Tears were now freely running down her cheeks and she kept wiping them away angrily with the back of her hand.

I stepped closer until we were toe to toe. She lifted her chin defiantly.

I shook my head and pinched the bridge of my nose before staring down at her. "You think I don't care? You think that's why I married you? Because I don't care?" I started and before I could stop myself, I confessed the only thing I told myself I wouldn't.

I took a deep breath and grabbed her head with both hands, bending my head closer to hers. "Of course I fucking do," I said, my voice coming out harsher than I intended. "I love you. I am in love with you. You're the love of my fucking life, but *this*"—I let go of her and gestured between us—"was never your choice. It's *because* I love you that I can't be selfish. I can't lose you again, and loving me, *being* with me will do that. So please, baby, just sign the damn papers."

I kissed her forehead and prepared myself to leave her when she spoke again.

"No," she whispered.

That damn fucking word.

"Sienna, wh—"

She wiped another stray tear. "No," she said sternly, squaring her shoulders. "You've said what you wanted to say and it's my turn to speak now. When I'm done, then you can talk again. But now, let me because I don't want to speak over you or interrupt your nonsense about signing divorce papers."

She took a shaky breath and stepped closer.

"My whole life, I've done what other people expected of me, what *they* wanted me to do. My life has been dictated by everyone else *but* me. But now, now that I finally realized that I deserve to be selfish and put myself first instead of everyone else, I get to make my own decisions. To decide what makes *me* happy. Do whatever the hell *I* choose."

She lifted her hand and rested it against my cheek. My eyes closed on their own as she traced my cheekbone with her thumb. "And what I choose is you."

I opened my eyes and looked straight into the ones of the woman I'd fallen in love with, bewildered by her words.

"You're the one I want to wake up to and go to bed with

and do everything in between with. I get a choice now. I get to choose and I choose you Jamal Menelik Aguerd."

"Your turn," she said, like we were in some sort of debate and it was my time to present my arguments.

My lips parted, but she added, "Oh, actually, one more thing. Stop with the nonsense about protecting me. We're stronger together, not apart. Okay, *now* I'm done. You can speak if you'd like."

I studied her, a million things running through my head. I wanted to say so much, yet any existing word in the vocabulary would fail to properly convey my love for this woman. This conversation didn't go the way I'd planned, but this was a better outcome, the outcome I'd wanted deep down.

This beautiful woman was stubbornly mine. She would always be.

Her hand was still against my cheek, so I placed mine over hers and bent down until only a few inches separated her beautiful face from mine.

"You're stubborn, you know that?" I finally said, my eyes dipping to her lips.

She put her hand on my chest and peered at me through her lashes. "I know what I want. There's a difference."

I shook my head and brought my lips even closer. I reached up and tucked a piece of hair behind her ear, my fingertips lingering on the skin beneath her ear, right above her pulse point. "I love you, you know?"

She gave me a small nod, her chest rising and falling faster. "I love you, too."

I pressed my body against her and smiled against her lips.

Then, because I couldn't wait any longer, I kissed my wife and I would kiss her every day after that.

EPILOGUE

"ONCE AGAIN, UNDETERRED, CYNARA CRUZ, OUR championship leader, crosses the line and makes it another win for her to extend her Championship lead in the F1 Academy as we head into the final round," the commentator on the screen announced.

"Yes!" I yelled, jumping off the couch.

I heard chuckles from behind me and whipped around.

"What's so funny?" I asked, raising an eyebrow.

Shareef quickly looked away from where my husband was sitting behind me, stifling his laughter. "You're just… very enthusiastic," Shareef said from his spot on the other side of the couch where he and Kenna were snuggled.

Kenna swatted at his chest and glared at him, muttering something to him under her breath in Yorùbá. Then she turned her attention to me. "What my dear husband meant was that your joy and involvement in this sport is a beautiful thing to watch," Kenna said, her eyes glimmering with amusement.

Shareef placed a hand on her belly and kissed her cheek. "Yes, what my beautiful wife said."

I huffed out a laugh, shaking my head. These two were sickly adorable and he would agree to anything she said, especially now that she was pregnant.

Kenna had found out the news three months ago. When two pink lines had shown up on the stick, she'd immediately video called our group chat, freaking out from her bathroom floor.

She and Shareef had planned to wait until she had completed her residency to start trying, but after a two-hour-long conversation, her fear turned into an overwhelming joy, happy tears flowing freely when she truly realized that she was becoming a mom.

And to say Shareef was happy about becoming a father would be an understatement.

"But you did almost step on me with that *enthusiasm*," Kai claimed from where he was sitting on the floor, his elbow propped on the couch where we were all sitting.

I glanced down at him and mouthed a sorry before I took my seat again.

The man beside me tightened the arms I loved around me and made a noise that had me glancing at him out of the corner of my eye. He had his head cocked to look at me, a playful smile that both annoyed me and made my heart beat faster plastered on his face.

I lifted my legs and draped them over his lap, earning me a kiss on the top of my head before we both faced the screen again, watching Cynara pop her winning bottle and spraying the sparkling wine onto the other two winners.

We were all in Jamal's and my living room for our monthly gatherings. We'd started these about two months ago, alternating between here and Kenna and Shareef's new place they'd bought after finding out they were becoming parents.

To my luck, this month's get-together just happened to be on race day, which meant more time for me to convert them into F1 lovers. They'd even agreed—okay, I'd forced them—to wear Matrix Motorsports for the race later today.

The doorbell suddenly rang as the post-race interviews started. Kai got up and headed out of the living room and to the front door.

When he opened it, Esra rushed inside with a brown box in one hand while brushing off the snow from her brown hair that was tied in a low bun with the other. Kai quickly closed the door once she was inside to avoid the frigid November air.

"God, I'm *so* sorry I'm late," she huffed out, bending down to take off her high-heeled boots with one hand while balancing the box in the other. "I was supposed to leave work an hour ago, but as usual, Mr. Asshole delayed my plans."

She successfully removed one boot, but when she reached for the other, she almost fell. Kai helped her stay upright and offered to grab the box from her. She tilted her head up and gave him a small smile before handing it to him.

He walked back into the living room and placed the pastry-filled box on the table among the other food and beverages we'd laid out.

Esra followed shortly after, her coat draped on her forearm. "So," she started, draping her trench coat on the backrest and settling on the armchair next to where Kai was seated since Valentina was occupying the one on the opposite side. "What did I miss?"

"Oh, nothing," Kai drawled, twisting to look at Esra. "Just Sienna almost knocking me over."

Esra reached for the box and Kai grabbed it to bring it closer to her. Their hands briefly brushed and Kai blushed, quickly pulling back after Esra grabbed a croissant from the box.

Out of curiosity, I cast a glance over at where Valentina was sitting, only to find her scowling at Esra and sipping on her red wine to hide it.

Esra settled back in her seat, tucking her feet under her. "She got too eager again when her favorite won?" She took a bite, her mischievous eyes locking with mine.

Knowing what she was about to say because she *loved* to tell the story, I gave her a warning look. "Esra, you better n—"

She ignored me and averted her gaze, focusing her attention back on Kai. "Did she ever tell you that one time she gave me a black eye because I stood too close to her when Isaiah King won his first championship?"

I stared at her in disbelief. "It was an accident and I have apologized many times," I grumbled.

Esra just laughed, flakes of croissant spilling out of her mouth. She pressed her palm to her mouth, muttering sorrys as she swallowed. "Yes, but I still had to sport a black eye for a week at school."

I cocked my head to the side and pinned her with a glare, my finger pointing at her. "It led to Max asking you out because he felt bad and wanted to make you feel better. Whom might I remind you, you spent the majority of your senior year in college crushing on."

She held her palms up, admitting defeat. "Touché."

Esra and Kai shared more stories about my *burst of enjoyment* when it came to Formula One, Kenna interjecting here and there, and I watched their conversation with amusement.

A sense of happiness washed over me as I watched my friends blend so well with Jamal's.

Like my husband knew exactly what I was thinking, he bent down and whispered in my ear, "I love you."

My gaze met his and I gripped his chin, his dark stubble rough under my fingertips. I tugged him closer to press a kiss on his lips. "*Jamais plus que moi.*" His eyes filled with an abundance of emotions as I pressed another kiss to his lips.

It had been five months since Jamal and I had remarried. A week after I'd refused to sign his ridiculous divorce papers, he'd proposed with the ring I thought I'd lost when Mateo removed it from my finger.

Our second wedding had been an intimate ceremony on the beach along the coast of Sardenya and this time there were no unannounced interruptions. Most importantly, this time we were surrounded by the people we loved.

Our friends and Jamal's uncle, Noah, were in attendance. My sisters had shown up, but I'd asked my parents not to come. Our relationship was still strained and although guilt had gnawed at my insides announcing to them that they weren't invited, I knew it was for the best.

I'd spent my life dousing my happiness for the comfort of others, but this time, for what was meant to be one of the happiest days of my life, I wanted to put myself first despite how others, my parents in this case, would feel.

Maybe one day I'd let them back in and work toward having a relationship with them, but for now, I wanted to break the vicious cycle I'd found myself in constantly.

For now, I'd enjoy the company of people who didn't only seem to care for me if I had something to give back to them. People who cared for who *I* was.

As I looked around the room that was filled with people I loved—yes, even Valentina—my heart filled with warmth.

I might not have had somewhere to call home before, but I'd made one for myself with my husband and I planned to make the most of it.

Especially with the new addition that would join our monthly gatherings in nine months.

EIGHT YEARS LATER

"Selim, what overalls do you want to wear today? The brown ones or the blue and white striped ones?"

My son sat on his bed in only his diaper and a cream long-sleeved shirt that said "Atlas Racing" in bold black letters with a Formula One car drawing underneath it.

Courtesy of Sienna. She wanted to make sure that our children would follow in her footsteps when it came to her love for the sport.

He watched attentively the two options I was displaying for him, then pointed his chubby finger to the brown one. "*Hado.*"

"Good choice, *zin dyali*," I said, then dropped to one knee.

As he lay on his bed, I slipped his legs through the

pants, then helped him up to tuck his shirt inside and fasten the buckles. While he was still cooperative, I took the opportunity to slip on his socks and cream-colored shoes.

Might not be the best outfit for him to sludge around in dirt at the park, but he was a kid, so no matter what clothing I put on him, he would find a way to dirty them.

"Ready?"

My son's smile widened as he used both of his hands to grab my cheeks and squeeze them, one of his new habits. "Yes!" Then he gave me a kiss on my cheek filled with drool. "Thank you, *Baba*."

I lightly tickled him on his belly and kissed his forehead. "You're welcome, my beautiful boy."

"Should we go find Selena and see if she's ready to go?"

I stood from the ground, letting him put his hand in mine.

"Yes, let's go see Lena," he answered, looking up at me with wide and excited hazel eyes.

I led him to his older sister, only to find her ready and waiting at her doorstep as we turned the corner of the hallway that led to her room.

"Hey, *kbida dyali*, you ready?"

"Yes, *Baba*, I'm all ready to go," she said, giving me her little smile that melted my heart.

I grabbed her small hand in mine, that wasn't so small anymore, and headed for the door. How the hell was she already seven? It felt like it was just yesterday when I held her in my arms for the first time.

Sienna had gotten pregnant a few months after our second wedding. It'd been hard on her at the beginning because of her severe morning sickness, but as soon as her first trimester had ended, she'd felt much better and was able to resume working as she did before, only slowing down when she approached her due date.

We then had Selim five years later and her pregnancy was much smoother the second time around. Whether it was because she was carrying a boy or it was her second time was still to be determined.

We both had wanted more kids, but I knew she wanted to focus on her career and I was already beyond happy with the family we'd created.

I hadn't had the chance to grow up with a big family and had always hoped that once I was older, I'd get the chance to create my own.

I was eternally grateful that Sienna came into my life. She already made it better, but being graced with being a father at her side made it even better. If that was possible.

"Oh, we forgot to say bye to Mama," Selim announced, letting go of my hand.

"She's sleeping," I tried to say, but he was already beelining for our bedroom at the end of the hall to find his mom before I could stop him.

Selena shook her head and let out a laugh. "He's so energetic."

"That he is," I said, making our way there too.

Sienna had a day off today and I'd planned on taking our kids to the park so she could sleep and enjoy a relaxing morning.

Guess that's out the window now.

The thump of his feet hitting the hardwood floors followed by the slam of doors bursting open and cracking against the wall echoed in the house.

Since his legs were still short, his sister and I got there just as he flew to the bed and climbed on. Sienna rose from her sleep at the intrusion and opened her arms wide to welcome him.

"Mom!" he squealed, trying to wrap his arms around her neck.

"Morning, my beautiful son," she said over the sound of Selim's giggles as she peppered a million kisses on his face.

"Selim, your shoes," I reprimanded him.

"Sorry, Daddy," he apologized and pushed against the heels of his slip-ons to remove them, letting them fall on the floor.

Selena let go of my hand and joined them in bed as I stood at the door and watched my wife scoop both of our children in her arms.

This was easily my favorite view.

My entire world was looking right back at me. This was a family I'd longed for, dreamed of, and I'd never felt more complete than at this moment.

"Morning, princess," she said to our daughter as she gave her a kiss on her cheek.

"Morning, Mommy."

They both snuggled on each side of her and she looked over at me, beaming.

I grinned, my heart expanding to the point of hurting from the happiness I was experiencing. I was the luckiest person in this world.

"What do we think about Daddy joining us?" she asked both of our children.

I didn't need to be told twice.

I crawled into the bed and placed my hands on either side of her face, caging my wife in. Then I put my weight on her and pressed a kiss on her lips, conveying that I'd teach her a lesson later for calling me Daddy in front of the kids.

Selena groaned next to us and I turned my head to look at her.

"You know," my daughter announced, her palm shielding her eyes, "kissing is gross, Baba. You and Mama shouldn't do it in front of us."

"Oh, yeah?" I asked, pressing another kiss on Sienna's lips. "We kiss to show affection and love." I sat on my heels. "Just." I inched closer to her. "Like." I moved another inch closer. This," I finished before darting for her. I scooped her up in my arms and rolled onto my back, tickling her ribs and smothering her in kisses.

She squealed. "Okay, okay," she huffed out, her laughter increasing.

I stopped and snuggled her, sandwiching her between her mom and me. Her laughter subsided and she reached for her brother's hand, tangling her fingers to his and bringing him closer to whisper something in his ears.

Whatever she told him wouldn't lead to anything good. They were great kids, but when they combined their minds together, they were outright mischievous.

I looked over Selena's head and found Sienna staring at me, her chocolate brown eyes full of happiness.

"I love you," she said.

"*Jamais plus que moi*," had barely left my mouth when our kids jumped and attacked us with kisses.

Guess our trip to the park would have to wait.

Thank You!

Hey lovely,

Thank you so much for reading *Ashes*! If you enjoyed this book, I would be grateful if you could leave a review on the platform(s) of your choice.

One review can make all the difference !

Xo, Seraya

Also by SeRaya

THE VENDETTA SERIES

A series of interconnected standalones

Nemesis

Ashes

The Vendetta Series Book #3

Keep in touch with Seraya

Here's where you can chat all things SeRaya and get access to first looks, exclusive giveaways, and the best place to connect with me!

Reader Group: facebook.com/groups/serayaswarriors

Website: authorseraya.com

Instagram: www.instagram.com/authorseraya/

Tiktok: www.tiktok.com/@serayawrites

Goodreads: goodreads.com/authorseraya

Acknowledgments

We did it...Again!

I wouldn't be able to write this if it wasn't for you. Without your unconditional support and love for Nemesis and my words, I wouldn't have been able to write Ashes. So, I wanted to thank you for taking a chance on my debut and giving it so much love.

To my beautiful friends, you know who you are—I am eternally grateful for every single one of you. You have supported me and became the family I never thought I'd have. The love and encouragement you have given throughout the time we've known each other is something that I will never forget. Thank you for being there every step of the way, for being my ride or dies and some of the best people I've ever known.

To my second half, my found sister—I would have never thought that I'd meet a complete stranger and they'd become one of the most important people in my life. I love you so much sweet girl.

To my brain twin—There is so much to say, so I'll keep it short and start by saying thank you. Thank you for being there for me, for showing up for me everyday and literally sharing brain cells. Without you, none of this journey would be possible & I hope we get to do more of life together.

To Jess, Kylie, Lola, Salma and Shania—I am so

grateful for your input in this story. I'm so lucky to have people on my team that care about my characters and my stories as much as I do. Your feedback helped make Sienna & Jamal shine, and making the final version of this story.

To Genesis, my best friend—Where do I even start? Thank you for always supporting me through thick and thin. You've always been one of my biggest cheerleader and I'm so lucky to have you in my life. I can't thank you enough for sharing your knowledge and insights into Dominican culture. Sienna wouldn't be the same without you.

To Rania—Seeing you react to Sienna & Jamal was my favorite thing! Your excitement and suggestions helped highlight Jamal's background. I'm so thankful for your help and you wanting to be a part of my process.

To Cat—You always create magic and I'm so happy to have you bring my stories to life. I'm obsessed with you and love you!

To Emily—Thank you for making my words shine and making this story the best it could be. I couldn't do this without you!

And last but not least, to you the reader—Thank you for taking a chance on me and my stories. This story was very special to me and I hope you fell in love with these two just as I did writing them. None of this journey would be possible without you lovelies and I cannot wait to see where we go next!

xo, Seraya

About the Author

SeRaya is an author of romance books that are both dark and steamy, aiming to write stories that will give you the best of both worlds.

She has a weakness for morally grey characters and happy endings. while darkness is what she loves most, she's a hopeless romantic at heart (but will deny it if you ask).

Besides being cozied up with a good romance book, she enjoys rewatching her favorite tv shows and discovering new food places.

She's happily single (because never settle for less), but busy with her many book boyfriends.

9 781738 935321